flash and bones

Kathy Reichs is vice president of the American Academy of Forensic Scientists; a member of the RCMP National Police Services Advisory Council; forensic anthropologist to the province of Quebec; and a professor of anthropology at the University of North Carolina at Charlotte. Her first book, *Déjà Dead*, catapulted her to fame when it became a *New York Times* bestseller and won the 1997 Ellis Award for Best First Novel. *Flash and Bones* was an instant *Sunday Times* bestseller and is the fourteenth novel featuring Temperance Brennan. For more about the author, please visit www.kathyreichs.com

D0207627

Praise for Kathy Reichs

'Reichs is the queen of pathology thrillers'
Independent

'Completely engrossing . . . drags the reader into a different
world where dialogue is tense, dead men tell the best tales and
the ice will freeze the bones. Read this and you'll know why
the word "thriller" was invented'
Frances Fyfield

'Reichs has proved that she is now up there with the best'
Marcel Berlins, *The Times*

'The forensic detail is harrowing, the pace relentless and the
prose assured. Kathy Reichs just gets better and better and is
now the Alpha female of the genre' *Irish Independent*

'A long way from your standard forensic thriller:
all the excitement you crave, indefatigably expert.
But conscience-generated and compassionate too'
Literary Review

'A brilliant novel . . . fascinating science and dead-on
psychological portrayals, not to mention a whirlwind
of a plot . . . a must-read'
Jeffery Deaver

Tempe Brennan . . . is smart, resourceful and likeable . . . an
investigator to follow' *Daily Telegraph*

'It's becoming apparent that Reichs is not just "as good as"
Cornwell, she has become the finer writer . . . the
ever-accelerating unfolding of the plot has all the élan of
Kathy Reichs at her most adroit'
Daily Express

Also available by Kathy Reichs

Kathy
Reichs
flash and bones

arrow books

Published by Arrow Books in 2012

2 4 6 8 10 9 7 5 3 1

Published by arrangement with the original publisher, Scribner,
an imprint of Simon & Schuster, Inc.

First published in Great Britain in 2011 by William Heinemann

Arrow Books
The Random House Group Limited
20 Vauxhall Bridge Road, London, SW1V 2SA

www.randomhouse.co.uk

Addresses for companies within The Random House Group Limited can be
found at: www.randomhouse.co.uk/offices.htm

The Random House Group Limited Reg. No. 954009

A CIP catalogue record for this book is available from the British Library

ISBN 978-0-099-57095-0

The Random House Group Limited supports The Forest Stewardship
Council® (FSC®), the leading international forest-certification organisation.
Our books carrying the FSC label are printed on FSC®-certified paper.
FSC is the only forest-certification scheme supported by the leading
environmental organisations, including Greenpeace. Our
paper procurement policy can be found at
www.randomhouse.co.uk/environment

MIX
Paper from
responsible sources
FSC® C016897

Typeset in Berling LT Std by SX Composing DTP, Rayleigh, Essex, SS6 7XF

Printed and bound in Great Britain by Clays Ltd, St Ives plc

For
Declan Rex Reichs
Born July 1, 2010

Acknowledgments

Flash and Bones would not have been possible without the help of Barry Byrd. *Muchas gracias*, Byrdman! I owe you.

Scott and Tiffany Smith invited me into their home and included me with the Race Week gang. Thanks. You created a new fan. Marcus Smith and Bryan Hammond welcomed me to the Charlotte Motor Speedway and answered endless questions about NASCAR and the track. Chad Knaus, Jimmie Johnson's awesome crew chief, provided information on cars and race teams. Marty Smith of ESPN offered the perspective of a media insider. Bruton Smith's hospitality in the owner's suite was greatly appreciated.

Drs. Jane Brock, Patty McFeeley, and Mike Graham responded to my queries about ricin. Dr. William C. Rodriguez and Mike Warns answered a million questions each. Sergeant Harold (Chuck) Henson, Charlotte-Mecklenburg Police Department, helped with details on policing and law enforcement.

D. G. Martin shared an article on the history of stock car racing, and David Perry graciously donated *Real NASCAR: White Lightning, Red Clay, and Big Bill France*, by Daniel

S. Pierce, University of North Carolina Press, Chapel Hill.

I appreciate the continued support of Chancellor Philip L. Dubois of the University of North Carolina-Charlotte.

I am grateful to my family for their patience and understanding. Amazing how they still put up with my grumpy phases.

Deepest gratitude to my agent, Jennifer Rudolph Walsh, and to my genius editors, Nan Graham and Susan Sandon. I also want to thank all those who work so very hard on my behalf, including: Katherine Monaghan, Paul Whitlatch, Rex Bonomelli, Kara Watson, Simon Littlewood, Gillian Holmes, Rob Waddington, Glenn O'Neill, Kathleen Nishimoto, Lauren Levine, Tracy Fisher, Michelle Feehan, Cathryn Summerhayes, and Raffaella De Angelis. I am also indebted to the Canadian crew, especially to Kevin Hanson, Amy Cormier, and David Millar.

And, of course, I am grateful to my readers. Without you, what's the point?

If I have forgotten to thank anyone I am truly sorry. Though I tried to be careful, if the book has errors they are my fault.

1

Looking back, I think of it as Race Week in the Rain. Thunderboomers almost every day. Sure, it was spring. But these storms were over the top.

In the end, Summer saved my life.

I know. Sounds bizarre.

This is what happened.

Bloated, dark clouds hung low to the ground, but so far no rain.

Lucky break. I'd spent the morning digging up a corpse.

Sound macabre? Just part of the job. I'm a forensic anthropologist. I recover and analyze the dead that present in less than pristine condition—the burned, mummified, mutilated, dismembered, decomposed, and skeletal.

OK. Today's target wasn't actually a corpse. I'd been searching for overlooked body parts.

Short version. Last fall a housewife vanished from her Cabarrus County home in rural North Carolina. A week ago, while I was away on a working vacation in Hawaii, a trucker admitted to strangling the woman and burying her body in a sandpit. Impatient, the local cops had sallied forth with shovels and buckets. They delivered the bones in a Mott's applesauce carton to my employer, the Medical Examiner's Office, in neighboring Mecklenburg County.

Yesterday, my aloha tan still glowing, I'd begun my analysis. A skeletal inventory revealed that the hyoid, the mandible, and all of the upper incisors and canines were missing.

No teeth, no dental ID. No hyoid, no evidence of strangulation. Dr. Tim Larabee, the Mecklenburg County medical examiner, asked me to have a second go at the sandpit.

Correcting screwups usually makes me cranky. Today I was feeling upbeat.

I'd quickly found the missing bits and dispatched them to the MCME facility in Charlotte. I was en route to a shower, a late lunch, and time with my cat.

It was 1:50 p.m. My sweat-soaked tee was pasted to my back. My hair was yanked into a ratty knot. Sand lined my scalp and undies. Nevertheless, I was humming. Al Yankovic, "White & Nerdy." What can I say? I'd watched a YouTube video and the tune lodged in my head.

Wind buffeted my Mazda as I merged onto southbound I-85. Slightly uneasy, I glanced at the sky, then thumbed on NPR.

Terry Gross was finishing an interview with W. S. Merwin, the U.S. poet laureate. Both were indifferent to the conditions outside my car.

Fair enough. The show was produced in Philadelphia, five hundred miles north of Dixie.

Terry launched into a teaser about an upcoming guest. I never caught the name.

Beep! Beep! Beep!

The National Weather Service has issued a severe-weather warning for parts of the North Carolina piedmont, including Mecklenburg, Cabarrus, Anson, Stanly, and Union counties. Severe thunderstorms are expected to move through the area within the next hour. Rainfall of one to three inches is anticipated, creating the potential for flash flooding. Atmospheric conditions are favorable for the development of tornadoes. Stay tuned to this station for further updates.

Beep! Beep! Beep!

I tightened my grip on the wheel and goosed my speed to seventy-five. Risky in a sixty-five-mile-an-hour zone, but I wanted to reach home before the deluge.

Moments later Terry was interrupted again, this time by a muted *whoop-whoop*.

My eyes flicked to the radio.

Whoop!

Feeling stupid, I checked the rearview mirror.

A police cruiser was riding my bumper.

Annoyed, I pulled to the shoulder and lowered my window. When the cop approached, I held out my license.

"Dr. Temperance Brennan?"

"Looking somewhat worse for wear." I beamed what I hoped was a winning smile.

Johnny Law did not beam back. "That won't be necessary," indicating my license.

Puzzled, I looked up at the guy. He was mid-twenties, slim, with an infant mustache that appeared to be going nowhere. A badge on his chest said R. Warner.

"The Concord Police Department received a request from the Mecklenburg County medical examiner to intercept and divert you."

"Larabee sent the cops to find me?"

3

"Yes, ma'am. When I arrived at the recovery site, you'd left."

"Why didn't he call me directly?"

"Apparently he couldn't get through."

Of course not. While digging, I'd locked my iPhone in the car to protect it from sand.

"My phone is in the glove compartment." No need to alarm Officer Warner. "I'm going to take it out."

"Yes, ma'am."

The numbers on the little screen indicated three missed calls from Larabee. Three messages. I listened to the first: "Long story, which I'll share when you're back. The Concord PD received a report of a body at the Morehead Road landfill. Chapel Hill wants us to handle it. I'm elbow-deep in an autopsy. Since you're in the area, I hoped you could swing by to check it out. Joe Hawkins is diverting that way with the van, just in case they've actually got something for us."

The second message was the same as the first. Ditto the third, but more terse. It ended with the inducement: You're a champ, Tempe.

A landfill in a storm? The champ was suddenly not so chipper.

"Ma'am, we should hurry. The rain won't hold off much longer."

"Lead on." I could not have said this with less enthusiasm.

Warner returned to his cruiser, whoop-whooped, then pulled into traffic. Inwardly cursing Larabee, Warner, and the landfill, I palm-slapped the gearshift and followed.

Traffic on I-85 was unusually heavy for Thursday, mid-afternoon. As we approached Concord, I could see that the Bruton Smith Boulevard exit ramp was a parking lot.

And realized what a nightmare this little detour of Larabee's would be.

The Morehead Road landfill is back-fence neighbor to the Charlotte Motor Speedway, a major stop on the NASCAR circuit. Races would be held there this weekend and next. Local print and broadcast coverage was extensive. Even I knew that tomorrow's qualifying would determine which lucky drivers made the cut for Saturday's All-Star Race.

Two hundred thousand avid fans would pour into Charlotte for Race Week. Looking at the sea of SUVs, campers, pickups, and sedans, I guessed that many had already hit town.

Warner rode the shoulder. I followed, ignoring the hostile glares of those cemented in the logjam.

Lights flashing, we snaked through the bedlam on Bruton Smith Boulevard, past the dragway, the dirt track, and a zillion fast-food joints. On the sidelines, the tattooed and tank-topped carried babies, six-packs, coolers, and radios. Vendors sold souvenirs from folding tables beneath improvised tents.

Warner looped the surrealistic geometry of the Speedway itself, made several turns, then rolled to a stop outside a small structure whose siding might once have been blue. Beyond the building loomed a series of mounds resembling a Martian mountain range.

A man emerged and issued Warner a yellow hard hat and a neon orange vest. As they talked, the man pointed at a gravel road rising sharply uphill.

Warner waited while I received my safety gear, then we proceeded up the slope. Trucks rumbled in both directions, engines churning hard going in, humming going out.

When the road leveled, I could see three men standing by an enormous Dumpster. Two wore coveralls. The third wore black pants and a long-sleeved black shirt over a white tee. Joe Hawkins, longtime death investigator for the MCME. All three featured gear identical to that lying on my passenger seat.

Warner nosed up to the Dumpster and parked. I pulled in beside him.

The men watched as I got out and donned my hard hat and vest. Fetching. A perfect complement to my current state of hygiene.

"We gotta quit meeting like this." Joe and I had parted at the sandpit barely an hour earlier.

The older man stuck out a hand. "Weaver Molene." He was flushed and sweating and filled his coveralls way beyond their intended capacity.

"Temperance Brennan." I'd have skipped the handshake, given the black moons under Molene's nails, but didn't want to be rude.

"You the coroner?" he asked.

"I work for the medical examiner," I said.

Molene introduced the younger man as Barcelona Jackson. Jackson was very thin and very black. And very, very nervous.

"Jackson and I work for the company that manages the landfill."

"Impressive pile of trash," I said.

"Site's got a capacity of over two and a half million cubic meters." Molene ran a dingy hankie across his face. "Friggin' weird Jackson stumbled onto the one square foot holding a stiff. Or maybe not. Probably dozens out there."

Jackson had mostly kept his eyes down. At Molene's words, he raised and then quickly dropped them back to his boots.

6

"Tell me what you found, sir."

Though I spoke to Jackson, Molene answered.

"Probably best we show you. And quick." He pocket-jammed the hankie. "This storm's coming fast."

Molene set off at a pace I would have thought impossible for a man of his bulk. Jackson scampered after. I fell into line, paying attention as best I could to the uneven footing. Warner and Hawkins brought up the rear.

I've excavated in landfills, am familiar with the aroma of eau de dump, a delicate blend of methane and carbon dioxide with traces of ammonia, hydrogen sulfide, nitrogen, hydrogen chloride, and carbon monoxide added for spice. I braced for the stench. Didn't happen.

Good odor management, guys. Or maybe it was Mother Nature. Wind swirled dirt into little cyclones and tumbled cellophane wrappers, plastic bags, and torn paper across the landscape.

Our course took us the length of the active landfill, down a slope, then around a series of what appeared to be closed areas. Instead of raw earth, the tops of the older mounds were covered with grass.

As we walked, the rumble of trucks receded, and the whine of fine-tuned engines grew louder. Based on the changing acoustics, I figured the Speedway lay over a rise to our right.

After ten minutes, Molene stopped at the base of a truncated hillock. Though tentative grass greened the top, the side facing us was scarred and pitted, like a desert butte gouged by eons of wind.

Molene said something I didn't catch. I was focused on the exposed stratigraphy.

Unlike the sandstone or shale that make up metamorphic rock, the mound's layers were composed of flattened

7

Pontiacs and Posturepedics, of squashed Pepsis, Pop-Tarts, Pringles, and Pampers.

Molene pointed to a crater in a brown-green layer eight feet above our heads, then to an object lying about two yards off the base of the mound. His explanation was lost to a clap of thunder.

Didn't matter. It was obvious Jackson's "stiff" had dropped from the mound, probably dislodged by the previous day's storm.

I crossed to the thing and squatted. Molene, Warner, and Hawkins clustered around me but remained standing. Jackson kept his distance.

The object was a drum, approximately twenty inches in diameter and thirty inches high. Its cover lay off to one side.

"Looks like a metal container of some kind," I said without looking up. "It's too rusted to make out a logo or label."

"Flip it," Molene shouted. "Jackson and I turned the thing bottom up to protect the stuff inside."

I tried. It weighed a ton.

Hawkins squatted, and together, we muscled the drum upright. Its interior was filled with a solid black mass.

I leaned close. Something pale was suspended in the dark fill, but the pre-storm gloom obscured all detail.

I was reaching for my Maglite when lightning sparked.

A human hand flashed white in the electric brilliance.

Dissolved to black.

2

I ran my beam over the inky matrix.

The white inclusion was unquestionably a human hand.

The fill was rock-hard but crumbling at the exposed edges. I suspected asphalt. The size of the drum suggested a thirty-five-gallon capacity.

Thirty seconds of discussion, and we had a plan.

Warner and Jackson would stand guard while the rest of us returned to the management office. Though Jackson's look said he'd rather be elsewhere, he offered no protest.

The clouds burst as Hawkins, Molene, and I picked our way back. We arrived mud-coated and thoroughly soaked.

To my dismay, two vehicles waited a short distance down the dirt road, motors idling, wipers slapping. I recognized the driver of the Ford Focus.

"Sonofabitch," I said.

"What?" Behind me, Molene was breathing hard.

"Reporters." I waved a hand in the direction of the cars.

"I didn't talk to no one. I swear."

"Their scanners probably picked up the radio transmission from the cops to the ME."

"You're kidding."

"It's Race Week." I made no attempt to hide my irritation. "A murder at the Speedway would make splashy headlines."

Seeing us, the reporters emerged from their cars and slip-slid to the checkpoint. One was a mushroom-shaped man holding an umbrella. The other was a woman in a slicker and pink vinyl boots.

The guard looked a question in our direction. Molene gestured "no" with both hands.

Denied access, the pair shouted through the downpour.

"How long has the body been out there?"

"Is it the kid who went missing from Bar Carolina?"

"Any tie-in to the Speedway?"

"Dr. Brennan—"

"Is the ME planning to—"

Hawkins, Molene, and I hurried into the office. The door slammed, cutting off the barrage of questions.

"Any chance it *could* be the Leonitus kid?" Hawkins referred to a young woman who'd vanished two years earlier after a night of barhopping with friends.

"How old is that sector?" I asked Molene.

"I'll have to check the records."

"Ballpark." I removed my hard hat and vest and held them at arm's length. Not that it mattered. I was dripping as much as they were.

"We stopped dumping in that area in 2005. That layer, I'd say late nineties to maybe 2002."

"Then the vic ain't Leonitus," Hawkins said.

Or parts of her, I thought.

While Hawkins and Molene drove a motorized cart back out to retrieve the drum, I phoned Larabee. He said what I expected: See you tomorrow.

10

So much for lounging with my cat.

Thirty minutes later Jackson's prize sat on plastic sheeting in the ME van, oozing muddy water and flecks of rust. Five minutes after that, it was making its way to Charlotte along with the Cabarrus County sandpit teeth and bones.

Officer Warner escorted me back to the interstate. After that I was on my own.

Between the downpour, rush hour, and the Race Week frenzy, vehicles were backed up to Minneapolis. Fortunately, that was opposite to my direction of travel, though westbound traffic was also heavy. While lurching and braking my way toward home, I wondered about the person we'd just recovered.

A whole body? A tight fit for a thirty-five-gallon container, but not impossible. Dismembered parts? I hoped not. A partial corpse would mean a return to the landfill for a systematic search.

That prospect was decidedly unappealing.

Friday promised a repeat of Thursday. Hot and sticky with more afternoon storms.

Wouldn't affect me. I'd be stuck in the lab all day.

After a quick breakfast of granola and yogurt, I drove downtown. Or uptown, as Charlotteans prefer.

The Mecklenburg County medical examiner occupies one end of a featureless brick box that spent its early years as a Sears Garden Center. The box's other end houses satellite offices of the Charlotte-Mecklenburg Police Department. Devoid of architectural charm save a slight rounding of the edges, the building is located at College and Tenth, just a hair outside the fashionable heart of uptown. Though plans exist to develop the site and move the facility, so far the MCME has stayed put.

Works for me. The place is just ten minutes from my town house.

At 8:05 I parked in the small tentacle of lot facing the MCME entrance, gathered my purse, and headed for the double glass doors. Across College, a half-dozen men sat or leaned on a wall bordering a large vacant lot. All wore the hodgepodge of ratty clothing that is the uniform of the homeless.

Beyond them, a black woman was muscling a stroller along the sidewalk toward the county services building, struggling with the uneven pavement.

The woman stopped to tug upward on her tube top. Her eyes drifted in my direction. I waved. She didn't wave back.

Entering the vestibule, I tapped on a window above a counter to my left. A chubby woman turned in her chair and peered through the glass. Her blouse was sharply pressed, her hair permed and fixed primly in place.

Eunice Flowers has worked for the MCME since sometime back in the eighties, when it moved from the basement of the old Law Enforcement Center to its present location. Monday through Friday, she screens visitors, blessing some with entry, turning others away. She also types reports, organizes documents, and keeps track of every shred of information generated throughout the analysis of the dead.

Smiling, Mrs. Flowers buzzed me in. "You were a busy lady yesterday."

"Very," I said. "Anyone else here?"

"Dr. Larabee will be in shortly. Dr. Siu is lecturing at the university. Dr. Hartigan is in Chapel Hill."

"Joe?"

"Gone to collect some poor soul from a Dumpster. Bless his heart. It's gonna be another hot one today." Mrs.

Flowers's vowels could have landed her a role in *Gone With the Wind*.

"Is the landfill body getting any attention?"

"Made the *Observer*. Local section. I've answered a half-dozen calls already."

Mrs. Flowers's tidiness includes not just her person but everything around her. At her workstation, Post-it notes hang equidistant, paper stacks are squared, pens, staplers, and scissors are stowed when idle. It is an orderliness of which I am incapable. Unnecessarily, she adjusted a photo of her cocker spaniel.

"Do you still have the paper?"

"I'd like it back, please." She handed me her neatly folded copy. "The Belk ad is good for twenty percent off on linens."

"Of course."

"The consult requests are on your desk. I believe Joe placed everything in the stinky room before he left."

The facility has a pair of autopsy rooms, each with a single table. The smaller of the two has special ventilation to combat foul odors.

For decomps and floaters. My kind of cases.

Good choice, Hawkins. Though the sandpit bones would be relatively aroma-free, there was no telling about the landfill vic. And I was uncertain how best to free the remains from the asphalt. Depending on their condition, things could get messy.

Passing the cubicles used by the death investigators, I checked the erasable board on the back wall. Five new arrivals had been entered in black Magic Marker. A newborn found dead in her bed. A man washed ashore at Mountain Island Lake. A woman bludgeoned with a frying pan in her kitchen on Sugar Creek Road.

13

My sandpit recovery had been designated MCME 226-11. Though the bones and teeth were probably those of the missing housewife, that assumption could always prove false. Thus, a new case number was assigned.

The landfill remains had been designated MCME 227-11.

My office is in back, near those of the three pathologists. The square footage is such that, were I not on staff, the space might have been used for the storage of buckets and mops.

Unlocking the door, I tossed the newspaper onto my desk, dropped into the chair, and placed my purse in a drawer. Two consult requests lay on the blotter, both signed by Tim Larabee.

I started with the *Observer*. The article was on page three of the local section, just six lines of copy. The byline said Earl Byrne, the mushroom guy I'd spotted in the Focus.

My name was mentioned, and the fact that remains had been transported from the Morehead Road landfill to the ME office. I figured Byrne had seen Hawkins and Molene load the drum into the van. Combining that with the radio transmission from the Concord cops, he'd decided the story was solid.

Fair enough. Maybe exposure would help with an ID.

I pulled a pair of forms from plastic mini-shelving on a filing cabinet at my back, filled in the case numbers, and wrote brief descriptions of each set of remains and the circumstances surrounding their discoveries. Then I went to the locker room, changed to surgical scrubs, and crossed to the stinky room.

The sandpit bones were on the counter, in the brown evidence bag in which I'd placed them.

The landfill drum sat atop its mud-caked sheeting on a morgue gurney.

Since the missing housewife was higher up the queue, I decided to start there.

After assembling camera, calipers, clipboard, and a magnifying lens, I accessorized with a paper apron and mask and snapped on latex gloves. No match for the hard hat and vest, but the look was elegant in its own way.

By ten-fifteen I was done. X-rays, measurement, and gross and microscopic observation revealed that the bones and teeth were compatible with the rest of the sandpit skeleton. Dental analysis would confirm the finding, but I was confident the parts I'd recovered belonged to the missing housewife.

And that she had indeed been murdered.

The hyoid, a delicate U-shaped bone from her throat, showed fractures on each of its wings. Such trauma almost always results from manual strangulation.

I was finalizing my notes when the phone rang in a cadence that indicated the call was internal.

"I have a gentleman here who wishes to see you." Mrs. Flowers sounded flustered.

"Can't Joe deal with him?"

"He's still out."

"I'm trying to focus on these cases," I said.

"The gentleman says he has information that is extremely important."

"Information about what?"

"The body from the landfill."

"I can't discuss that yet."

"He thinks he knows who it is." Hushed but excited.

"D. B. Cooper has finally turned up?" Snarky, but I'd heard this line many times before.

15

There was a moment of prim silence.

"Dr. Brennan. This man is not a crackpot."

"What makes you so sure?"

"I've seen his picture in *People* magazine."

3

Generation? Upbringing? Hormones? I've no clue the reason, but in the presence of attractive Y-chromosomers, Mrs. Flowers blushes and her voice goes breathy.

"Dr. Brennan, I'd like to present Wayne Gamble."

I looked up.

Standing in my doorway was a compact man with intense brown eyes and dark blond hair cut short and combed straight back. He wore jeans and a black knit polo with a Hilderman Motorsports logo stitched in red.

I laid down my pen.

Gamble stepped into the office and held out a hand. His grip was firm but not a testosterone crusher.

"Please have a seat."

I gestured at a chair on the far wall. Meaning six feet from my desk. Gamble dragged it forward, sat, and planted his palms on his knees.

"Can I get you anything?" Marilyn crooning birthday wishes to the prez. "Water? A soft drink?"

Gamble shook his head. "No, ma'am."

Mrs. Flowers remained fixed in the hall.

"Perhaps it's best if you close the door," I said gently.

Cheeks flaming, Mrs. Flowers did as requested.

"What can I do for you, Mr. Gamble?"

For a moment the man just stared at his hands. Reconsidering? Choosing his words?

I wondered at his reticence. After all, he'd come to me. Why such caution?

"I'm the jackman for Stupak's fifty-nine car."

My confusion must have been obvious.

"The Sprint Cup Series? Sandy Stupak?" he said.

"He's a NASCAR driver."

"Sorry. Yeah. Stupak drives the fifty-nine Chevy for Hilderman Motorsports. I'm on his pit crew."

"Thus your photo in *People*."

Gamble gave a self-deprecating grin. "They did a spread on racing and I got caught in some of the shots. The photographer was aiming at Sandy."

"You're in town for the Coca-Cola 600?" Flaunting my minuscule knowledge of NASCAR.

"Yeah. Actually, I live in Kannapolis, just down the road. Raised there." Again Gamble hesitated, obviously uncomfortable. "My sister, Cindi, was two years older than me."

The verb tense clued me where this was going.

"Cindi went missing her senior year of high school."

I waited out another pause.

"I read in the paper you found a body in the dump out by the Speedway. I'm wondering if it could be her."

"When did your sister disappear?"

"1998."

Molene thought the drum holding our John/Jane Doe had eroded from an area of the landfill active at that time. I kept this fact to myself. "Tell me about her."

Gamble pulled a snapshot from his pocket and flipped it onto my desk. "That was taken just a couple of weeks before she went missing."

Cindi Gamble looked like she could have modeled for yogurt ads. Her teeth were perfect, her skin flawless and lousy with health. She had a blond pixie bob and wore a silver loop in each ear.

"Are those cars on her earrings?" Returning the photo.

"Cindi wanted to be a NASCAR driver in the worst way. Drove go-karts from the time she was twelve, moved up to legends."

Again, I must have looked lost.

"Little single-seat cars for beginners. Legends driving trains kids so they can advance to real short-course racing."

I nodded, not really understanding.

Gamble didn't see. His eyes were on the photo still in his hand. "Funny how life turns out. In high school I was all about football and beer. Cindi hung with the science geeks. Loved cars and engines. NASCAR was her dream, not mine."

Though anxious for Gamble to get on with his story, I didn't interrupt.

"The summer before her senior year, Cindi started dating another wannabe driver, a guy named Cale Lovette. That fall, Cindi and Cale both vanished. Bang. Gone without a trace. No one's seen them since."

Gamble's eyes met mine. In them I saw apprehension. And resurrected pain.

"My folks went crazy. Posted flyers all over town. Handed them out in malls. Nothing." Gamble wiped his palms on his jeans. "I've got to know. Could that body be my sister?"

"What makes you think Cindi is dead?"

"The police said the two of them left town together. But Cindi's whole life was NASCAR. I mean, she was on fire to drive. What better place to do that than Charlotte? Why would she just pick up and leave? And she's never turned up anywhere else."

"There was an investigation?"

Gamble snorted in disgust. "The cops poked around for a while, decided Cindi and Cale took off to get married. She was too young to do that without parental approval."

"You doubt that theory?"

Gamble's shoulders rose, fell. "Hell, I don't know what to believe. Cindi didn't confide in me. But I'm sure my folks would never have agreed to her marrying Cale."

"Why?"

"She was seventeen. He was twenty-four. And rolled with a pretty rough crowd."

"Rough?"

"White-supremacist types. Hated blacks, Jews, immigrants. Hated the government. Back then I suspected Cale's racist buddies might be involved. But what would they have against Cindi? I don't know what to think."

Gamble shoved the photo back in his pocket.

"Mr. Gamble, it's unlikely that the person we recovered is your sister. I'm about to begin my analysis. If you'll leave contact information, I'll inform you when I've finished."

I passed across pen and paper. Gamble scribbled something and handed them back.

"Should it prove necessary, could you obtain Cindi's dental records?"

"Yeah."

"Would you or another maternal relative be willing to provide a DNA sample?"

20

"It's just me now."

"What about Lovette?"

"I think Cale's father still lives around here. If I can find a listing, I'll give him a call."

Gamble got to his feet.

I rose and opened the door.

"I'm truly sorry for your loss," I said.

"I just keep pedaling to stay out front."

With that odd comment, he strode down the hall.

I stood a moment, trying to recall news stories about Cindi Gamble and Cale Lovette. The disappearance of a seventeen-year-old kid should have generated a headline or two. Angel Leonitus certainly had.

I could not remember seeing anything on Gamble.

Vowing to research the case, I headed back to the stinky room.

The landfill drum was as I'd left it. I was circling the gurney, considering options, when Tim Larabee pushed through the door wearing street clothes.

Mecklenburg County's chief medical examiner is a runner. Not the healthy knock-out-three-miles-in-the-neighborhood variety but the train-for-a-marathon-in-the-Gobi-Desert zealot. And it shows. Larabee's body is sinewy and his cheeks are gaunt.

"Oh boy." Larabee's deep-set eyes were pointed at the gurney.

"Or girl," I said. "Take a look." I indicated the open end of the drum.

Larabee crossed to it and peered at the hand. "Any idea how much more is in there?"

I shook my head. "Can't x-ray because of the metal and the density of the fill."

"What's your take?"

"Someone stowed a body or body parts, then filled the drum with asphalt. The hand was up top and became visible when the lid came off and the asphalt eroded."

"Tight fit for an adult, but I've seen it done. Any dates on the sector where they found this thing?"

"A landfill worker said that area of the dump closed in 2005."

"So it's not Leonitus."

"No. She's too recent."

"As of Monday, we got us another MP. Man came from Atlanta to Charlotte for Race Week. Wife reported him missing." Larabee was studying the drum. "How will you get it out?"

How will *I* get it out?

Great.

Though I'd never freed remains from asphalt, I had liberated corpses from cement. In each case, because fats from the surface tissues had created a nonbinding surface, a small void had surrounded the body. I anticipated a similar situation here.

"The drum is no problem. We'll cut through that. The asphalt is trickier. One option is to saw at horizontal and lateral planes to the block, then use an air hammer to create propagation cracks."

"Or?"

"The other option is to chisel away as much asphalt as possible, then dip the block in solvent to dissolve what remains."

"What kind of solvent?"

"Acetone or turpentine."

Larabee thought a moment, then, "Asphalt and cement

work damn well as sealants, so there might be fresh tissue preserved in there. Go with Plan A. Joe can help."

"Joe's out on a call."

"He just got back." Larabee changed the subject. "Have you examined the new sandpit bones?"

"Everything is consistent with the rest of the skeleton."

"Music to my ears." Larabee chin-cocked the drum. "Let me know how it goes."

I was taking photos when Hawkins entered the autopsy room and strode to the gurney.

Cadaver-thin, with dark circles under puffy lower lids, bushy brows, and dyed black hair combed straight back from his face, Joe Hawkins looks like an older and hairier version of Larabee.

"How we going to crack this sucker?" Hawkins rapped gnarled knuckles on the drum.

I explained Plan A.

Without a word, Hawkins went in search of the necessary tools. I was finishing with overview shots when he returned, dressed in blue surgical scrubs identical to mine.

Hawkins and I donned goggles, then he inserted a blade, plugged in, and revved the handheld power saw.

The room filled with the whine of metal on metal and the acrid smell of hot steel. Rust particles arced and dropped to the gurney.

Five minutes of cutting, then Hawkins laid down the saw and tugged and twisted with his hands. The segment came free.

More cutting. More tugging.

Eventually a black lump lay on the gurney, and an exoskeleton of torn metal lay on the floor.

Joe killed the saw. Raising my goggles to my forehead, I stepped forward.

23

The asphalt cast was the exact shape and size of the drum's interior. Objects grazed its surface, pale and ghostly as morgue flesh.

The curve of a jaw? The edge of a foot? I couldn't be sure.

Hawkins switched to the air hammer and, with some direction from me, began working downward toward the body parts. As cracks formed, I freed chunks of asphalt and placed them on the counter. Later I would examine each and take samples so chemists could determine their elemental composition.

Maybe useful, maybe not. Better to be safe. One never knew what would later prove significant.

Slowly, the counter filled.

One hunk. Three. Nine. Fifteen.

As the cast shrank, its contour changed. A form took shape, like a figure emerging from a block of marble being sculpted.

The top of a head. An elbow. The curve of a hip.

At my signal, Joe set down the chisel. Using hand tools, I went at the remaining asphalt.

Forty minutes later a naked body lay curled on the stainless steel. The legs were flexed with the thighs tight to the chest. The head was down, the forehead pressed to the upraised knees. The feet pointed in opposite directions, toes spread at impossible angles. One arm L'ed backward. The other stretched high, fingers spread as though clawing for escape.

A sweet, fetid odor now rode the air. No surprise.

Though shriveled and discolored, overall, the cadaver was reasonably well preserved.

But that was changing fast.

4

Hawkins bent sideways and squinted through black-framed glasses that had gone in and out of vogue many times since their purchase.

"Dude's hanging a full package."

I joined him and checked the genitals.

"Definitely male," I said. "And adult."

I shot close-ups of the outstretched hand, then asked Hawkins to bag it. The fingers first spotted by Jackson were now in pretty bad shape, but those embedded deeper in the asphalt retained significant soft tissue. And nails, under which trace evidence might be found.

While Hawkins sealed the hands in brown paper sacks, I filled out a case marker and adjusted camera settings. As I moved around the body, shooting from all angles, Hawkins brushed away black crumbs and positioned the card.

"Looks like this will be one for Doc Larabee."

Pathologists work with freshly dead or relatively intact corpses to determine identity, cause of death, and postmortem interval. They cut Y-incisions on torsos and remove skullcaps to extract innards and brains.

Anthropologists answer the same questions when the flesh is degraded or gone and the skeleton is the only game left. We eyeball, measure, and x-ray bone, and take samples for microscopic, chemical, or DNA analysis.

Hawkins was guessing that a regular autopsy might be possible.

"Let's see how he looks stretched out," I said.

Hawkins snugged the gurney to the autopsy table, and together we transferred MCME 227-11 and rolled him to his back. While I pulled on his ankles, Hawkins pushed downward on his legs. It took some effort, but eventually the John Doe lay flat on the stainless steel.

The man's face was grotesque, the features distorted by a combination of hot asphalt and subsequent expansion and contraction while in the landfill. His abdomen was green and collapsed due to the action of anaerobic bacteria, the little buggers that start working from their home base in the gut once the heart stops beating.

Based on the amount of surface decomp, I guessed gray cells and organs might remain.

"I think you're right, Joe."

I pried loose the hand that had been twisted behind the man's back. The fingers had shriveled, and the tips had suffered some skin slippage.

"We might get prints. Try rehydrating for an ink and roll."

I was asking Hawkins to plump the fingertips by soaking and then injecting them with embalming fluid. Hopefully, he could obtain ridge detail for submission to national and state databases.

Hawkins nodded.

"Let's get height," I said.

Hawkins positioned a measuring rod beside the body,

and I read the marker. As I jotted my estimate, he pried open the jaws. After thirty-five years on the job, he needed no direction.

MCME 227-11 had not been big on oral hygiene. His dentition contained no fillings or restorations. A molar and a premolar were missing on the upper left. Three of the remaining molars had cavities that could have housed small birds. The tongue side of every tooth was stained a deep coffee brown.

"The wisdom teeth have all erupted, but the first and second molars show very little wear," I observed aloud.

"Young fella."

Nodding agreement, I added my age estimate to the case form, completing a preliminary biological profile.

Male. White. Thirty to forty years of age. Five feet seven. Smoker. Dental records unlikely.

Not much, but a start for the pathologist.

"Finish with the photos, shoot some full-body and dental X-rays, then put him back in the cooler for Dr. Larabee. And let's send a sample of asphalt over to the crime lab," I said.

I stripped off my mask, apron, and gloves, tossed them in the biohazard pail, then went to update my boss.

Larabee was in his office, talking to a man with salt-and-pepper hair and an NFL neck. Tan sport jacket, open-collar blue shirt, no tie.

Seeing that Larabee had a visitor, I started to move on. Blue Shirt's words caused me to linger. He was asking about MCME 227-11, the John Doe whom Hawkins and I had just examined.

"—body from the landfill could be Ted Raines, the guy who went missing earlier this week."

"The man visiting from Atlanta."

"Yeah. He came to make business calls, but mainly for Race Week. Bought tickets for the All-Star Race tomorrow night, the Nationwide and Coca-Cola 600 next weekend. Visited clients, as planned, on Monday. After that he stopped calling home or answering his cell phone. Wife's gone apeshit. Thinks something bad happened in Charlotte."

"We haven't begun the autopsy." Larabee sounded anxious to be rid of the guy. "An anthropologist will first assess the condition of the remains."

A rubber sole squeaked on the tile behind me. I turned. Hawkins was staring past me toward Larabee's half-open door, scowling deeply.

"Next of kin are coming out of the woodwork," I said, feeling guilty at having been caught eavesdropping.

Still scowling, Hawkins continued down the hall.

Allrighty, then.

I photocopied my case form and gave it to Mrs. Flowers to deliver to Larabee.

My watch said 1:48 p.m.

I considered my options. I'd finished with the sandpit bones. The landfill John Doe was now Larabee's problem. Since I work only when anthropology cases come in, and there was nothing to keep me at the MCME, the afternoon was mine to spend as I chose.

I chose to placate my cat.

Birdie was miffed. First I'd dumped him with a neighbor while I was away in Hawaii. Then, his first day home, I'd abandoned him to dig up a sandpit.

Or maybe it was the thunder rumbling again. Birdie hates storms.

"Come on out." I waggled a saucer at floor level. "I've got lo mein."

Birdie held position, entrenched beneath the sideboard.

"Fine." I placed the noodles on the floor. "It's here when you want it."

I pulled a Diet Coke from the fridge, served myself from the little white carton I'd picked up at Baoding, and settled at the kitchen table. Opening my laptop, I Googled the names Cindi Gamble and Cale Lovette.

The results were useless. Most led to fan sites for Lyle Lovett.

I tried Cindi Gamble alone. The name generated links to a Facebook page, and to stories about a woman mauled to death by a tiger.

I paused to consider. And to slurp lo mein.

Local disappearance. Local paper.

I tried the online archives of *The Charlotte Observer.* 1998.

On September 27 a short article updated the case of a twelve-year-old girl missing for nine months. Nothing on Cindi Gamble.

More lo mein.

Why would the disappearance of a seventeen-year-old kid receive no coverage?

I began checking sites devoted to finding MPs and to securing names for unidentified bodies.

Neither Cindi Gamble nor Cale Lovette was registered on the Doe Network.

I switched to the North American Missing Persons Network.

Nothing.

I was logging on to NamUs.gov when thunder cracked

and lightning streaked big-time. A white blur shot from beneath the sideboard and disappeared through the dining room door.

The kitchen dimmed and rain came down hard. I got up to turn on lights and check windows.

Which didn't take long.

I live on the grounds of a nineteenth-century manor-turned-condo-complex lying just off the Queens University campus. Sharon Hall. A little slice of Dixie. Red brick, white pediment, shutters, and columns.

My little outbuilding is nestled among ancient magnolias. The Annex. Annex to what? No one knows. The two-story structure appears on none of the estate's original plans. The hall is there. The coach house. The herb and formal gardens. No annex. Clearly an afterthought.

Guesses by family and friends have included smokehouse, hothouse, outhouse, and kiln. I'm not much concerned with the architect's original purpose. Barely twelve hundred square feet, the Annex suits my needs. Bedroom and bath up. Kitchen, dining room, parlor, and study down.

Finding myself suddenly single over a decade ago, I'd rented the place as a stopgap measure. Contentedness? Laziness? Lack of motivation? All these years down the road, I still call it home.

Hatches battened, I returned to my laptop.

For naught. Like the other sites, NamUs had nothing on Gamble or Lovette.

Frustrated, I gave up and shifted to e-mail.

Forty-seven messages. My eyes went to number twenty-four.

Flashbulb image. Andrew Ryan, Lieutenant-détective, Section des crimes contre la personne, Sûreté du Québec. Tall, lanky, sandy hair, blue eyes.

I am forensic anthropologist for the Bureau du coroner in *la Belle Province*. Same deal as with the MCME. I go to the lab when an anthropology consult is requested. Ryan is a homicide detective with the Quebec provincial police. For years Ryan and I have worked together, with him detecting and me analyzing vics.

From time to time we have also played together. And Ryan plays *very* well with others. Many others, it turned out. Ryan and I hadn't been an item for almost a year.

Currently, Ryan's only child, Lily, was in Ontario, enrolled in yet another drug rehab program. Daddy had taken leave to be there with daughter.

I read Ryan's e-mail.

Though witty and charming, when it comes to correspondence, Monsieur le Détective is not Victor Hugo. He wrote that he and Lily were well. That his short-term rental apartment had crappy pipes. That he would phone.

I responded in kind. No nostalgia, no sentimentality, no personal updates.

After hitting send, I sat a moment, a tiny knot tightening in my gut.

Screw prudence.

I dialed Ryan's cell. He answered on the second ring.

"Call a plumber."

"*Merci, madame.* I will give your suggestion serious consideration."

"How's Lily?"

"Who knows?" Ryan sighed. "The kid's saying all the right things, but she's smart and a champ at working people. What's new in North Carolina?"

Share? Why not? He was a cop. I could use his input.

I told Ryan about the sandpit and landfill cases. About

31

the landfill's proximity to the Charlotte Motor Speedway. About my conversation with Wayne Gamble.

"Gamble is jackman on Sandy Stupak's crew?"

"Yes."

"The Sprint Cup Series driver?" Finally Ryan sounded a wee bit animated.

"Don't tell me you're a NASCAR fan."

"*Bien sûr, madame.* Well, to be accurate, I'm a Jacques Villeneuve fan. I used to follow Indy and Formula One. When Villeneuve made the switch to NASCAR, I went with him."

"Who's Jacques Villeneuve?"

"Seriously?" Ryan's shock sounded genuine.

"No. I'm testing to see if you're bullshitting me."

"Jacques Villeneuve won the 1995 CART Championship, the 1995 Indianapolis 500, and the 1997 Formula One World Championship, making him only the third driver after Mario Andretti and Emerson Fittipaldi to accomplish that."

"What's CART?"

"Championship Auto Racing Teams. It's complicated, but it was the name of a governing body for open-wheel cars, the kind that race the Indy. The group doesn't exist under that name now."

"But you're not talking stock cars."

"Hardly."

"I'm going to go out on a limb here and guess Villeneuve is Quebecois."

"Born in Saint-Jean-sur-Richelieu, he still has a home in Montreal. You know the course out on Île Notre-Dame?"

Ryan was referring to a track at Parc Jean-Drapeau on Île Notre-Dame, a man-made island in the Saint Lawrence

River. Each year during Grand Prix Week, you could hear the whine of Formula 1 engines even miles away at our lab.

"Yes," I said.

"Jacques's father, Gilles, also drove Formula One. He was killed during qualifying for the 1982 Belgian Grand Prix. That year the track on Île Notre-Dame was renamed Circuit Gilles Villeneuve in his honor."

"It's a road course, not an oval, right?"

"Yes. The Formula One Canadian Grand Prix is run there. So are the NASCAR Canadian Tire Series, the NASCAR Nationwide series, and a number of other events."

Grand Prix Week in Montreal is like Race Week in Charlotte. Bucks flow like water, making merchants, restaurateurs, hoteliers, and bar owners giddy with joy.

"You surprise me, Detective. I'd no idea you follow auto racing."

"I'm a man of many talents, Dr. Brennan. Find us a backseat and I'll race your—"

"Keep me in the loop on Lily."

After disconnecting with Ryan, I deleted twelve other e-mails, ignored the rest.

I was considering alternate ways to research Cindi Gamble's disappearance when the landline rang.

"How you doing, sugar britches?"

Great. My ex-husband. Or almost ex. Though we'd been separated for over a decade, Pete and I had never bothered with paperwork or courts. Weird, since he's a lawyer.

"Don't call me that," I said.

"Sure, butter bean. How's the Birdcat?"

"Totally freaked by the storm. How's Boyd?"

Boyd is typically the reason I hear from my ex. If I'm in Charlotte, I take care of the chow when Pete has to travel.

"Unhappy with the current divisive climate in Washington."

"Is he coming for a visit?"

"No. We're cool."

A few months back, almost-fifty Pete had slipped a ring onto the finger of twentysomething-D-cup Summer, creating the need for an unmarital status that was legal and official. Currently, that was the second most frequent reason I heard from Pete.

"I've yet to receive papers from your lawyer," I said. "You need to goose—"

"That's not why I'm calling."

I know Janis Petersons like I know the inside of my ear. Twenty years of marriage will do that to people. He sounded tense.

I waited.

"I need a favor," Pete said.

"Uh-huh."

"It's about Summer."

Warning bells clanged in my brain.

"I want you to talk to her."

"I don't even know her, Pete."

"It's probably just the wedding. But she seems"— silver-tongued Mr. Petersons searched for a descriptor— "unhappy."

"Marriage planning is stressful." True. But if *Bridezilla* held auditions in Charlotte, Summer would be a shoo-in.

"Could you feel her out? See what's up?"

"Summer and I—"

"It's important to me, Tempe."

"I'll give her a call."

"It might be better if you invite her to your place. You know. 'Girls sharing a glass of wine' kind of thing?"

"Sure." Masking my horror at the thought. And my annoyance at Pete's failure to bear in mind that I'd popped my final cork years ago.

"Who knows, buttercup?" Relief put a bounce in Pete's tone. "You might find you like her."

I'd have preferred hemorrhoids to a conversation with Pete's dimwit fiancée.

5

That night's storm made Thursday's look like a fairyland sprinkle. I awoke to windows papered with soggy magnolia leaves and blossoms.

And a Chet Baker ringtone.

Relocating Birdie to my left side, I picked up my iPhone. Through one half-raised lid, I could see that the caller was Larabee. I clicked on.

"Hello." I did that thing you do when trying to sound wide awake.

"Were you sleeping?"

"No. No. What's up?"

"We didn't get a chance to talk before you left."

"I had errands to run."

"Listen, a guy came to see me yesterday. He's wondering if the landfill John Doe could be this Ted Raines guy who went missing earlier this week."

I sat up and stuffed a pillow behind my head. Birdie stretched all four legs and spread his toes.

"I seriously doubt that drum went into the landfill this week. What's Raines's story?"

"He's a thirty-two-year-old white male. Married, one kid. Lives in Atlanta, works for CDC."

Larabee was referring to the government's Centers for Disease Control and Prevention.

"How tall is he?"

"Five-eight."

Males tend to embellish their actual height, and measurements taken from corpses are often inaccurate. The extra inch wasn't a problem. Raines fit my profile. But Larabee knew that. So why was he calling?

"Didn't Mrs. Flowers give you my prelim?" I asked.

"I wanted your take."

"Given what you say, there's nothing to exclude him based on physical characteristics."

Birdie recurled into a very small ball.

"What about PMI?" Larabee wanted to know how long I thought the John Doe had been dead.

"Other than Molene's speculation that the drum came from a sector of the landfill active during the late nineties, and the fact that the thing is old and rusty, I've nothing more to go on. Could be a month. Could be a decade. But I doubt it was less than a week."

"Do you have a gut?"

"You were right about the asphalt. It created an airtight envelope and kept scavengers away from the body, so the vic is in pretty good shape. But the drum is toast. Given its condition and location, I think the guy was in there a while."

"He have anything with him? Clothes, personal items, maybe a social security number?"

"Zip."

"Guess I can rule out natural death."

"Did Hawkins manage to get prints?" I asked.

"Six. I'll have them run through AFIS." The Automated Fingerprint Identification System, a national database.

"Can Raines's wife get dental records?"

"I wanted to be sure there was a point before asking."

"Was he a smoker?"

"I'll find out."

"You're doing the autopsy this morning?"

"As soon as I hang up."

I remembered the man in Larabee's office the previous afternoon. "Who was the next of kin?"

"Big guy, arms like caissons?"

"Yeah."

"He wasn't family. That was Cotton Galimore, head of security for Charlotte Motor Speedway."

That surprised me. "What's Galimore's interest?"

"Damage control."

"I'm sure you'll explain that."

"Think about it. Raines tells his wife he'll be at events connected with Race Week. He goes missing. A body turns up spitting distance from where two hundred thousand fans will be parking their butts."

"NASCAR wants to avoid distractions. Especially negative distractions."

"NASCAR. The Speedway. The Chamber of Commerce. I can't name the prime mover. But if there's a chance Raines went to the Speedway and ended up dead, the powers that be want to spin the situation in the best light possible. Galimore was ordered to get the lowdown."

Birdie got up, arched his back, and began nudging my chin with his head.

"I've got to go," I said.

"One other thing." I heard paper rustle. "A guy named Wayne Gamble has left four messages for you."

"Saying what?"

"'I need to talk to Dr. Brennan.' Who is he?"

"A member of Sandy Stupak's pit crew." I told Larabee about Cindi Gamble and Cale Lovette.

I waited out a pause. Then,

"You think the age is too far off for our John Doe to be Lovette?"

"Probably. But I can't exclude him."

"Give Gamble a ring," Larabee said. "I'm going to need a cold hose for Mrs. Flowers if she keeps taking his calls."

Larabee read off a number. I wrote it down.

"Phone if you need me." My tone set a new standard for insincere.

"I'll do some cutting, see what the John Doe's got going inside."

After disconnecting, I threw on jeans and a tee and headed downstairs. Birdie padded behind.

While Mr. Coffee did his thing and Birdie crunched little brown pellets, I retrieved the paper from the back stoop. Even the *Observer* had gone Race Week–crazy. The front page featured photos of Richard Petty, Junior Johnson, and Dale Earnhardt. Hall of Fame candidates or some such. Full color. Above the fold.

Point of information. My hometown is Mecca for NASCAR fans.

Why Charlotte, you ask?

During Prohibition, moonshiners in the Appalachian Mountains of North Carolina used innocent-looking sedans to distribute illegal hooch produced in their stills. To outrun the cops, they modified their vehicles for greater speed and

39

better handling. Many got a rush driving breakneck down twisty mountain roads.

So they started racing each other for fun.

Though the repeal of Prohibition eliminated the need for illicit booze, it seems Southerners had developed a taste for "shine." Drivers who continued "runnin'" now needed to evade revenuers trying to tax their operations.

More tinkering.

More speed.

More competition.

By the 1940s, tracks had sprung up all over Dixie. In places like Wilkes County, North Carolina, stock car racing became the hottest entertainment in town.

But things were messy back then. Schedules weren't organized, so fans never knew where their favorite drivers would be. Neither cars nor tracks were subject to safety rules. And some promoters were less than honest.

Bill France, Sr., a driver and race promoter himself, thought this was a lousy way to run a sport. In 1948 he founded NASCAR, the National Association for Stock Car Auto Racing.

France's idea was simple. NASCAR would establish racing series, sort of like baseball leagues or football conferences. In each series, a group of drivers would compete in a set number of events and follow a common set of rules. At the end of each season, using a uniform scoring system, one champion would be crowned.

Out of chaos came order.

Today NASCAR sanctions the Sprint Cup, the Nationwide Series, and the Camping World Truck Series. There are also some touring competitions, but I've no idea their names.

In 1948 the first NASCAR race took place in Daytona Beach, Florida, using the beach for one straightaway and a narrow blacktop highway for the other. Fourteen thousand fans showed up.

NASCAR's top races were originally known as the Strictly Stock Car Series; then for twenty years as the Grand National Series; then for thirty-plus years as the Winston Cup Series. It was the NEXTEL Cup Series from 2004 to 2007 and has been the Sprint Cup Series ever since. In 2007 nearly 250 million viewers tuned their TVs to watch Sprint Cup events. Those numbers place NASCAR second only to the NFL in popularity.

A lot of the players set up shop in Charlotte.

In May 2010 the NASCAR Hall of Fame opened its doors just a few miles from where I was sitting. The project cost the Queen City two hundred million dollars and hosted ten thousand visitors its first week of life.

All because Americans love their cars and their booze.

I know the names of some drivers. Jimmie Johnson, Jeff Gordon. And some former drivers. Richard Petty, Junior Johnson. Hell, many of them live in and around my zip code. Otherwise, that's the extent of my NASCAR knowledge.

Normally I'd have skipped the Race Week hype in favor of NBA playoff coverage. Because of the landfill John Doe, I flipped to the racing section.

That day the Charlotte Motor Speedway was hosting a barbecue. That night, in addition to the All-Star Race, events would take place, the nature of which was a mystery to me.

I skimmed the paper's front and local sections. There was no mention of Raines or the landfill John Doe.

I ate some cornflakes. Gave Birdie the milk leavings.

Took my bowl and cup to the sink, rinsed, and placed them in the dishwasher. Wiped the table. Watered the small cactuses that live on my windowsill.

The clock said 10:08.

Out of excuses for further delay, I phoned Summer.

"Hello. I'm Summer's answering machine. Please tell me your name. I'm sure Summer would love to call you back."

Eyeballs rolling, I disconnected and dialed the number Larabee had provided.

Wayne Gamble picked up on the first ring.

"This is Dr. Brenn—"

"Any news?" In the background I could hear the roar of engines and the tinny sound of electronically enhanced announcements.

"Dr. Larabee will perform an autopsy this morning. But I can tell you that the victim from the landfill is male."

"I'm being followed." Gamble spoke in a hushed, clipped way.

"Sorry?" Surely I'd heard incorrectly.

"Hang on."

I waited. When Gamble spoke again, the background noise was muted.

"I'm being followed. And I'm pretty sure my back door was jimmied last night."

"Mr. Gamble, I realize you're anxious—"

"It happened then, too. To my parents, I mean. I used to see guys hanging around outside our house. Odd cars parked on our street or following us when we drove."

"This occurred when your sister disappeared?"

"Yes."

"Did your parents tell the police?"

"My parents contacted the Kannapolis PD and the

Cabarrus County Sheriff. And the FBI. Maybe the Charlotte PD. The local cops had asked Charlotte for help. No one took them seriously. Everyone wrote it off as paranoia."

"Why the FBI?"

"The feds took part in the investigation."

"Because?"

"It was the nineties. Lovette was hanging with right-wing wackos."

It took me a moment to grasp Gamble's meaning.

In 1995 Timothy McVeigh blew up the Alfred P. Murrah Federal Building in Oklahoma City. In 1996, during the summer Olympics, a bomb exploded in Centennial Olympic Park in Atlanta. In 1997 the target was an abortion clinic in Sandy Springs, Georgia. That same year bombs were planted at the Otherside Lounge, a lesbian bar in Atlanta. A year later it was an abortion clinic in Birmingham, Alabama.

In 1998, when Gamble and Lovette disappeared, the FBI was focused full-bore on domestic terrorism. If Lovette was known to associate with anti-government extremists, I wasn't surprised the bureau was keeping an eye out.

"Regretfully, I see no link between your sister and the victim found in the landfill. As I stated, my preliminary findings suggest that the individual is male and that he was older than twenty-four."

"Then why is some jackass tailing me?" Very angry.

"Calm down, Mr. Gamble."

"I'm sorry. I feel like crap, probably some kind of flu. Really bad timing."

"If you'd like to reopen the investigation into your sister's disappearance, you could try contacting the Charlotte-Mecklenburg PD Cold Case Unit."

"Will they admit to the cover-up back in 'ninety-eight?"

"What do you mean?"

"The cops formed a task force, made a public show of looking, then shoved the whole thing under the rug."

"Mr. Gamble, I'm a forensic anthropologist. I'm not sure how I can help you."

"Yeah. That's what I expected." Coating his anger with disdain. "Cindi wasn't a congressional intern or some bigwig's kid. No one gave a rat's ass then, no one cares now."

My first reaction was resentment. I started to respond.

Then I thought of Katy, just a few years older than Cindi. I knew the agony I'd feel if my daughter went missing.

How much time could a little poking around take?

"I can't promise anything, Mr. Gamble. But I'll ask a few questions." I reached for pen and paper. "Who was lead on the investigation into your sister's disappearance?"

The name shocked me.

6

Cotton Galimore. The man who'd visited Larabee. The head of security for Charlotte Motor Speedway.

"Anyone else?"

"A detective named Rinaldo, or something like that."

"Rinaldi?"

"That's it. You know him?"

"I do." After so much time, cold fingers still grabbed and twisted my gut.

Eddie Rinaldi spent most of his career with the Charlotte-Mecklenburg PD Felony Investigative Bureau/ Homicide Unit. The murder table. We'd worked many cases together. Two years back, I'd watched Rinaldi gunned down by a manic-depressive who'd skipped his meds.

Gamble's words brought me back. "Rinaldi seemed like a stand-up guy. You'll talk to him?"

"I'll see what I can find out," I promised.

Gamble thanked me, and we disconnected.

I sat staring at the page on which I'd written nothing.

For decades Rinaldi had partnered with a detective

named Erskine Slidell. Skinny. I wondered why he was working with Galimore in the fall of 'ninety-eight.

Call Slidell? Galimore?

Though a good cop, Skinny Slidell tends to grate on my nerves.

But something in my brain was cautioning against Galimore.

I checked my address book, then dialed.

"Slidell."

"It's Temperance Brennan."

"How's it hangin', Doc?" Slidell views himself as Charlotte's answer to Dirty Harry. Hollywood cop lingo is part of the shtick. "Found us a rotter?"

"Not this time. I wonder if I could pick your brain for a minute." Generous. A second was plenty to search Skinny's entire neocortex.

"Your dime, your time." Spitty. Slidell was chewing on something.

"I'm interested in a couple of MPs dating back to 'ninety-eight. Eddie worked the case."

There was a long moment with neither reply nor sounds of mastication. I knew Slidell's insides were clenching, as mine had.

"You there?" I asked.

"Fall of 'ninety-eight I was TDY on a training course up in Quantico."

"Did Eddie partner with someone while you were away?"

"A horse's ass name of Cotton Galimore. What the hell kinda name is Cotton?"

Typical Skinny. He thinks it, he says it.

"Galimore is now in charge of security for Charlotte Motor Speedway," I said.

Slidell made a noise I couldn't interpret.

"Why did he leave the force?" I asked.

"Got too close to a buddy name of Jimmy Beam."

"Galimore drinks?"

"Booze is what finally got him booted."

"I gather you don't like him."

"Ask me? You can cut off his head and shit in his—"

"Did Eddie ever mention Cindi Gamble or Cale Lovette?"

"Give me a hint, Doc."

"Gamble was a high school kid, Lovette was her boyfriend. Both went missing in October of 'ninety-eight. Eddie worked the case. The FBI was also involved."

"Why the feds?"

"Lovette had ties to right-wingers. Possible domestic terrorism issues."

I waited out another pause. This one with a lot of slurping and popping.

"Kinda rings a bell. If you want, I can pull the file. Or check Eddie's notes."

Cops hang nicknames on each other, most based on physical or personality traits. Skinny, for example, hadn't seen a forty-inch waistline in at least twenty years. Other than excessive height, a taste for classical music, and a penchant for pricey clothes, Rinaldi had exhibited no quirks at which to poke fun. Eddie had remained Eddie throughout his career.

Rinaldi's one singular peculiarity was his habit of recording the minutiae of every investigation in which he took part. His notebooks were legendary.

"That would be great," I said.

Slidell disconnected without a good-bye or any query concerning the nature of my interest in a case now over a dozen years cold. I appreciated the latter.

I played with Birdie. Made the bed. Took out the trash. Loaded laundry. Read the e-mails that I'd ignored. Checked a freckle on my shoulder for signs of melanoma.

Then, with a level of enthusiasm I reserve for flossing and waxing, I again phoned Summer.

To my dismay, she answered.

"Hi. This is Tempe." I could hear voices in the background. Regis and Kelly? "Pete's ex. Well, any day now."

"I know who y'all are." Summer had a drawl you could pour on pancakes.

"How's it going?"

"Good."

"Are you still working at Happy Paws?" Desperate for subject matter.

"Why wouldn't I be?" Defensive. "I'm a fully trained veterinary assistant."

"It must be exhausting having a full-time job while trying to plan a big wedding."

"Not everyone can be superwoman."

"How right you are." Cheerful as hell. "It's going well?"

"Mostly."

"Have you hired a planner?" I'd heard that she and Pete were inviting only a few thousand people.

I heard a quavery intake of breath.

"Is something wrong?"

"Petey's being a grumpy-pants about every little thing."

"I wouldn't worry. Pete's never been big on ceremony."

"Until that changes, Mr. Grumpy-Pants won't be foxtrotting at my prom. If you take my meaning."

So the groom-to-be had lost playground privileges.

"Pete thought it might be good if we got to know each other," I said.

48

Nothing but Regis and Kelly.

"If there's any way I can help . . ." I let the offer hang, expecting a frosty rebuff.

"Could you talk to him?"

"About?"

"Showing proper interest." Little-girl petulant. "When I ask what kind of flowers he wants, he says whatever. Cream or white linens on the tables? Whatever. Tinted or clear glass in the hurricane lamps? Whatever. He acts like he doesn't care."

Who would? I thought.

"I'm sure he trusts your judgment," I said.

"Pretty please?"

I pictured Summer with her overdeveloped breasts and underdeveloped brain. Marveled again at the folly of middle-aged men.

"OK," I said. "I'll talk to him."

The line beeped. I checked the screen. Slidell.

"I'm sorry, Summer. I have to take an incoming call."

I couldn't disconnect fast enough.

"I pulled Eddie's book for the fall of 'ninety-eight. Your MPs are in there. Cindi Gamble, seventeen, Cale Lovette, twenty-four. Last seen at the Charlotte Motor Speedway on October fourteenth. They were attending some big-ass race."

"The Speedway is located in Cabarrus County," I said. "Why did Eddie and Galimore catch the case?"

"Apparently the girl's parents called it in here. Then Kannapolis asked the Charlotte PD to stay in. You want to hear this or what?"

As frequently happened when dealing with Slidell, my upper and lower molars started reaching for each other.

"Gamble and Lovette were an item. He worked at the track. She was a senior at A. L. Brown High in Kannapolis."

Slidell paused. I could tell he was skimming, which meant this might take the rest of the morning.

"The girl's parents are listed as Georgia and James Gamble. Brother Wayne. According to the mother, Cindi left home around ten that morning to go to the track." Pause. "Good student. No problems with drugs or alcohol. That checked out solid.

"The boy's mother is listed as Katherine Lovette. Father's Craig Bogan. Kid left home at his normal time, seven a.m. Records showed he clocked in for the job, didn't clock out.

"A maintenance worker name of Grady Winge saw the MPs around six that night. Lovette was talking to a male subject unknown to Winge. Gamble and Lovette drove off with the subject in a 'sixty-five Petty-blue Mustang with a lime-green decal on the windshield on the passenger side. What the hell's Petty blue?"

"Was the car traced?" I asked.

"Winge didn't get a plate."

Pause. I could almost hear Skinny reading with his finger.

"Lovette hung with a group of right-wing nutballs called themselves the Patriot Posse. Militia types. The feds had him and his buddies under surveillance. I'm guessing they were hoping for a lead to Eric Rudolph."

Slidell referred to a suspect in the bombings at Centennial Olympic Park, the lesbian bar, and both abortion clinics. In May 'ninety-eight Rudolph made the FBI's Ten Most Wanted list and became the subject of a million-dollar reward. For five years, while federal and amateur teams searched, Rudolph lived as a fugitive in the Appalachian wilderness, evading capture with the assistance of white-supremacist, anti-government sympathizers, only to be caught almost accidentally by a local town cop. Rudolph was scavenging a supermarket Dumpster for food.

"—Special Agents Dana Reed and Marcus Perenelli."

I jotted down the names.

"What the hell makes them special? Think I'll start calling myself Special Detective Slidell."

I heard a sharp inhalation followed by *thwp*. I knew a wad of Juicy Fruit was sailing into a flowerpot on Slidell's desk.

"Wayne Gamble said a task force investigated the disappearances."

"Yeah. Made up of the two specials, Rinaldi, and Galimore. They interviewed the usual wits, family, known associates, yadda yadda. Searched the usual places. Ran the usual loops. Six weeks out, they handed in a report saying Gamble and Lovette most likely took off."

"Why?"

"Maybe to get married. The girl was underage."

"Took off where?"

"Theory was the Patriot Posse piped them in to the militia underground."

"Wayne Gamble didn't buy that theory. Still doesn't."

"Ditto Gamble's parents." Slidell paused. "Gamble had a teacher, Ethel Bradford. Bradford swore there was no way the kid would leave on her own."

I thought about that. "I searched but found no news coverage of the incident. That strikes me as odd, given that a seventeen-year-old girl had vanished."

"Eddie says in here there was a lot of pressure to keep things under wraps."

"Out of the papers."

"Yeah. He also hints there was a real squeeze to roll with the party line."

"Squeeze from whom?"

"He don't say."

"Did he disagree with the task force's finding?"

A full minute passed as Skinny picked through Rinaldi's notes.

"Not straight out. But I can tell from his wording he thought something didn't smell right."

"What does he say?"

Slidell has an annoying habit of sidestepping questions.

"I've gotta do some canvassing on a domestic. Soon as I'm back, I'll pull the original case file."

"How's Detective Madrid?" I asked.

Following Rinaldi's death, Slidell had been assigned a new partner. Feeling he needed a tune-up in the area of cultural diversity, the department had paired him with a woman named Theresa Madrid. Boisterous, bodacious, and weighing almost as much as Skinny, Madrid referred to herself as a double-L: Latina lesbian.

Madrid turned out to be a crackerjack detective. Despite Skinny's initial horror, the two got along well.

"Get this. The broad's on frickin' maternity leave. Can you believe it? She and her partner adopted a kid."

"You're working solo?"

"Ain't it grand."

As before, Slidell disconnected without an *adieu*.

The phone was still pressed to my ear when it rang again.

"Just finished the autopsy on your John Doe." Larabee's voice sounded odd. "Damned if it makes sense to me."

7

"You want details or the short version?"

"Short."

"The guy had lesions in his airways and pulmonary edema. The organs were pretty far gone, but I saw hints of multifocal ulceration and hemorrhage in the gastric and small-intestinal mucosa."

"Meaning he died of natural causes?"

"Meaning his lungs were full of fluid and something was screwing with his vascular system. But it's not that simple. He'd also taken a blow to the left side of the head, resulting in hemorrhage into the temporal lobe."

"The man either fell or was struck."

"If the tox screen comes back negative, MOD goes down as undetermined." Larabee used the acronym for one of the five categories of manner of death: natural, homicide, suicide, accidental, or undetermined.

"So how'd the guy end up in a barrel of asphalt?"

"In my report I'll note suspicious circumstances."

"What about ID?"

"Nothing. Even though you think it's unlikely the PMI

works, I'm following up on Raines. According to the wife, his last dental checkup was in 2007. The dentist died in 2009, and no one knows what happened to his files."

"Any hit on the prints?"

"No. The landfill guy's not in any system."

I told Larabee about my conversations with Wayne Gamble and Skinny Slidell. "I suppose the John Doe could be Cale Lovette." I didn't really believe it.

"Your age estimate looks pretty solid. At least dentally, the landfill guy looks older than twenty-four. How about you get Lovette's profile, maybe a photo, then check the John Doe's skeletal markers, try to narrow the range?"

"Today?"

"Galimore phoned twice this morning. The folks at the Speedway are pissing their shorts for resolution on this."

My eyes met Birdie's. The cat was giving me an accusatory look. I think.

"Is Joe working this afternoon?"

"Yes."

"I'll be there shortly." Resisting the impulse to sigh theatrically.

"You're a trouper."

I checked my list of incoming calls, scrolled down, hit dial. I'd been on the phone so long, the handset was now the same temperature as my liver.

Wayne Gamble answered after two rings. Background noise told me he was still at the track.

"Can you describe Cale Lovette?" I asked.

"Dirtbag."

"His physical appearance."

"Brown hair, brown eyes, wiry, maybe a hundred and sixty pounds."

"How tall?"

"Five-six or -seven. Why? What's happened?"

"Nothing. I just need descriptors."

"I saw the little snake who's been tailing me. First at the hauler, then by Sandy's trailer. Whenever I spot him, he cuts into the crowd."

"Mr. Gamble, I—"

"Next time I'll twist his balls until he tells me what the hell's going on."

"Thank you for the information."

Driving to the MCME, I pondered Larabee's closing "attagirl." Wondered. Was "trouper" a promotion or demotion from "champ"?

When I arrived, Larabee had left a photocopied picture on my desk. The name Ted Raines was written at the bottom.

Raines wasn't exactly a looker. His weak chin and prominent nose made me think of a bottlenose dolphin.

Hawkins had already rolled the John Doe to the stinky room and plugged in the Stryker saw. With his help, I removed the collarbones and the pubic symphyses, the little projections that meet at the midline on the belly side of the pelvis.

While Joe stripped flesh from the harvested bones, I retracted the scalp to observe the cranial surface.

The adult skull is composed of twenty-two bones separated by twenty-four sutures that appear as squiggly lines. Throughout adulthood, these gaps fill in and disappear. Though progress varies from person to person, the state of suture closure can provide a very general sense of age.

The John Doe's squiggles suggested he was a middle-aged adult.

The pubic symphyseal faces also undergo change throughout adulthood. Those of the John Doe were smooth and had raised edges rimming their perimeters, suggesting an age range centering on thirty-five.

The epiphysis, or little cap at the breastbone end of each clavicle, fuses to the shaft somewhere between the ages of eighteen and thirty. Both the John Doe's caps were solidly attached.

Bottom line. My first estimate was dead-on. In all probability, the John Doe was in his fourth decade when he died.

A bit old for Cale Lovette, but not impossible.

"So," I said, stripping off and tossing my gloves. "It's probably not Lovette."

"Who's Lovette?"

Hawkins was at the sink, untying his apron. I told him about the MPs from 1998.

"Don't remember hearing talk of 'em." His tone was brusque.

"Apparently no one does. Anyway, Galimore will be happy."

Hawkins winged his wadded apron toward the biohazard receptacle. It bounced off the edge and landed on the floor. He made no move to retrieve it.

"You have issues with Galimore?" I asked.

"Damn right I have issues with Galimore."

"You want to tell me?"

"The man can't be trusted." Hawkins's mouth was crimped as though he'd tasted something bitter.

"Are you referring to his alcohol problem?"

"Suppose that's as good a starting place as any."

Hawkins crossed to the pail, pounded the pedal with his heel, snatched up and tossed the apron inside. Letting the lid slam, he strode from the room.

After changing to street clothes, I went in search of my boss. He was not at his desk, in the kitchen, out front, or in the large autopsy room.

I returned to my office, jotted Larabee a note about my refined age estimate, then headed out.

The afternoon was featuring the season's current default weather. The sky was pewter, the thunderheads dark and fat as overripe plums.

On the way home, I thought about the man entombed in asphalt. Had someone filed a missing person report? When? In Charlotte or elsewhere? Had a girlfriend or wife or brother gone to a station, filled out forms, then waited for a call that never came?

I felt in my gut that the man had spent years in the drum. Wondered. Was someone still waiting? Or had all those who'd known him long since forgotten and moved on with their lives?

The first drop hit my windshield as I pulled in at the Annex. I was locking the car when I noticed the doors open on a Ford Crown Vic parked by the coach house ten yards away.

Two men got out. Each wore a dark suit, blue tie, and eye-blistering white shirt. I watched the pair walk toward me.

"Dr. Brennan?"

"Who's asking?"

"I'm Special Agent Carl Williams." Williams flashed a badge. He was small and compact, with mahogany skin and nostrils that flared spectacularly.

I looked at Williams's badge, then at his companion.

"With me is Special Agent Percy Randall."

Randall was tall and pale, with wide-set gray eyes and a quarter-inch buzz. He nodded slightly.

Keys in hand, I waited.

"I suppose you know why we're here." While Williams took the lead, Randall observed me closely.

"I have no idea." I didn't.

"Two days ago you recovered a body from the Morehead Road landfill."

I neither confirmed nor denied the statement.

"You've been asking about Cindi Gamble and Cale Lovette."

Didn't expect that. Had Wayne Gamble contacted the FBI? Slidell? Galimore? How would Galimore know what names I'd queried?

"What is it you want?" I asked.

"We can't help wondering if the man from the dump is Cale Lovette."

"I'm not at liberty to discuss medical examiner files. You'll have to speak to Dr. Larabee."

"We're trying to contact him. In the meantime, we hoped you could save us some shoe leather." Williams did something with his mouth that might have been a smile.

"Sorry," I said.

A drop hit my forehead. Backhanding the moisture, I glanced skyward.

"I wasn't involved in the Gamble-Lovette inquiry back in 'ninety-eight." Williams ignored my not so subtle hint. "Those special agents are now gone from North Carolina. But I can assure you, the task force carried out a thorough and comprehensive investigation."

"I've no reason to doubt that, but I understand they didn't locate either live persons or bodies."

"Wayne Gamble was a child at the time. He didn't fully understand the effort that went into searching for his sister. The task force concluded she had gone underground."

"Is there something specific you wish to discuss?" A steady rain was falling now.

"Task force members canvassed family, friends, teachers, students, coworkers—anyone who'd had even the most casual contact with Gamble or Lovette."

"Grady Winge?" Winge was the last to see Cindi and Cale alive. His name came out before I even thought about it.

Williams's lower lids pinched up ever so slightly. "Of course. Everyone searched until the trail went dead. The consensus was that Gamble and Lovette had left the area of their own volition."

"The parents didn't think so. Nor did Ethel Bradford." I tossed out the teacher's name, implying I knew more about the investigation than I actually did. Which was virtually nothing.

"Mr. Gamble is still upset." Williams's tone remained absolutely neutral. "And that is understandable. He lost his sister. The bureau has no problem with his wish to reopen the case."

If Williams wanted a response, I disappointed him.

"We prefer, of course, that he act with discretion."

"I can't stop him from talking to the press, if that's what you mean."

"Of course not. But we hope he might be discouraged from making unjustified allegations against the FBI."

Rain was dropping in earnest. Williams kept talking.

"If the case is reopened, the bureau will cooperate fully. But I'll be straight with you, Dr. Brennan. We don't know if Cindi Gamble and Cale Lovette are alive or dead."

"Thank you for your honesty."

"We know it will be reciprocated." Again, Williams might have smiled.

"Should the case be reopened, would the medical examiner and the CMPD have access to information gathered by the bureau back in 'ninety-eight?" I asked.

Williams and Randall exchanged glances.

"I don't want to dishearten you, Dr. Brennan. But I can't guarantee that the FBI will turn over all its files and internal notes to anyone. Please trust me when I say we have no idea what happened to Gamble and Lovette. They simply vanished."

I looked Williams straight in the eye. "You've spoken with members of that task force. What do you think happened to them?"

"I believe they left to join fellow extremists out West."

"Why?"

Williams hesitated. Debating whether to pony up some of that reciprocal honesty?

"The sieges at Ruby Ridge in 'ninety-two and Waco in 'ninety-three shot militia outrage sky-high. When Gamble and Lovette disappeared, the airways were full of anti-government chatter."

Williams referred to incidents in which U.S. agents stormed compounds occupied by fringe groups. In each case, people were killed, and those contesting the legitimacy of government were irate.

"From everything I've learned, Lovette was a virulent young man, and Gamble was very young, in love with him, and under his thumb," Williams said.

"So the two just slipped underground."

"That's the only theory that makes sense."

"Is that really so easy to do?"

"Rural Michigan, Montana, Idaho," Williams said. "These crackpots go so far off the grid, no one can find them."

One thing bothered me.

"The investigation lasted only six weeks," I said.

"Which is why Gamble thinks it was a sham. But his sister and Lovette vanished so completely from the outset, it was thought they'd probably gone underground. When the trail went cold, the FBI decided to disband the task force and rely on intel."

I remembered Slidell's comment. "You hoped Lovette might lead you to a bigger catch. Like Eric Rudolph."

"We considered that."

I hiked my purse back onto my shoulder. Which was soaked.

"Please go in out of the rain, Dr. Brennan." Williams flicked the maybe-smile. "And thank you for talking with us. Believe it or not, the bureau is as anxious to find out what happened as you are."

With that, Williams and Randall hurried to their car and drove off.

The conversation replayed in my mind as I changed clothes and towel-dried my hair. Had the visit been an attempt to dissuade me from helping Wayne Gamble?

I'd just slipped on sandals when the phone rang.

As usual, Slidell skipped the pleasantries.

What he said stunned me.

And tripped an anger switch in my brain.

8

"Gone?"

"Like a long dog."

"Gone where?"

"Snatched by the fart barf and itch." Slidell's voice was tight with fury.

"The FBI seized the entire Gamble-Lovette file?"

"Right down to the paper clips."

"At the conclusion of the inquiry?"

"No. Right now. Yesterday. Twelve years after the investigation, they came and grabbed the file."

"Who authorized that?"

"All I could pry loose was that word came from high up."

"What about Eddie's notes?"

"No friggin' way. They weren't part of the jacket." I heard a palm smack something solid. "Got 'em right here."

A body surfaced at the landfill on Thursday. Wayne Gamble came to see me on Friday. Shortly thereafter, a twelve-year-old file was suddenly confiscated. What the hell?

Silence hummed across the line as Slidell and I considered the implications. He broke it.

"Something stinks."

"Yes."

"No one fucks with Erskine Slidell." I'd seen Skinny angry. Often. But rarely with so much emotion.

"What are you going to do?" I asked.

"Call you right back."

Dead air.

Fifteen minutes later the phone rang again.

"You free?" Slidell asked.

"I could be."

"Pick you up in ten."

"Where are we going?"

"Kannapolis."

Ethel Bradford taught junior and senior chemistry at A. L. Brown High School from 1987 until her retirement in 2004. She still lived in the house she'd purchased upon landing that job.

Save for the blasting AC and angry air whistling in and out of Slidell's nose, the drive from Charlotte to Kannapolis passed in silence. Skinny alternated between drumming agitated fingers and gripping the wheel so tightly I thought he might crush it.

Though the temperature inside the Taurus was subarctic, the space was ripe with odors. Old Whoppers and fries. Cold coffee. The bamboo mat on which Skinny parked his ample backside.

Slidell himself. The man reeked of cigarette smoke, drugstore cologne, and garments long overdue for hamper or dry cleaner.

I was bordering on queasiness and hypothermia when Slidell pulled to the curb in front of a small brick bungalow with green shutters and trim. Hydrangeas bordered the foundation. Potted geraniums lined brick steps leading to the front porch.

"Is she expecting us?" I asked.

"Eeyuh."

Pushing off the seat back with an elbow, Slidell hauled himself from behind the wheel. I followed him up the walk.

The inner door swung open before Slidell's thumb hit the bell.

I'd formed a mental image, perhaps based on my own high school chemistry teacher. Ethel Bradford was younger than I expected, probably just a hair north of sixty-five, slim, with boy-cut auburn hair. Her pale blue eyes looked enormous behind thick round glasses.

Slidell made introductions and held his badge to the screen. Without studying it, Bradford stepped back and opened the outer door. I noted that she hadn't dressed up for our visit. She wore khaki shorts, a checked cotton blouse, and was barefoot.

Bradford led us down a hall lined with framed travel photos, then through an arched opening to the right. The living room had linen drapes and a tan Oushak rug overlying a gleaming oak floor. The brick fireplace was painted white to match the woodwork and flanking bookcases.

"Please." Bradford gestured at a leather sofa.

Slidell took one end. I took the other. Bradford sat in an armchair on the far side of a steamer trunk doing duty as a coffee table.

Before Slidell could begin, Bradford started asking questions.

"Have you found Cindi?"

"No, ma'am."

"Is she dead?"

"We don't know that."

"Has new information emerged?"

"No, ma'am. We'd just like to ask a few questions."

"Just seems odd, that's all. After so much time." Bradford twisted sideways and tucked her bare feet up under her bum.

"Yes, ma'am. So you do remember Cindi Gamble?"

"Of course I do. She was an excellent student. There were far too few of those. I also knew her through STEM."

"STEM?" Slidell pulled a spiral pad from his pocket, flipped pages with a spitted thumb, and clicked a pen to readiness.

"The Science, Technology, Engineering, and Math Club. Cindi was a member. I was faculty adviser."

"You remember when she went missing?"

Slidell got a withering look from behind the Harry Potter lenses.

"I assume you were questioned at the time," he said.

"Briefly. The police lost interest because I couldn't really tell them much." Using one finger, Bradford shot her glasses up the bridge of her nose. They immediately dropped back into the groove in which they'd been resting.

"What did you tell them?"

"Cindi stopped coming to school."

"That's it?"

"That's all I knew."

"They talk to other teachers?"

"I suppose so. I'm really not sure."

While Slidell asked questions, I observed Bradford. I noted that her right hand grasped one ankle very tightly. Though trying to hide it, the woman was nervous.

"What about Lovette?" Slidell asked.

"What about him?"

"Did you know him?"

"I had no personal contact with Cale Lovette. He was not a student at A. L. Brown. Isn't this all on record somewhere? I've already answered these very same questions."

"Did you know that Cindi was dating Lovette?"

"Yes."

"She ever talk about him?"

"Not to me."

"Were you aware of Lovette's involvement with a group called the Patriot Posse?"

"I'd heard rumors." Bradford's gaze flicked toward the doorway, as though a noise or movement had startled her.

"Were the kids into that sort of thing?"

"What sort of thing?"

Slidell stared at Bradford, unmoving. I could sense his irritation.

"Cindi ever say anything about hating Negroes or Jews? Homosexuals?" Slidell pronounced it "homo-sectials."

"That would have been out of character."

"Abortionists? The federal government?"

"I don't think so."

"But you don't know." Slidell was losing patience.

"The sad truth is, teachers know very little about their students. About their private lives, I mean. Unless a student chooses to confide."

"Which Cindi did not."

Bradford stiffened at Slidell's accusatory tone. I met her eyes. Rolled mine, implying that I also found his attitude boorish.

Slidell tapped his pen on his pad, eyes locked on Bradford. She didn't blink.

The standoff was interrupted by Slidell's cell phone. Yanking it from his belt, he checked the number.

"Gotta take this." Slidell shoved to his feet and lumbered from the room.

I decided to continue with the good-cop ploy.

"It must have been dreadful losing a student like that."

Bradford nodded.

"Was there talk on campus?" I asked gently. "Among faculty and students? Speculation about what happened to them?"

"Frankly, there was surprisingly little. Lovette was an outsider. Other than STEM, Cindi wasn't a joiner. She wasn't"—Bradford hooked a half quotation mark with the fingers of her free hand—"popular."

"Kids can be cruel."

"Viciously cruel." Bradford was falling for my female-bonding shtick. "Cindi Gamble loved engines and wanted to be a race car driver. For a female, in those days, such an avocation did not make you prom queen, even in Kannapolis."

"I know it's hard to remember so far back. But was there any student with whom she was close?"

The free hand rose, palm up, in a gesture of frustration. "As I understood it, she spent all of her time at some track."

"Do you remember seeing Cindi with anyone in particular at school, maybe in the halls or the cafeteria?"

"There was one girl. Lynn Hobbs. Cindi and Lynn often ate lunch together."

"Did Lynn give a statement?"

"I'm not sure."

"Do you know where she lives today?"

Bradford shook her head.

"Would you mind telling me who interviewed you back in 'ninety-eight?" I asked.

"Two police officers."

"From the Charlotte-Mecklenburg PD?"

"Yes."

"Do you remember their names?"

"No."

"Can you describe them?"

"One was tall and thin. Very polite. His accent suggested he wasn't local. The other was coarser. He looked like a bodybuilder."

"Detectives Rinaldi and Galimore?"

"That sounds right."

Leaning forward, I lowered my voice to confide, girlfriend to girlfriend. "Anyone else?"

"What do you mean?"

"Were you questioned by the FBI?"

As before, Bradford's gaze jumped toward the archway behind me, then dropped. Clearly our presence was making her anxious. She nodded.

"Did you make a formal statement?"

"No."

"Did the special agent mention the Patriot Posse?"

"I don't recall details of the conversation."

"Did the FBI ask you to keep your discussions confidential?"

Before Bradford could answer, Slidell reappeared and tipped his head toward the door.

"One last question," I asked softly.

Bradford raised reluctant eyes to me.

"Do you think Cindi Gamble left on her own?"

"Not for a second," she said firmly. "I said so then, and I'll say it now."

Leaving our cards, Slidell and I headed out.

Back in the Taurus, I told him what I'd learned in his absence.

"Dame wanted us there about as much as a boil on her ass."

"She seemed uncomfortable."

"She knows more than she's saying."

"What reason could she have for withholding information?"

"The feebs probably fed her some bullshit about domestic terrorism and confidentiality and national security."

"Now what?" I asked.

"Who was the lunch buddy?"

"Lynn Hobbs."

"That name was in Eddie's notes."

"Think you can find her?"

"Oh, yeah." Slidell slid knockoff Ray-Bans onto his nose. "I'll find her."

9

Sunday, a miracle occurred. No rain.

Sadly, I had no one with whom to share the fine weather. Katy was in the mountains. Ryan was in Ontario. Harry, my sister, was at home in Texas. My best friend, Anne Turnip, was absorbed in a home renovation project. Charlie Hunt was hunkered in at the Mecklenburg County Public Defender's Office, preparing his closing argument for the trial of a woman accused of shooting her pimp.

How to label Charlie Hunt? My friend? Suitor? Wannabe squeeze? So far, that was as hot as things had gotten. My call, not his.

I celebrated the sunshine by running my long loop through Freedom Park and around all the Queens Roads. And Charlotte has a boatload. There's even an intersection of Queens and Queens.

In the afternoon I weeded the garden, then took Birdie onto the lawn for a session with the FURminator, removing several pounds of fur. After the grooming, he made himself scarce.

In the evening I caught up on paperwork, then grilled

a steak and ate it listening to Foghat and Devo full blast. Dove Bar for dessert.

I am an island. A rock. Whatever.

Ryan phoned around nine. I sensed from his tone that he preferred to keep the conversation light and away from the subject of Lily. His goal seemed to be educating me on NASCAR in Canada. Realizing his need for diversion, I mostly listened.

"Jacques Villeneuve is an officer of the National Order of Quebec and was inducted into Canada's Walk of Fame."

"Quite an honor for an athlete."

"To date, no other Canadian has won the Indianapolis 500 or the F One Drivers' title."

"Impressive—"

"Jacques Villeneuve has had over a dozen career NASCAR starts. Five in the Nationwide Series and three in the Sprint Cup Series."

"And the others?"

"Probably the Camping World Truck Series. I know he drove in the 2009 Canadian Tire Series. I was in the stands for that one."

"What team is he with?"

"He was driving the thirty-two Toyota for Braun Racing. Not sure now. I think he's trying to get back into Formula One, but the FIA World Motor Sport Council decided there won't be any new teams this year."

"Is Villeneuve the only Canadian NASCAR driver?"

"*Tabarnac*, no. Mario Gosselin drives in the Camping World Truck Series. Pierre Bourque, D. J. Kennington, though those guys are mostly part-timers. Jean-François Dumoulin and Ron Fellows are road-course ringers."

"Which means?"

"They drive road courses, not ovals." Pause. "Anything new on your landfill case?"

I briefed him on developments.

"You planning a return trip to the Speedway?"

"If necessary."

Ryan hesitated. "If you go, will you be anywhere near the Nationwide garage area?"

When I realized where he was going, I burst out laughing.

"You want Jacques Villeneuve's autograph, don't you?"

"The man's a legend."

"You're such a dork."

"It's not like I'm suggesting you steal the guy's jockeys."

"Lieutenant-détective Andrew Ryan, Villeneuve groupie."

"Dr. Temperance Brennan, all-around smart-ass." I could hear Ryan's blush flame across the line.

"You wear a cap with the number thirty-two and Jacques's picture stitched on the brim?"

"Forget it. I don't even know if Villeneuve's racing in Charlotte."

Ryan wished me *bonne chance*, then we disconnected.

I was settling on the sofa to watch *Boston Legal* reruns with my very dapper cat when the front doorbell bonged.

Birdie and I looked at each other in surprise. No one ever uses that entrance.

Curious, I crossed the living room and put an eye to the peephole.

And actually cringed.

Summer stood on the porch, digging in a purse the size of a mail pouch. Backlit by the carriage light, her hair looked like a nimbus of white cotton candy.

I considered a quick drop and a belly crawl to the stairs.

Instead, I turned the lock.

Summer's head popped up at the sound of the tumblers. Even in the dimness, I could see she'd been crying.

"Hey," she said.

"Hey."

"I know it's kinda late."

Kinda.

"Would you like to come in?" I stood back and opened the door wide.

Summer slipped past me, leaving a tsunami of Timeless in her wake. When I turned, she was extending a box of Tic Tacs in my direction.

"Breath mint?"

"No, thanks."

"I find the taste calmative."

"Yes," I agreed. Using a word like "calmative" was quite an undertaking for Summer.

Summer dropped the little dispenser into her purse and fingered the strap nervously. In her pink-sequined bra tank, pink pencil skirt, and murderous high heels, she looked like an ad for Frederick's of Hollywood.

"The study is more comfortable," I said.

"OK."

Summer clicked along behind me, head swiveling from side to side.

"Would you like something to drink?" I gestured at the sofa.

"Merlot, please."

"I'm sorry. I don't keep wine in the house."

"Oh." Summer's perfectly plucked brows V'ed down in confusion. "OK. I didn't really want it."

"So. What's up?" Suspecting this conversation was going

to be unpleasant, I dropped into the desk chair and assumed a listening attitude.

"I followed your advice."

"My advice?"

"I did exactly what you told me to do."

"Summer, I didn't—"

"I told Pete he had to show more interest in the wedding." Summer crossed one long tan leg over the other. "Or else."

"Wait. What? I—"

"I said, 'Petey, if this snideybutt attitude continues, I don't think things will work out between us.'"

Summer's double-D cups rose tremulously. Fell.

I waited.

The tearful account poured forth.

As I listened, short phrases winged in my brain.

Run, Pete.

Run fast.

Run far.

Mean. I know. But that's the response my gray cells offered.

I didn't let on. Just nodded as I supplied tissues and empathetic sounds.

The longer Summer talked, the more horrified I became. How could she have misinterpreted my comments so badly?

I imagined Pete's anger at my perceived culpability. What was Harry's favorite saying?

No good deed goes unpunished.

Yep. Serious castigation was barreling my way.

Finally the whole sad story was told. Ultimatum. Quarrel. Sobbing exit. Slamming door.

When she'd finished, I offered another tissue.

Summer dabbed beneath each lavishly mascaraed eye.

"So." She drew a wet breath. "What do I do?"

"Summer, I really don't feel comfortable—"

"You have to help me." The tears started anew. "My life is ruined."

"Perhaps I've done enough damage already." I didn't really believe it, but the conversation was going even worse than I'd anticipated.

"Exactly. That's why you have to fix it."

"I don't think that's my place," I said gently.

"You have to talk to Pete. You have to bring him to his senses." Summer was creeping closer to hysteria with every word. "You have to—"

"OK. I'll phone him in the morning."

"Honest to God?"

"Yes."

"Cross-your-heart promise?"

Merciful God.

"Yes."

For one awful moment I thought she would hug me. Instead she blew her nose. Which was now the color of my Christmas socks.

But the mascara remained flawless. I wondered about the brand.

I was still wondering when Summer's head tipped to one side.

"Oh, sweetie. You are booty-pooty-ful."

I followed her sight line.

Birdie had entered the room. He sat watching us, ears forward, tail curling around one haunch.

Summer wiggled her fingers and spoke in the same saccharine voice. "Oh, you just come here, you little precious thing."

Right. In addition to thunderstorms, my cat dislikes strangers and the smell of strong perfume.

To my astonishment, Birdie padded over and jumped onto the couch. When Summer stroked his back, he dropped onto his forepaws and raised his tail high.

Summer pursed up her lips and uttered another string of baby-talk gibberish.

The little traitor actually purred.

"I apologize, Summer. It's been a long day, and there are things I need—"

"You must think my mama taught me no manners at all." Pecking Birdie on the head, Summer gathered her purse and rose.

At the door, she swiveled and beamed me a smile. "One day we'll all laugh about this."

"Mm."

"Tempe, I take back every mean thought I ever had about you."

With that, Summer teetered off into the night.

Falling asleep, I wondered: Can one take back thoughts? Take them back from whom? To what end?

Monday morning, Birdie woke me by chewing my hair.

Fair enough. I'd FURminated off half of his undercoat.

After steeling myself with a quadruple espresso, toaster waffle, and wedge of cantaloupe, I phoned Pete.

"Summer came by my place last night."

"Did she."

"She was upset."

"I expect she was."

"Look, Pete. I did as you asked. She talked, I listened."

"Seems you did more than just listen."

"I offered no advice, rendered no opinion."

"That wasn't her take."

I struggled to be tactful. "Summer has her own way of viewing the world."

"You turned her into a crazoid."

She had a huge head start. I didn't say it.

"What did you do to make her so touchy?" Pete asked.

"She's concerned about your lack of interest in the upcoming nuptials."

"Who cares about napkin color? Or the flavor of frosting? Or the shape of a cake?"

"Your fiancée."

"It's like some monster has taken possession of her mind."

Not much to take. Again I kept it to myself.

"You shouldn't have told her I hate weddings," Pete said.

"I didn't. I simply said you weren't big on ceremony."

Pete had skipped his high school, college, and law school graduations. Our own marriage extravaganza was organized by my mother, Daisy Lee. Right down to the pearls on the napkin holders, which rested on the china, which complemented the linen tablecloths trimmed with alabaster lace. Pete had simply shown up at the church.

"What do you recommend?" Pete asked wearily.

Stun gun?

"Fake it," I said. "Pick ivory or white. Raspberry or cherry."

"She always disagrees with my choice."

"At least you've made the effort."

"I don't need this shit at my age."

Hell-o.

"Pete?"

"Yeah."

"Did she really call you a snideybutt?"

77

Dial tone.

After the bout with my ex, I needed physical exertion.

Birdie watched as I laced on my Nikes.

"What do you see in that bimbo?" I asked.

No response.

"She has the depth of a powder-room sink."

The cat offered nothing in his defense.

The weather was still August-hot. Eight-fifteen and already eighty-two degrees.

I opted for the short course and ran the loop up Queens and through the park. By nine-thirty I was back home, showered, and dressed.

Thinking Slidell might call with information on Lynn Hobbs, I worked through e-mail and paid some bills. Then I read an article in the *Journal of Forensic Sciences* on the use of amino acid racemization rates in dentition for the estimation of age. Light stuff.

By eleven the phone hadn't rung.

Needing a change of venue, I opted for the MCME. I'd finish my report on the landfill John Doe, then package the bone plugs. Should DNA analysis be needed, the specimens would be ready to go.

I'd barely hit my office when Tim Larabee burst through the door.

The look on his face told me something was wrong.

10

"Where's the John Doe?" Larabee's bloodstained scrubs suggested he'd already been cutting.

Not surprising. Mondays can be hectic for coroners and MEs. Especially Mondays coming off hot summer weekends.

"Sorry?"

"MCME 227-11. Barrel boy. When you finished on Saturday, what did you do with him?" There was a sharp edge to Larabee's voice.

"I told Joe to return the body to the cooler."

"It's not there."

"It has to be."

"It's not."

"Did you ask Joe?"

"He's off today."

"Call him."

"He doesn't answer."

Slightly annoyed, I hurried to the cooler and yanked the handle. The door whooshed outward, carrying with it the smell of refrigerated flesh.

Five stainless-steel gurneys sat snugged to the far wall. Four others occupied the sides of the room. Six held body bags.

As I stepped inside, Larabee watched from the hall, sinewy arms folded across his chest. Moving from bag to bag, I checked case numbers.

Larabee was right. MCME 227-11 was not present.

Shivering and goose-bumped, I exited and closed the door.

"Did you look in the freezer?"

"Of course I looked in the freezer. No one's in there but the old-man Popsicle we've had for two years."

"A corpse can't just walk away."

"Indeed."

"You didn't sign a release for removal of the body?" I asked. Stupid. But this was making no sense.

Larabee's scowl was answer enough.

"You did your autopsy Saturday morning. I finished with my skeletal analysis around four Saturday afternoon. The body must have been moved after that."

Tight nod.

My mind sorted through possibilities.

"It couldn't be a funeral-home mix-up. They don't do pickups on Sundays."

"And everyone else is accounted for."

"When did you notice the John Doe missing?"

"About an hour ago. I went into the cooler to collect a gunshot case."

"Was anyone in here over the weekend? Cleaning crew? Maintenance? Repair service?"

Larabee shook his head.

"Joe was on duty?"

"Yes."

When alone on night shift, Joe sleeps on a cot in the back of the men's room. Closed door. Bad ears. An army could march through and he wouldn't hear a thing.

"Is it possible someone broke in?" I asked.

"And stole a corpse?" Larabee sounded beyond skeptical.

"It happens." Defensive.

"Body snatchers would have needed to disarm the security system."

"And tinkering is supposed to trigger an alarm."

"*Supposed* to." Larabee's tone affirmed his cynicism about modern technology.

"Let's check for signs of forced entry."

We did.

Found none.

"This is insane." I was at a loss for more ideas.

"There's something I should tell you." Larabee and I were standing beside the roll-on scale at the receiving dock.

I looked a question at him.

"Let's go to my office." Now the ME sounded nervous.

We entered and Larabee closed the door. He sat behind his desk. I took a chair facing him.

"As I was leaving on Saturday, I got tagged by the FBI."

I took a wild guess. "Special Agents Williams and Randall?"

Larabee glanced at a paper lying on his blotter. "Yes. They were asking about the John Doe."

"What did you tell them?"

"I shared my autopsy findings and your bio profile. I said I'd collected samples for tox analysis and warned that a final report would take time."

"And?" I asked.

"Williams offered to deliver the samples personally. Said he'd try to get them bumped up the queue. I called the Charlotte field office. The two are legit, so it seemed kosher to me. I asked Joe to handle it." Larabee's brows dipped sharply. "A report faxed in around ten this morning."

"You're kidding." I was astonished. Normally it takes weeks, even months, to get lab results.

"My mention of pulmonary lesions and edema coupled with gut ulceration and hemorrhage must have triggered something for Williams. He had my specimens driven to the CDC and fast-tracked through immunochromatographic analysis."

Larabee referred to a type of immunoassay, a chemical test designed to detect organic substances. I wasn't an expert but knew a little about the process.

Short course.

Antigens are molecules recognized by our immune systems as outsiders. Could be toxins, enzymes, viruses, bacteria. A transplanted lung that looks wrong. Antibodies are proteins that attack and neutralize these foreign invaders.

Antibodies are present normally in our bodies or are produced in response to specific antigens. This is known as an immune reaction.

Immunoassay tests are based on the ability of antibodies to bind to specific antigens. Threat X triggers response Y. Gotcha! In forensics, the technique is used to identify and quantify unknown organic compounds in samples. This antibody reacted, so this substance must be present.

I waited.

"The test indicated the presence of ricin in two of my samples."

"Ricin?" I couldn't keep the surprise from my voice.

Ricin is a naturally occurring toxin derived from the beans of the castor-oil plant, *Ricinus communis*. One of the deadliest poisons known, it can cause death in thirty-six to seventy-two hours after exposure.

In addition to binding specificity, the other key feature of an immunoassay is that the test produces a measurable signal in response to a particular antigen-antibody hookup. In the case of ricin, a green light is given off. That's the chromatographic part of the long term.

The green light is measured by a spectrophotometer or similar piece of equipment. Basically, the brighter the glow, the more ricin there is in a sample.

Larabee nodded.

"That explains the fast turnaround time," I said.

In the past few years immunoassay testing has become quick and simple. There are now kits for the detection of ricin, anthrax, plague, tularemia, and many other biotoxins.

"But it doesn't explain how ricin got into our John Doe," Larabee said.

"That's the stuff that killed Georgi Markov." I referred to a Bulgarian journalist murdered in London in 1978.

"I doubt our John Doe was ass-stabbed with an umbrella."

"Markov was jabbed in the leg," I said.

Larabee gave me a look.

I thought a moment. If ingested, inhaled, or injected, ricin causes nausea, muscle spasm, severe diarrhea, convulsion, coma, and ultimately, death.

"Ricin poisoning would fit your autopsy finding," I said.

"And would explain the interest of the feds." The phone rang. Larabee ignored it. "The military has been studying ricin for years. They've tried coating bullets and artillery

83

rounds with it. They've tested it in cluster bombs. I did a quick check after this thing came in."

He flapped a hand at the fax. "Ricin is listed as a schedule-one controlled substance under both the 1972 Biological Weapons Convention and the 1997 Chemical Weapons Convention."

"But other toxins are much more effective bioweapons. Anthrax, for example. You'd need tons of ricin compared to a kilo of anthrax." I'd read that somewhere. "And ricin breaks down relatively quickly. Anthrax spores can remain lethal for decades."

"The average person can't lay his hands on anthrax. Or botulin. Or tetanus. The castor bean plant is a friggin' ornamental. Any loon can grow it in his garden."

I started to comment. Larabee wasn't finished.

"Close to a million tons of castor beans are processed every year. About five percent of that ends up as waste containing high concentrations of ricin."

"So how'd our John Doe die of ricin poisoning?" I asked.

"And end up in a barrel of asphalt in a landfill in Concord?"

"And where the hell is he?"

Without a word, Larabee put his desk phone on speaker and jabbed the buttons. Ten beeps, a buzzy ring, then Hawkins's voice answered.

"Can't survive without me, eh, Doc?"

"Sorry to bother you on your day off." Taut.

"No bother."

"This may sound odd. But we can't find the body from the landfill."

There was no response. In the background I could hear the cadence of a televised baseball game.

"You there?"

"I'm here. Just trying to figure the question."

"MCME 227-11. The man in the asphalt."

"I know who you mean."

"Dr. Brennan and I can't locate him."

"'Course you can't. He's gone."

"Gone?" Larabee was twisting and untwisting the receiver cord with his free hand.

"A funeral home came and got him."

"I didn't sign for release of the body," Larabee snapped.

Joe answered with silence.

"Sorry. I just want to understand."

"The FBI agent. I forget his name—"

"Williams."

"Yeah. Williams. You said give him what he needs. That's what I did."

"Meaning?"

"He took your tox samples on Saturday. Called Sunday, said a van was coming, that I should prepare the John Doe for transport. Took all the X-rays, too."

"The body left the morgue yesterday?"

"The paperwork's there, Doc."

Larabee's eyes met mine. "Thanks, Joe."

Larabee cradled the receiver.

Together we hurried to Mrs. Flowers's station.

"Did Joe leave a transfer form yesterday?"

Mrs. Flowers flipped through her in-box, pulled a paper, and handed it to Larabee.

"What the hell's SD Conveyance?" Larabee spoke as he read.

"Never heard of it," I said.

"Special Agent Williams signed for the body."

"Not a funeral home?"

"No." Larabee thrust the paper my way.

Behind us, Mrs. Flowers had gone very quiet. I knew she was listening.

"This is outrageous. The medical examiner must operate independently. I can't have government agents waltzing into my morgue and confiscating remains."

Sudden synapse.

"You said the government is interested in ricin as a potential bioweapon."

"So?"

"Ted Raines works for the CDC."

"The guy who went missing last week?"

I nodded.

Catching my implication, Larabee began pacing.

Mrs. Flowers watched, eyes shifting like a spectator's at a tennis match.

"Sonofabitch." Larabee's face had gone crimson.

"Don't have a heart attack," I said.

"How do I ID a body without the body? Or the X-rays?"

"Maybe the feds don't want this body identified."

We were gnawing on that when my brain cells fired up another offering.

"I cut bone plugs from the John Doe in case we decided to do DNA testing."

Larabee and I raced to the stinky room.

I checked the counter. The cabinets. The small refrigerator used for storage of specimens.

The large autopsy suite.

My office.

The shelves in the cooler.

The microscopy lab.

The bone plugs were gone.

11

I'd just returned to my office when the phone rang.

"I asked him to wait, but he wouldn't listen." Mrs. Flowers was peeved. "He never does."

Heavy footsteps alerted me to the source of her irritation.

"It's all right," I said.

I was replacing the receiver when Slidell appeared in my doorway. Today's jacket was tan polyester. The tie was black, the shirt orange.

Without invitation, Slidell entered and dropped into a chair.

"Please come in," I said.

"What's eating you?" Two scuffed loafers shot my way. The carroty socks matched the carroty shirt. Nice.

"Mrs. Flowers prefers to announce visitors," I said.

"She'll get over it."

"She sees it as part of her job."

"I've got places to be."

First the missing body. Now Slidell.

I drew a calming breath.

"Williams and Randall confiscated the John Doe."

Slidell drew in his feet and leaned forward at the waist. "No shit."

"No shit."

"Where'd they take him?"

"That's unclear. Larabee is phoning the FBI now."

"Any idea why?"

I told Slidell about the ricin.

"They thinking terrorism?"

I raised both palms. Who knows?

"How 'bout you?"

I debated. Share my conjecture? Why not.

"Ted Raines is employed by the CDC," I said. "Raines came to Charlotte for Race Week and vanished. Shortly thereafter a body turned up in a landfill smack next to the Speedway. That body is contaminated with a biotoxin."

Slidell's eyes narrowed in thought. Then, "How about this? Cale Lovette hung with right-wing loonies. Lovette disappeared in 'ninety-eight, the year anthrax threats started dropping into mailboxes at women's clinics. The same year Barnett Slepian was murdered."

"The abortion doctor."

"Yeah."

Not bad, Skinny.

"I think the landfill John Doe is too old to be Lovette," I said.

"You sure?"

"No. Age indicators vary from person to person. Lovette could fall at the extreme upper end of his chronological range."

For a few moments no one spoke. Finally Slidell placed his forearms on his thighs, leaned on them, and looked up at me from below puffy lids. The black tie dangled between his knees.

"Tracked down Grady Winge."

It took me a moment to make the connection. "The man who saw Cindi and Cale leave the Speedway the night they vanished."

"Yeah. Winge hasn't blazed what you'd call a fiery career path."

"Meaning?"

"The mope's still at the same job he had back then. I'm heading to Concord now."

I opened the drawer and grabbed my purse.

"Let's go," I said.

The Charlotte Motor Speedway accommodates a whole lot more than racing. In addition to the 1.5-mile quad oval track, the two-thousand-plus-acre complex contains grandstand seats, food concessions, restroom facilities, and campgrounds for the masses. The affluent enjoy luxury suites, a fifty-two-unit condo complex, and the Speedway Club, an exclusive dining and entertainment facility.

For drivers, there is a twenty-thousand-square-foot Sprint Cup garage area, a 2.25-mile road course, and a .6-mile karting layout in the infield. A quarter-mile oval utilizes part of the front stretch and pit road, and a one-fifth-mile oval sits outside turn three.

The seven-story Smith Tower is home to ticket and corporate offices, and a small industrial park houses motor-sports-related businesses.

The Speedway grounds also contain a natural wildlife habitat. And, of course, the landfill.

Grady Winge tended flowers throughout all but the latter two areas.

Given that it was Race Week, traffic was reasonable, and

Slidell and I made it to Concord in forty minutes. A young man met us outside the Smith Tower and offered to take us by golf cart to the infield. His name badge said Harley.

Slidell stated his preference to drive.

Harley explained the impossibility of maneuvering the Taurus through the throngs of people jamming the grounds. Slidell argued. Smiling but firm, Harley restated his willingness to transport us.

I resolved the issue by hopping onto the cart's backseat, the rearward-orienting position, so Slidell could at least face forward. Snorting in disgust, Skinny deposited his substantial bulk in front. Harley popped the brake, wove through the crowd, then plunged downward into the underground tunnel leading into the infield.

At midpoint, I glanced over my shoulder toward the front seat. Slidell was haloed by sunlight pouring through the opening at the tunnel's far end. One beefy hand gripped the upright as though bracing for passage through a 20-G centrifuge.

The infield campgrounds were crammed with the tents and motor homes of the devoted. Fans sweated on lawn chairs and atop trailers, many wearing far too little clothing and needing far more sunblock. Others crowded picnic tables outside concession stands, chowing on corn dogs, burgers, fries, and 'cue.

Harley glided to a stop beside a gray and blue building bearing the words MEDIA CENTER. Enormous haulers sat side by side in a fenced area opposite the building's main entrance.

Alighting, I heard Harley tell Slidell that the haulers belonged to Nationwide drivers. Not interested or not comprehending, Slidell offered no response.

Entering the Media Center was like stepping from a blast oven into a cooler. Harley indicated a man seated at the farthest in a cluster of round plastic tables off to the right. "That's Grady Winge."

Winge was enormous, perhaps six two, three hundred pounds, with thin brown hair tied into a pony at the nape of his neck. His khaki shirt was mottled with soil, its underarms darkened by large half-moons.

"Here's my cell phone number." Harley handed me a card. "Call when you're finished." Flashing a smile, he headed off into the building.

Slidell and I took a moment to observe our target. Winge's face was tanned and creased from hours in the sun, making it hard to pinpoint age. His cap lay on the table, sweat-stained to the belly of the number 3 centered over its brim. A cross hung from a chain around his neck.

In addition to size, the man's other striking feature was his stillness. Winge sat with fingers laced, eyes down, perfectly motionless.

Slidell and I approached. "Grady Winge?"

When Winge glanced up, Slidell badged him.

Winge looked at the shield but said nothing.

Slidell and I sat in the plastic chairs facing Winge.

"You know why we're here." Slidell laid it out as statement, not question.

Winge said nothing.

"I see you're a Dale Earnhardt fan." I gestured at the cap.

"Yes, ma'am."

"He was the best." I wasn't really sure.

"Yes, ma'am."

"Cindi Gamble and Cale Lovette disappeared from this Speedway on October 14, 1998." Slidell was in no mood for small talk. "According to the file, you were the last person to see them that day."

Again Winge offered nothing.

"You stated that Gamble and Lovette argued with a man around six that evening. The three then drove off."

"That's right."

"Did you recognize the man?"

"I'd seen him around."

"Are you sure the couple was Gamble and Lovette?"

A moment passed. Then, "I'm sure it was Lovette."

"How's that?"

"Lovette worked here."

"You ever see Lovette outside of the track?"

Winge shrugged. "I mighta."

"And where was that?"

"A place called the Double Shot."

"The Double Shot Tap in Mooresville?"

I figured Slidell knew the name from Rinaldi's notes.

"I had my trailer up by the lake, so I'd catch a beer there now and again."

"Lovette was a regular?"

"He'd drink with his buddies."

"Militia types."

Winge said nothing.

"Well?" Gruff.

"Well what?"

"Give me an answer."

"Give me a question."

"Don't screw with me, asshole."

"They mighta been."

"Let me ask you, Grady. You saddle up with the posse?"

Winge's Adam's apple bobbed. A moment passed. "I'm a different man now."

"You're a prince," Slidell said. "How about some names?"

"There was a guy named J.D. Another called Buster. Maybe an E-Man. That's all I remember."

"Good start. Real names? Last names?"

"J. D. Danner. That's the only one I ever caught."

Slidell wiggled his fingers in a "give me more" gesture.

"J.D. was the boss," Winge offered.

"What's that mean?"

"He said what to do."

"What did J.D. say to do?"

Winge dropped his chin and clasped the cross suspended from his neck. I could see dandruff coating the swath of shiny scalp bisecting his hair.

Noting the man's discomfort, I raised a silencing hand. Slidell sighed but yielded.

"Mr. Winge, we think something bad might have happened to Cale and Cindi."

Winge raised his eyes to mine.

"Did the Patriot Posse have a political agenda?" I asked.

"What's that mean?"

"When you met, what did you talk about?"

"Hating black people, Jews, people in Washington. Blaming our problems on everybody but our own selves."

"Did you ever consider violence?"

Winge's eyes took on a guarded look. He didn't answer.

"Did you ever discuss blowing things up? Setting fires? Planting poison?"

"No way."

"Do you know where we can find J. D. Danner?"

"No."

"Do you still see him at the Double Shot?"

Winge shook his head. "I took Jesus into my heart." His head dipped as his lips spoke the name. "The Lord don't approve of liquor. When I cast out Satan, I quit going to bars."

"Mr. Winge, do you think Cindi and Cale left on their own?"

The massive shoulders rose, then fell.

"Do you think J.D. and his posse had anything to do with their disappearance?"

Winge overshook his head. "No, ma'am. I don't."

Again I switched course.

"In your statement, you said Cale and Cindi got into a car."

"A 'sixty-five Petty-blue Mustang with a lime-green decal on the passenger-side windshield."

"Had you seen the car before?"

"No. But that was one sweet ride. And that color. I met Richard Petty a couple of times. Primo racer. Cool dude."

"Can you describe the driver?"

"Nothing special. Medium height, dark hair. Not real tall, not real short. I suppose he could have been black."

Out of ideas, I posed the same question I'd posed to Williams and Randall. "What do you think happened to Cale and Cindi?"

"I pray to the sweet Lord Jesus their souls found peace."

12

"Prick just wasted an hour of my life."

"The time wasn't wasted."

Slidell and I were back in the Taurus. He was whacking the AC so hard I was sure he'd break one of the levers.

"Maybe Danner still drinks at the Double Shot."

"Life should be that easy."

A rivulet of sweat broke from Slidell's hairline as he yanked his mobile from his belt and punched in digits.

In minutes we had an answer. The Double Shot was still pouring from noon until two a.m. daily.

Mooresville edges up to a meandering man-made body of water called Lake Norman. Situated roughly twenty-five miles from Charlotte, in Iredell County, the little hamlet is home to twenty-five thousand citizens and a buffalo ranch.

Along with the surrounding towns of Huntersville, Cornelius, Kannapolis, and Concord, Mooresville is also home to a truckload of NASCAR team shops. Bobby Labonte. Martin Truex, Jr. Brian Vickers. Thus the burg's self-selected moniker: Race City, U.S.A.

We found the Double Shot on a narrow strip of two-lane a mile and a half east of I-77. Located on neither the lakeshore nor the interstate, the place in all likelihood depended on the business of locals who were regulars.

Curb appeal was definitely not the draw. The building was a 1950s-style ranch with red siding turned salmon by years of sun. DOUBLE SHOT had been hand-lettered on the highway-facing wall sometime this century, then never touched up.

Four motorcycles formed a line outside the front entrance. Two pickups sat at careless angles in the gravel lot.

I must watch too much TV. When Slidell and I entered, I expected every eye to swing our way. Didn't happen.

To the left, two men played pool while a third watched, legs straddling, arms draping a back-turned chrome and vinyl chair. At the bar, a pair of beer drinkers continued their conversation. At the opposite end, another customer focused on his burger.

Painted windows kept the Double Shot's interior dim. Overhead fans created a jumpy, surreal effect by dancing the neon oranges, reds, and blues glowing from wall-mounted beer signs.

As my eyes adjusted, my mind logged detail.

Three wooden booths ran the wall to the right of the entrance. A pointing-finger sign indicated that toilets lay somewhere beyond the booths.

Straight ahead, tables filled floor space fronting the bar. Behind it, a gray-bearded man washed mugs by moving them on a brush fixed upright beside the sink.

Every patron was male. Three were heavily tattooed. Four badly needed a trip to the barber. Two had shaved heads. Despite the ninety-degree heat, all wore jeans and heavy leather boots.

Slidell's eyes probed every shadow as we crossed to the bar. The tension in his shoulders told me he was locked and loaded.

Though Gray Beard never raised his head, I knew he was tracking us. Slidell and I stopped in front of him and waited.

Gray Beard continued his piston-cycle moves with the glassware.

"You want I should flash the shield, impress your upscale clientele?" Slidell said, not all that quietly.

"They know who you are." Gray Beard set down a mug. Picked up and started cleaning another.

"That so?"

"They can smell cop."

"Look at me, dipshit."

Gray Beard's eyes rolled up. In the gloom, their whites looked urine-yellow.

"We can chat here," Slidell said. "Or we can chat someplace nice and official. And while we're gone, I can have every inspector north of Aiken checking this dump out."

"How can I help you, Officer?" Faux-polite.

"How about we start with your name."

"Posey. Kermit Posey."

"That a joke?"

"I don't joke."

"This your joint?"

Posey nodded.

"I'm interested in a guy name of J. D. Danner."

Posey set the mug beside others sitting on a blue-and-white-checkered towel.

"I'm waiting, asshole." Slidell's tone was dangerous. "But not very long."

"This look like a place folks trade business cards?"

"J. D. Danner."

"I might have heard the name."

"I have a witness says Danner was a regular here back in 'ninety-eight."

"That was a long time ago."

"Says Danner rolled with a group called themselves the Patriot Posse."

Posey hiked one shoulder. So what? Could be? Who knows?

Reaching across the bar, Slidell grabbed Posey's beard and pulled the man's face to within inches of his own. "Having trouble hearing me, Kermit? That better?"

Posey gagged and braced both hands on the bar. To either side, conversation and burger consumption halted. Behind us, pool balls stopped clicking, and the banter went still.

"Danner still enjoying a brew now and then?"

Posey nodded as best he could, then a wet sound rose from his throat, half gag, half cough.

"Where can I find him?"

"I only heard rumors."

"Indulge me," Slidell said.

"Word is he lives in Cornelius." Posey cough-gagged again. "Honest to God, that's all I know."

Slidell released his grip.

Posey tumbled backward, fingers clawing the counter for purchase. The towel flew. Mugs hit the floor in an explosion of glass.

Slidell chin-cocked the shards.

"Saved you some washing."

Back in the Taurus, Slidell again attacked the AC. While he phoned headquarters, I dialed the MCME.

Larabee told me that the landfill John Doe had been confiscated under a provision of the *Medical Examiner/Coroner's Guide for Contaminated Deceased Body Management.*

"Because of the ricin," I said.

"Which is bullshit. The ricin toxin can't spread from person to person. You've got to breathe or eat the stuff."

Or get jabbed with an umbrella.

Slidell barked something, then tossed his phone onto the dash.

"Where was the body taken?" I asked Larabee.

"The FBI is stonewalling on that. But I'll find out. I'll goddamn well find out."

Slidell positioned the mock Ray-Bans, clicked his seat belt, and shifted into gear.

"Keep me in the loop," I said, then disconnected.

Gravel flew from our tires as Slidell gunned from the lot.

"Get an address for Danner?" I asked.

"They're working on it."

Knowing Slidell would share when ready, I held my tongue. It was pointless to press.

A minute later he was ready.

"Lynn Marie Hobbs attended NC State from 'ninety-eight until 2001. Didn't graduate. Married a guy named Dean Nolan in 2002, now goes by Lynn Nolan."

Static spit from the radio. Slidell reached out and twisted the knob.

"After leaving school, Nolan returned to the old homestead. Works for an outfit called the Cryerton Respiratory Research Institute. CRRI. Headquarters is in some sort of industrial park near China Grove."

I thought a moment. "The Southeast Regional Research Park?"

"That's it."

China Grove is a stone's throw from Kannapolis.

"I assume we're heading there now?"

"Eeyuh."

"Is Nolan expecting us?"

"I figure a surprise might liven things up."

"What does CRRI do?"

"Call me crazy, but I'm guessing they spend a lot of time thinking about lungs."

Pointedly, I turned my face toward the window.

Corn rows marched to the horizon, dark and shimmery in the afternoon heat. Above them, a red-tailed hawk looped lazy circles low in the sky.

Instead of returning to I-77, Slidell cut east on NC-152. Just before China Grove, he made three right turns, then a left onto a wide paved road.

No cornfields here. Wild flowers as far as the eye could see. A veritable Monet ocean of color.

A quarter mile up the blacktop, redbrick walls stretched to each shoulder, and large iron gates blocked access to manicured grounds beyond. A stone plaque identified the Southeast Regional Research Park.

Slidell stopped at the guardhouse and lowered his window. A uniformed young man emerged with a clipboard. "May I help you?"

"We're looking for Lynn Nolan."

"Yes, sir. I'll check the list."

"We aren't on it."

"I'm sorry, but—"

Slidell held out his badge.

The man studied it earnestly. "Do you have a warrant?"

"Why? Something going on here gonna cause problems?"

"I'll have to call for clearance."

"No," Slidell said. "You won't. Nolan works for CRRI. Where do I find her?"

"Building Three. Second floor."

"You have a real special day." Slidell hit a button and his window hummed up.

The man retreated, the gates opened, and Slidell drove through.

The Southeast Regional Research Park looked like a small college campus in Mississippi. Brick buildings fronted by broad steps, Greco-Roman pillars, porticos, and pediments. Covered parking garages. Well-groomed gardens. Boisterously green grass which seemed to stretch for several hundred acres. Small lake complete with ducks, geese, and a swan.

Yet nothing stirred. The effect was like one of those disaster movies in which a virus destroys life but leaves the hardscape intact.

Building 3 was a four-story number on Progress Avenue. Flanking both sides were half-completed foundations, suggesting progress had been less than desired.

Ignoring the no-parking signs, Slidell pulled to the curb. We got out and entered Building 3 through tinted glass doors.

The lobby was all gleaming rosewood and marble, with a futuristic stone sculpture parked in the center. A directory verified that CRRI was located in 204.

A spotless elevator took us to the second floor. There the decorator's palette had been labeled something like sand or wheat. Beige walls, beige trim, beige carpet, beige chairs, each shade just a hair off the others. The only color came from framed black and whites with highlighted details.

A woman's red lips. A green umbrella. A blue and yellow tail dangling from a kite.

Room 204 was halfway down on the right.

A woman occupied a desk directly opposite and facing the door. She was tiny, with caramel eyes, sun-bronzed skin, and long brown hair spilling from a barrette atop her head.

When we entered, the woman's eyes widened. A manicured hand flew to her mouth. "Are you really going to arrest me?"

So much for the guard not announcing our presence.

13

The woman watched us cross to the desk, her body rigid with apprehension.

"Lynn Nolan?" Not a bark, but close.

Nolan nodded, lavender-tipped fingers still pressed to her lips.

Slidell flipped his badge. "Got some questions about Cindi Gamble."

Nolan's eyes now went impossibly wide.

"You remember Cindi Gamble?"

Nolan nodded again.

"You want we should do this standing?"

The hand left Nolan's mouth and fluttered toward two desk-facing chairs.

As we sat, Nolan's gaze flicked to me, but she said nothing.

While Slidell started the interview, I looked around.

The furnishings were standard reception-room walnut and tweed, including Nolan's desk, our chairs, and a love seat centered on the back wall. Fronting the love seat was a coffee table heaped with magazines. Every title contained the terms "air," "atmosphere," or "energy." As in the corridor, beige ruled.

Above Nolan's head, a mural displayed the CRRI logo, a stylized windmill with greenery twining the central post. Three words circled the blades: GENOMICS. PROTEOMICS. METABOLOMICS.

"You the receptionist?" Slidell produced his spiral, more for effect than note-taking, I suspected.

Another nod.

"What goes on here?"

"Research."

Slidell stared at Nolan. She stared back.

"Why am I getting the impression you're not enjoying our visit?"

"Into air pollution."

By my count, that brought Nolan's total word count to four.

"Research for who?" Slidell positioned his pen.

"Industrial consortia, clinical trials companies, R and D firms, consulting groups." The answer sounded rote. Nolan had obviously given the spiel before.

Slidell jotted something, then got to the point.

"You attended A. L. Brown High with Cindi Gamble?"

Nolan nodded again. She was very good at it.

"Tell me about her."

"Like what?"

"Dig deep, Miss Nolan."

"It's Mrs."

"Uh-huh."

"I hardly knew her. Like, Cindi wanted to drive race cars. That wasn't my thing."

"But you were friends."

"Just at school. Sometimes we, like, ate lunch together."

Nolan was gouging a cuticle on one thumb with the acrylic nail on the other. I wondered why a visit from the cops was unnerving her so badly.

"And?" Slidell prodded.

"And then she disappeared."

"That's it?"

"We didn't hang out senior year."

"Why was that?"

"Like, her boyfriend was a jerk."

"Cale Lovette."

Major-league eye roll. "The guy gave me the creeps."

"Why was that?"

"The whole shaved-head-and-tattoo thing. Gross."

"That what turned you off? Lovette's sense of style?"

Vertical lines dented the bridge of Nolan's nose. Then, "He and his psycho-loser friends were always talking about guns. They thought it was cool to crawl around in the woods and play soldier. I thought it was dumb."

"That it?"

"They had all these weird ideas."

"Like what?"

"Like the Japanese blew up that building in Oklahoma. I mean, how dumb is that? Oh, and the United Nations was going to take over the government. There were people, like, setting up concentration camps in national parks."

"In your statement back in 'ninety-eight, you said you overheard Lovette discussing poison with someone."

"Another gross-o."

"Bald and inked?"

"No. Old and hairy."

"Did you know the guy?"

"No."

"You stated that Lovette and his buddy were talking about poisoning something."

Nolan's eyes dropped to the cuticle. Which was now bleeding. "I could have got it wrong. I wasn't, like, *trying* to eavesdrop. But they were pretty—" Nolan circled both hands in the air. "What's that word for when people, you know, gesture a lot?"

"Animated?" I suggested.

"Yeah. Animated. I passed them when I went to the ladies'."

"What were they saying?" Slidell.

"Something about poisoning a system. And an ax or something."

"Where did this conversation take place?"

"A really lame bar up by Lake Norman."

"Name?"

"I don't remember."

"Why were you there?"

"Cindi wanted to hook up with Cale, but she knew her parents would flip out, you know, about her being in a bar. She told them there was a school party and talked me into going along to back up the lie. The place was, like, scuzz city."

"This was a couple of months before Lovette and Gamble went missing."

"It was summer. That's all I remember."

"You think Lovette and his buddies were plotting something illegal?"

"Like robbing a bank?" The caramel eyes were now perfectly round.

"Let's think here, Lynn. Poison?" Nolan's dim-wittedness was wearing on Slidell.

"I don't know. Maybe. Cale was mean as a snake."

"Tell me about that."

"Cindi showed up at school one time with bruises on her arms. Like fingerprints, you know?" Nolan was becoming more expressive, using her hands for emphasis. "She never said so, but I think Cale was smacking her around."

Slidell rotated one hand. Go on.

"Sometimes he talked to her like she was stupid. Cindi wasn't stupid. She was in STEM. Those people were all, like, scary smart." A lavender nail jabbed the air. "There's someone might know more than me. Maddy Padgett. She was in STEM, too. Maddy was totally into cars and engines. I think she and Cindi were tight."

Slidell scribbled a note. Then, "Why'd Gamble put up with Lovette treating her like crap?"

"She loved him." As though the question confused her.

"You think she went off with him?"

"Huh-uh."

"What's your take?"

Nolan looked from Slidell to me, then back. Her response was delivered with breathy affect. "I think Cale killed her, then ran away."

Humid air pressed our skin as Slidell and I walked back to the Taurus. The sun was a silver-white disc in the sky. An anemic breeze carried the smell of hot brick and mowed grass.

"Brain power of a newt."

I suspected Slidell was underestimating the amphibian. Didn't say so.

"What was that shit above her head?"

I wasn't sure if he meant Nolan's updo or the logo. I went

with the latter. "Genomics is the study of the genomes of organisms."

"Like figuring out their DNA?"

"Yes. Proteomics is the study of proteins. Metabolomics is the study of cellular processes." Oversimplified but close enough.

"How's all that fit in with air pollution?"

"I'll Google CRRI."

Slidell and I got into the car. The heat was worthy of Death Valley.

"What do you think of Nolan's theory?" I asked after securing my belt.

"That Lovette killed Gamble? The thought crossed my mind."

"Really?"

Slidell didn't elaborate until he'd turned the key, maxed the air-conditioning, and unwrapped and popped a stick of Juicy Fruit into his mouth.

"In his notes, Eddie mentions a guy name of Owen Poteat." Slidell made a U-ey toward the main drag. "Back in 'ninety-eight, Poteat claimed he saw Lovette at the Charlotte airport on the twenty-fourth of October."

The implication was clear.

"That was ten days after Lovette and Gamble disappeared from the Speedway. How did Poteat know it was Lovette?"

"He'd seen a photo on a flyer. Said the tats and bald head caught his attention."

"Was Poteat considered credible?"

"The task force thought so. According to Eddie, Poteat's statement played heavy into the conclusion that Lovette and Gamble took off."

"What about Cindi?" I asked.

"What about her?"

"Did Poteat see her at the airport with Lovette?"

"Apparently he wasn't so sure. But here's the thing."

Slidell flipped a wave at the guard as we exited the gates. The young man watched us roll through but didn't wave back.

"At the back of the notebook, Eddie had a page marked with big question marks."

"Meaning?"

"Meaning he had questions." Slidell reached out and smacked the AC control with the heel of one hand.

Easy, Brennan.

"Questions about Poteat?" I asked oh-so-precisely.

"Who the hell knows? For that entry, he used one of his codes. Means nothing to me." Slidell yanked his spiral from a shirt pocket and tossed it to me. "I copied the stuff into there."

ME/SC 2X13G-529 OTP FU

Wi-Fr 6–8

When hurried or feeling the need for discretion, Rinaldi used a form of shorthand known only to him. The cryptic notations were typical.

"Maine and South Carolina?" I guessed, looking at the longer entry.

Slidell shrugged.

I played with the alphanumeric combo. "Could it be a license plate?"

"I'll run it."

"FU probably means follow up."

I played some more. Came up blank.

"Can I have this?"

"Yeah, sure."

I tore the page free and slipped it into my purse. Then, "Who is Owen Poteat?"

"I'll know soon."

I settled back and closed my eyes. The heat and the car's motion acted like drugs. I was dropping off when my mobile sounded.

Joe Hawkins.

I clicked on.

"Hey, Joe." Sluggish.

"Forensics called with a prelim on the goop from the barrel. Good old asphalt, just like we thought."

"Not very useful."

"Maybe no, maybe yes. The sample contained an additive called Rosphalt, a synthetic dry-mix material made by Royston. Provides waterproofing, skid resistance, protects against rutting and shoving, thermal fatigue cracking, that kind of thing."

"Uh-huh." Stifling a yawn.

"Rosphalt comes in three types. One's used mainly for roadways and tunnels, another's used on airport runways. You still there?"

"I'm here." Though struggling to stay awake.

"Your sample contained the third type, R50/Rx. That one's used mostly by motor speedways."

My brain reengaged. "At the Charlotte Motor Speedway?"

"Knew you'd ask, so I gave a call out there. The track has some pretty steep banking. What with the sun and cars screaming around the curves, the asphalt can heat up, go liquid, and sink right down. They use Rosphalt to provide better holding power."

"I'll be damned. So the asphalt in the barrel probably came from the Speedway."

"Seems logical to me. The track's right there."

"Thanks, Joe."

I disconnected and told Slidell. "The Rosphalt connects the landfill John Doe to the track." I was totally pumped.

"Whaddya saying? The victim was killed at the Speedway, stuffed in a barrel, sealed in, and dumped at the landfill?"

"Why not? Thirty-five-gallon oil cans are common at speedways."

While Slidell was gnawing on that theory, my phone sounded again. This time it was Larabee.

"These assholes have gone too far!"

"Which assholes?"

"They won't get away with this."

"Get away with what?"

"The goddamn FBI torched our John Doe!"

14

The buzzing in my phone was so agitated that Slidell kept glancing my way. Again and again I gestured his eyes back to the road.

Peppered with expletives, the story came out.

Through multiple calls, many threats, and the intervention of the chief ME in Chapel Hill, Larabee had finally pried loose information on the whereabouts of MCME 227-11. Since the presence of ricin suggested the possibility of bioterrorism, the landfill John Doe had been confiscated under a provision of the Patriot Act and taken to a lab in Atlanta. There the body had been re-autopsied and new samples collected.

Far from standard protocol but understandable.

Then the bombshell.

Due to an unfortunate combination of circumstances, including a mix-up in paperwork, understaffing, and an error on the part of an inexperienced tech, instead of back to the cooler, the landfill John Doe had accidentally been sent for cremation.

Larabee was livid. Before disconnecting, he threatened

complaints to the governor, the Department of Justice, the director of the FBI, the secretary of Homeland Security, the White House, maybe the pope.

I decided it was a bad time to mention the Rosphalt.

As Slidell maneuvered through rush-hour traffic, I told him about the fate of the John Doe.

"That smell right to you?" I asked.

"As right as a barrel of week-old fish."

Slidell said nothing further until we were parked beside my car at the MCME. Then he grasped the wheel and rotated toward me. "What's your take, Doc?"

I ticked off points on my fingers.

"A couple vanishes in 1998. Family and associates disagree with a task force finding that the two left voluntarily. The missing couple has ties to and is last seen at a motor speedway. Years later a body turns up in a barrel of asphalt. That barrel is discovered in a landfill adjacent to said speedway, in a sector and layer dating from the late nineties to 2005."

I moved to my other hand.

"The asphalt in the barrel contains an additive commonly used at speedways. An autopsy finds that the body is contaminated with ricin, a poison once favored by anti-government extremists. The male member of the missing couple belonged to a right-wing militia. When the ricin is reported to the FBI, the body is confiscated and destroyed."

Slidell was silent for so long, I was certain he was about to blow me off. He didn't.

"You're thinking the landfill John Doe is connected to the Gamble-Lovette disappearance?"

I nodded.

"How?"

"I don't know."

"Who was the stiff?"

"I don't know."

"Lovette?"

"The age indicators are off, but I can't rule him out."

"What about this guy Raines from Atlanta?"

"The barrel looked way too old. And the sector it came from doesn't fit with a recent body dump."

"But your voice is telling me you can't rule him out, either."

"No. I can't."

Again Slidell went quiet. Then, "Maybe Cindi Gamble's baby brother isn't crackers after all."

"About a cover-up back in 'ninety-eight?"

Slidell ran a hand over his jaw. Did it again. Then, "Those fucking suits picked the wrong cop to screw with."

"What do you propose?"

"First off, another heart-to-heart with your NASCAR buddy."

I was approaching my kitchen door, lugging a Harris Teeter bag, when a silver RX-8 turned in to the circle drive at Sharon Hall. Thinking it was probably my ex, and not thrilled with the prospect of another go-round concerning Summer, I paused.

The Mazda looped the front of the manor house and headed toward me. As it neared, I could see the driver's head in silhouette. Oddly pear-shaped, its crown barely cleared the wheel.

Definitely not Pete.

Curious and a little wary, I watched the car pull to the same piece of curb occupied by Williams and Randall on Saturday.

The man who got out had a pompadour that brought his height to maybe five-four. Grecian Formula had turned the do a dead-lemur brown.

The man's clothes looked expensive. Ice-green silk shirt. Tommy Bahama linen pants. Softer-than-a-newborn's-bum leather loafers. Armani sunglasses perched on a hawklike nose.

"Good evening, Dr. Brennan." The man proffered a hand sporting a sapphire the size of Birdie's paw. "J. D. Danner."

"Do I know you, sir?"

"Word is you know *of* me." Despite the smile, Danner had a hostile, intimidating air.

Ping.

"You were an associate of Cale Lovette. A member of the Patriot Posse."

"I was commander of the posse, ma'am."

I adjusted my grip on the groceries.

Danner took a step toward me. "May I help with that?"

"No. Thank you."

Two palms came up. "Just offering assistance."

"Do you have information about Cale Lovette or Cindi Gamble?"

"No, ma'am. Nice kids. I hope they found what they were looking for."

"And what was that?"

"Life. Liberty. Happiness. Isn't that what we're all seeking?"

"What can I do for you, Mr. Danner?"

"Get off our backs."

"Meaning?"

"The Patriot Posse took Cale Lovette under its wing. Provided support. Guidance. A family. When he vanished, we

115

were the first ones in the crosshairs." Again the insincere smile. "The posse had nothing to do with whatever happened to Lovette and his girlfriend."

"Why would Lovette need the posse's support?"

"The kid was floundering. High school dropout. Dead-end job. Estranged father. Loony-tune mother."

That was the first I'd heard of Lovette's home life.

"Making him easy prey for your conspiratorial anti-American ideology," I said.

Danner crossed his arms and spread his feet. Which were small, like the rest of him. An image of Napoleon popped in my brain.

"Back then we were undisciplined, perhaps naive in many ways. But we were far from anti-American."

"Were?"

"The Patriot Posse disbanded in 2002."

"What was the group's purpose?"

"The posse functioned as an unorganized militia."

Typical right-wing fascist-speak. In federal and state law, the term "unorganized militia" refers to the nominal manpower pool created a century ago when federal law formally abandoned compulsory militia service.

"I prefer the army, navy, air force, and marines," I said.

"The Patriot Posse was, like other organizations of its kind, equivalent to the statutory militia. It was a legal, constitutional arm of the government. But the posse was not *controlled* by the government." A diminutive finger wagged back and forth in the air. "That's the difference. The posse existed to oppose the government should it become tyrannical."

"You believe the government might become tyrannical?"

"Dr. Brennan, please. You are an intelligent woman."

"Indeed I am."

"Recent history speaks for itself. The elections of Bill Clinton and Barack Obama. The Rodney King riots. The North American Free Trade Agreement. The dozens of bills currently under consideration that would rob us of our firearms. The murders at Ruby Ridge and Waco."

"Murders."

"Of course."

"Those compounds were stockpiled with enough fire-power to take out a city."

Danner ignored that. "The government will stop at nothing to eliminate people who refuse to conform. Independent militias must exist to protect the freedoms that our founding fathers died to ensure."

Knowing argument was pointless, I switched topics. "Tell me about Cale Lovette's parents."

Danner dropped his chin. Drew a breath. Let it out through his nose. "I don't like to speak badly, but Katherine Lovette was not what you'd call a lady. She was, how should I put it? A NASCAR groupie. If you take my meaning."

"I don't."

"Some women whore themselves to rock stars. For Kitty Lovette, it was NASCAR. Owners. Drivers. Mechanics. Didn't much matter. She worked the whole circuit back in the seventies."

"Meaning she slept around." Danner's holier-than-thou attitude irritated me.

Danner nodded. "Of course she got pregnant. Named the baby after Cale Yarborough. He was winning a lot of races back then."

"Are you saying Yarborough was Cale's father?"

"No, no. Nothing like that. For years Kitty never said.

117

But the baby grew to be the spitting image of a track hangaround name of Craig Bogan. Red hair. Blue eyes. Dimpled chin. By the time he was six, the kid looked like a clone. When Kitty finally fingered Bogan, he moved in with her. But the relationship was doomed from the outset."

"How so?"

"Bogan was in his mid-twenties. But smart. Ambitious. Kitty hadn't seen thirty in quite some time. And she—" Danner gave a tight shake of his head. "Well, enough said."

"How did Kitty support herself?"

"Sold herbs and vegetables grown at her house. Barely made enough to feed herself and the kid. Bogan actually turned the venture into a reasonable business, eventually bought it from her, house and all. Branched out. Added services like delivering produce to your door, planting flowers and shrubs in your garden."

"You knew both of them?"

Did I imagine it, or did Danner stiffen a bit at my question?

"I steered clear of Kitty."

"Go on," I said.

"By the time Cale was twelve, Kitty was heavy into booze and drugs. She finally OD'ed his freshman year of high school. Rumor was the kid found her." Again the head shake. "Things grew tense. Two years after Kitty's death, Bogan and Cale had a big throw-down, the kid dropped out of school, left home for good."

"Where did he go?"

"Cale had a passion for stock car racing, probably the only thing he got from his parents. He'd spent a lot of time hanging around dirt tracks, made some friends. Small-timers, wannabes. He mostly bunked with them."

I thought a moment. "Does Bogan still live in the area?"

Danner shrugged. Who knows?

"Tell me about Cindi."

"Girl-next-door. Real clean and shiny."

"Could you be more specific?"

"She was smart enough, if that's what you mean. And focused. All she talked about was driving NASCAR. Seemed her parents spent a lot of money on making that happen. Got her into Bandolero racing."

"Which is?"

Danner gave me a pitying look. "Entry level. A Bandolero car is built like a miniature stock car, with a tube frame and a sheet-metal cage. The driver enters through the roof. I guess you could say it falls somewhere between a kart and a car."

I must have looked lost.

"Like a kart, a Bandolero car has left-foot braking and a centrifugal clutch, so there's no gearshifting to worry about. The whole idea is simplicity and economy. Just one hundred and fifty parts make up the whole package."

"How fast do these cars go?"

"Upwards of seventy miles per hour. But they accelerate relatively slowly."

"They're for kids?"

"Most Bandolero drivers are from eight to sixteen years old, but there's no rule against older folks."

"They race on real tracks?"

"One-quarter-, three-eighths-, and four-tenths-mile ovals, some road courses, some dirt tracks. There are three divisions. Cindi Gamble raced Beginner Bandit."

I was glad Katy hadn't learned about this when she was a kid. She'd have loved roaring around at seventy miles per hour.

But I was off topic.

"Did Cindi seem committed to Lovette?" I asked.

"I'd say so."

"Where did they meet?"

"Concord Speedway, out in Midland. That's where she and Lovette spent most of their time."

"How did Lovette treat her?"

"Fair enough."

"What does that mean?"

"They came from different worlds. Cindi was a high school kid from the burbs. Lovette's mother was a dead junkie, and his father was a truck farmer. Cale wanted to race as much as Cindi did, but his folks weren't footing the bill."

"Did Lovette resent Gamble because her parents were supporting her financially?"

I got another shrug.

"Did Cindi have potential?"

"Oh, yeah. She was good. Won her share of races." Danner wagged his head. "Gal probably could have made it."

"How did you come to know Craig Bogan and Kitty Lovette?" I asked.

"In those days I went to the track now and then."

Danner glanced at his watch. Which resembled a ship's barometer.

"I hope this has been helpful. But the purpose of my visit was to reiterate what I said back in 'ninety-eight. The Patriot Posse had nothing to do with whatever became of those kids."

Danner pulled a brochure from the pocket of his Tommy Bahamas and held it out. I repositioned the bag and took it.

The thing had been printed on a home computer. A cheerful logo topped the front page, an eagle holding the American flag in its beak. Above the eagle were the words LOYALIST MOVEMENT.

Below the eagle was the phrase: DO THE RIGHT THING. Below that was a photograph showing young men standing in very straight lines. Each wore camouflage fatigues and held a rifle on his shoulder.

"I head an organization that represents almost four thousand citizens in twelve states," Danner said. "Every one is a patriot."

Every one is white and male, I thought, glancing at the faces.

"We have nothing to hide, Dr. Brennan. Didn't then. Don't now. We're proud of what we do."

"Which is?"

"We protect this country from those who would destroy it."

With that, Danner turned and walked to his car.

15

That night brought another storm. As usual, Birdie rode it out in the crook of my knee.

Tuesday morning dawned gray and soggy. Outside the kitchen window, the brick in my garden looked dark with moisture. Mist coated the spiderwebs draping the ivy and ferns.

Slidell phoned at eight. The Coca-Cola 600 was fast approaching, and issues with Stupak's car required Gamble's presence in the pit. We'd meet him at the Speedway.

By nine we were in the Taurus, rolling toward Concord. Before picking me up, Slidell had hit a Bojangles'. The air was thick with the smell of biscuits and sausage.

As he drove one-handed, I described my encounter with J. D. Danner. Slidell said he'd check out the Loyalist Movement. He'd already located Lovette's father. CB Botanicals sold flora from a Weddington property once deeded to Katherine Lovette.

Since it was Tuesday and between races, the scene at the Speedway was much calmer than on the previous Thursday. Though tents and trailers still packed the campgrounds, few fans were in evidence. I guessed a lot of moms were hitting the outlet malls, and a lot of dads were sleeping off hangovers.

Wayne Gamble met us outside the Smith Tower and drove us by car to the Sprint Cup garage area. His face looked sallow. The console between us held Pepto-Bismol and a mound of wadded tissues. Empty water bottles lay on the floor at my feet.

Great. Microbes coming my way. Without being obvious, I kept my head turned toward the window.

Gamble's fellow crew members were busy with the #59 Chevy, so we settled in the empty lounge in Stupak's hauler. Gamble slumped on the built-in sofa as if his muscles were linguine.

After introducing himself, Slidell recounted our conversation with Lynn Nolan. Then he got straight to the point. "Nolan thinks Lovette was knocking your sister around."

A flush blossomed in the hollow at the base of Gamble's throat.

"She thinks Lovette killed her."

The flush spread up Gamble's jaw and across his face. Still he said nothing.

"Nolan saw bruising on Cindi's arms. You ever notice anything along those lines?"

"Oh, Jesus." Gamble shot to his feet. "Oh, Jesus."

"That mean no?"

"I'd have killed the guy."

Seeing Gamble's agitation, I spoke in a tone I hoped would be calming. "Did Cindi change her habits that summer and fall? Alter her normal routine?"

"How would I know?" Gamble threw up both hands.

123

"She was sixteen. I was twelve. We traveled in different galaxies." He began pacing.

"How about her demeanor? How did she act?" I asked.

"Scared of her own shadow."

I gestured for him to continue.

"She was always looking around, you know? Like she was afraid someone was following her. And sometimes she'd bust my balls for no reason. That wasn't like her."

"Go on."

Gamble stopped. To gauge our reactions? "Looking back I always suspected she might have kicked Lovette to the curb."

"What makes you think that?"

"A couple weeks before she vanished, Cindi told our mother she'd lost her keys and asked to have all the locks changed at home."

"And?"

"She hadn't lost her keys. I saw them in her backpack. Why would she make up a story like that?"

"Why do you think?" I asked.

"I think she dumped Lovette, and it pissed him off. That's what was making her jumpy. She was afraid he'd come for her. She invented the key thing to be sure the house was secure."

Gamble resumed pacing, moving like a caged animal in the small space.

"Sit down," Slidell said.

Unable to stand still, Gamble ignored him.

"You report all this to the cops back then?" Slidell.

"I told some big guy."

"Galimore?"

Gamble shrugged. "Beats me. I was a kid. I learned later

124

that Galimore was on the task force. I don't know the guy, but I hear he works security here."

"Did the cops follow up?"

"Who knows?"

"How about the FBI?"

"I keep telling you. I was a kid. And my parents weren't on anyone's speed dial."

Footsteps clanged up metal stairs, then a door opened at the far end of the hauler. A jumpsuited man leaned in. He was sweating and breathing hard. "We've got a problem exiting turn three. The right-rear pressure needs tweaking."

"Gimme five," Gamble snapped.

"Stupak's going apeshit."

"Five!"

The man withdrew.

"Did you discuss Cindi's nervousness with your folks?" I asked.

"You think they sought my middle school views on my high school sister's mood swings?"

Point taken.

"Your parents have passed on, that right?" Slidell asked.

Gamble nodded. "Mom blew an aneurysm in 2005. Two years later Dad was killed in a hit-and-run on the road outside our house. That was fucked up. He'd walked that stretch every day for ten years."

Slidell's mobile sounded. Without looking, he reached to his belt and clicked the silencer.

"What do you know about J. D. Danner?" Slidell changed direction.

"Never heard of him. Who is he?"

"Guy ran the Patriot Posse."

Gamble's forearm muscles flexed as his fingers curled into fists. "I'm going to find the bastards who did this."

"Just calm down. You know anything about Danner and his cronies?"

"Look. I keep telling you. I was twelve. I was mostly focused on not getting zits."

"Your folks ever talk about it?"

A frown creased Gamble's forehead. Which looked clammy despite the AC.

"I may have heard the name during one of their screaming matches with Cindi."

"What was said?"

Gamble gave a tight shake of his head. "There was a lot of fighting going on that summer. I used video games to tune it out. All I know is the scenes were always about Lovette."

"How about a guy named Grady Winge?"

"He works here at the track. Not too bright but OK. Why? Was Winge involved?"

"Cool down. We're just working the names." Slidell stifled a pork-sausage belch. "How about Ethel Bradford?"

"She taught chem at A. L. Brown. You found Mrs. B.? What'd she say?"

"She doubts Cindi left on her own."

"Look. I'm not crazy. Everyone thought the same thing. Didn't matter. The FBI was telling the cops what to do. And for them, the flag had already dropped."

Slidell asked a few questions about Maddy Padgett and Lynn Nolan.

Gamble had no memory of Padgett, only a vague one of Nolan. While not flattering, his recall seemed spot-on. Body by *Playboy*, brains by Mattel.

* * *

Rather than hopping onto I-85, Slidell wound through town on Sharon Amity Road en route to the MCME.

Note about Charlotte. At least a zillion streets are named for a person or place called Sharon. Sharon Road. Sharon Lane. Sharon Lakes. Sharon Oaks. Sharon Hills. Sharon View. Sharon Chase. Sharon Parkway. Don't know the gal's story, but it must be a doozy.

For several miles the only sound in the car was radio static. Slidell and I were both turned inward, considering what Gamble had said.

Had Cindi been murdered? According to Nolan, Cale had treated her badly. Because he resented the support she was getting from her parents? Had she finally rebelled? Had Cale killed her because she'd broken off their relationship? Had Cale then disappeared, perhaps assumed a new identity? Had the Patriot Posse helped him slip underground?

Had Cindi and Cale both been murdered? If so, by whom? The Patriot Posse? Why?

Had the task force conclusion been correct? Had Cindi and Cale disappeared voluntarily? If so, why? Where had they gone? Was the Patriot Posse involved?

Were Gamble's suspicions legitimate? Had the FBI controlled the investigation? Concealed the truth about Cindi and Cale? If so, for what reason?

I thought about the question marks in Rinaldi's notes. Had Eddie known that something was off? Had Galimore?

My mind bounced like an untethered balloon on the wind, bobbing from one conjecture to another.

I finally broke the silence.

"Cindi was a kid. Cale was far from worldly. If the two left willingly, how did they cover their tracks so effectively?

127

I mean, think about it. Not one single slipup or sighting in all these years?"

"Except for Owen Poteat."

"The guy at the airport."

Slidell nodded.

"You learn anything about him?"

"I will."

"Suppose Gamble's right. Why would the FBI initiate a cover-up?"

"I've been poking at that."

Slidell made a right onto Providence Road before continuing.

"Say the FBI turned Lovette."

"Got him to work as a confidential informant?"

Slidell nodded. "Maybe the posse discovered he'd been flipped and capped him and his girlfriend."

I rolled that around in my head.

"Or maybe the CI was Cindi," I said. "Maybe she'd had it with Lovette's abuse and agreed to spy on the posse for the FBI. That would explain her nervousness."

"Eeyuh."

"Or what about this? Cindi or Lovette is working from the inside. Their cover is blown. The FBI pulls them both and pipes them into witness protection."

Slidell didn't answer.

"We should talk to Cotton Galimore," I said.

Slidell made that throat sound he makes when disgusted. He disliked Galimore. So did Joe Hawkins. Why?

"What's Galimore's story?" I asked.

"He dishonored the badge."

"By drinking? Other cops have had issues with the bottle."

"That was part of it."

"Galimore was bounced from the force. Isn't that punishment enough?"

The faux Ray-Bans swiveled my way. "That asshole betrayed all of us. And what did he get? A deuce and out."

"Galimore spent two years in jail?" I hadn't heard that. "On what charges?"

"Accepting a bribe. Obstruction of justice. The guy's scum."

"He must have straightened himself up."

"Once scum, always scum."

"Galimore is now head of security at a major speedway."

Slidell's jaw hardened, but he said nothing.

I remembered seeing Galimore in Larabee's office. Recalled his interest in the body from the landfill. The body later confiscated by the FBI.

Coincidence?

I don't believe in coincidence.

I reminded Slidell. As I was speaking, his cell rang again. This time he answered.

Slidell's end of the conversation consisted mostly of interrogatives. How many? When? Where? Then he clicked off.

"Sonofabitch."

"Bad news?"

"Double homicide. You want I should take you home?"

"Yeah. Then I'll head over to the MCME, tell Larabee about the Rosphalt, and see what else he's learned about the missing John Doe."

Though I went, that didn't happen.

But another issue resolved itself.

16

A carefully penned Post-it explained that Mrs. Flowers had left the MCME at 11:50, that she was lunching at Alexander Michael's pub, and that she would return at one p.m.

Hearing a cough, I moved toward the cubicles assigned to death investigators. Inside the second sat a new hire named Susan Volpe. We'd met only once.

Volpe's head popped up when I appeared at her entrance. She had mocha skin and curly black hair cut in an asymmetric bob. Maybe twenty-five, she was all snowy white teeth and lousy with enthusiasm about her new job.

According to Volpe, Larabee and Hawkins were at a homicide scene. I'd just missed them. The other two pathologists were also away. She didn't know where.

The erasable board logged three new arrivals. My initials were in a little box beside the number assigned to the third, indicating the case was coming to me.

Walking to my office, I wondered if Hawkins and Larabee had gone to the same address to which Slidell had been called.

A consult request lay on my desk. MCME 239-11. After depositing my purse and laptop, I glanced at the form.

A skull had been found in a creek bed near I-485. Larabee wanted a bio-profile, and especially PMI.

First, lunch.

I went to the kitchen for a Diet Coke to accompany the cheddar-and-tomato sandwich I'd brought from home. I'd barely loosened the wrapping when my landline rang.

Volpe. A cop wanted to see me. I told her to send him through.

Seconds later footsteps echoed in the hall. I turned, expecting Skinny.

Whoa!

Standing in my doorway was a man designed by the gods on Olympus. Then broken.

The man stood six-three and weighed around 240, every ounce rock-solid. His hair was dark, his eyes startlingly green, what Gran would have called black Irish. Only two things kept Mr. God a notch below perfect: a scar cut his right brow, and a subtle kink belied a healed nasal fracture.

My expression must have telegraphed my surprise.

"The lady said to come on back." Cotton Galimore punched a thumb in the direction of Volpe's cubicle.

"I was expecting Detective Slidell."

"Sorry to disappoint." Grin lines creased the perfect face.

Without awaiting invitation, Galimore entered and foothooked a chair toward my desk. My nose registered expensive cologne and just the right hint of male perspiration.

"Sure," I said. "Come on in."

"Thanks." He sat.

"What can I do for you, Mr. Galimore?"

"You know who I am?"

"I know who you are."

"That a plus?"

"You tell me."

"You working with Skinny?"

I nodded.

"Condolences." Again the boyish grin.

I didn't smile back.

"I'm guessing Slidell's not one of my fans," Galimore said.

"He's not."

I looked at my sandwich. So did Galimore.

"These tight bastards not paying you enough?"

"I like cheese."

"Cheese is good."

"I can't discuss the body from the landfill, if that's why you're here."

"That's partly why I'm here."

"Sorry."

"You know you'll have no choice."

"Really?"

"Really. Sooner or later you'll have to deal with me."

Astonished at the man's arrogance, I simply stared.

Galimore stared back. His hair was grayer at the temples, his face more deeply creased than I'd noticed at first.

Mostly I noticed his eyes. They held me in a way I couldn't explain.

Galimore looked away first. Glancing down, he drew a pack of Camels from his pocket, slipped one free, and offered it to me.

"This is a no-smoking facility," I said.

"I don't like rules." Sliding matches from beneath the cellophane, he lit up, took a long pull, and slowly exhaled. Acrid smoke floated over my desk.

"Aren't we the rebel." Cool.

Galimore shrugged.

I fought the urge to grab the cigarette and stub it out on his forehead.

"My office. My rules," I said with an arctic smile.

"In that case, happy to comply."

Galimore took another draw, exhaled, then extinguished the Camel on the side of my wastebasket. When he straightened and exhaled, another noxious gray cloud drifted my way.

"Detective Slidell is not known for his objectivity," he said.

I couldn't argue with that.

"Did he give you the full story?"

"He told me you drank."

"I did. But never on the job."

"And that you went to jail."

"I had that delight."

"For accepting a bribe."

"I was set up."

"Of course."

"You want to know what happened?"

I flipped a palm. Whatever.

"The week before my arrest, I'd busted a junkie name of Wiggler Coonts. Real fine citizen. The cops wanted me more than they wanted Wiggler, so they talked his lawyer into wearing a wire. The scumbag tracked me to a bar and started buying. I said some stupid things. No question. But it was textbook entrapment."

"Doesn't sound like a basis for a criminal conviction."

"A wad of cash turned up in a storage bin in the basement of my condo complex."

"Hardly incriminating."

"It was my bin."

"But not your wad."

"Never saw it before."

"You saying the cops planted it?"

"You saying they didn't?"

"Why?"

"They were looking for cause to boot me."

"Seems pretty extreme."

"That was just part of it."

Galimore crooked his right ankle onto his left knee. His tan slacks rode up to reveal one sockless calf.

"This came down while the Gamble-Lovette disappearances were topping the call sheet. There was a lot of pressure to clear the case. I was considered, shall we say, an impediment to swift closure."

"Why was that?"

Galimore gestured at my sandwich. "How about we find something better than cheese. I'll tell you all about it."

My libido gave an immediate thumbs-up.

My neocortex took time to consider.

Slidell would go ballistic. Hawkins would sulk. Larabee would object.

But Galimore had been part of the Gamble-Lovette task force. It was possible he had useful information. Probable.

"I'll meet you at Bad Daddy's in twenty minutes," I said.

"I can't discuss the landfill John Doe." I'd said it earlier but wanted to make myself clear.

Galimore was at the back of the restaurant, working on a sweaty glass of iced tea.

"Understood."

I slid into the booth.

"What did you tell Skinny?"

"I do not clear my actions with Detective Slidell." Sharp.

Galimore laughed and shook his head. "You're as feisty as they say."

"Thanks."

A waitress appeared with menus and introduced herself as Ellen. "Fill-up?"

Galimore nodded.

To me, "Sweet tea?"

"Diet Coke, please."

When Ellen returned with my drink, I ordered the Mama Ricotta burger. Galimore went for a make-your-own salad and chose a score of ingredients.

When Ellen withdrew, I decided to take control.

"Are you implying you were framed for refusing to go along with the task force conclusion on Cindi Gamble and Cale Lovette?"

"I'm not implying, I'm saying it straight out."

"Why?"

"There were a number of reasons the cops wanted me out of the way. Yeah, I was drinking. And I'd made some enemies on the force. For a while I thought that was it. I believed the DA really bought in to the bribe thing. The tape was damned incriminating, then the money sealed it."

Galimore's eyes swept the room, came back to me.

"Jail's not like prison. It's a holding tank. Since there's nothing to do, you spend a lot of time thinking. The more I thought, the more things started to bug me."

"Things?"

"Loose ends that didn't tie up."

A couple of teens moved toward the booth beside ours. He wore a tank and basketball shorts that hung to his knees. She featured a floopy little skirt that struggled to cover her bum.

"The Gambles refused to accept that their daughter left on her own," I said. "Are you saying they were right?"

"Maybe."

"Did you share your doubts with them?"

"Wasn't my place."

"Why are you telling me?"

"In retrospect, I realize that the investigation left holes big enough for a Humvee."

"Loose ends."

Galimore nodded. "That summer, Cindi asked to have the locks changed at home. Her kid brother thought it was because she was afraid of Lovette."

"What did you think?"

"I thought it was because she was afraid of *something*. When I shared this information with the FBI, they blew me off. For me, that doesn't skew right. When you learn a missing kid was scared, you find out why."

Ellen arrived with our food. For a moment we focused on dressing and condiments.

"Something else bugged me. In my initial canvas, I turned up a guy who claimed he saw Gamble and Lovette at the Speedway the night they disappeared."

"Grady Winge."

Galimore shook his head. "Eugene Fries. Fries swore he sold Gamble and Lovette corn dogs at a concession stand around eight p.m."

"Winge said they left the Speedway at six."

"Yeah."

"Did anyone interview Fries?"

"Our FBI brethren said the guy was a crackhead and unreliable."

"Did you share this with Rinaldi?"

Galimore nodded. "He agreed the contradiction was troublesome."

"Did either of you follow up?"

"We tried, but by then Fries was in the wind. Then my life started falling apart. I got busted, went to jail, lost my job, my marriage imploded."

Galimore took a forkful of lettuce, chewed.

"For a long time I was a very bitter man. Hated the cops, the FBI, my slut wife, life in general. The Gamble-Lovette file was like a festering wound. The only way I could move on was to put it behind me."

"I'm confused. You're revisiting the case now because your employer wants to know about the landfill John Doe? Or because you think the victim could be Cale Lovette?"

Galimore leaned forward, eyes intense. "Fuck my employer. Those dickwads locked me up so I couldn't follow through on a case that mattered to me. I want to know why."

"Did Rinaldi pursue the leads after you left the task force?"

"I don't know."

"Is it possible you're being paranoid?"

"We're talking the friggin' FBI. You don't think, with all their resources, they couldn't have cracked this case if they wanted to?"

That same thought had occurred to me.

"But it wasn't just the FBI and the cops." Galimore pointed his fork at his chest. "I was also part of the problem."

I let him continue.

"The Gambles were good people caught between bad alternatives. Either their daughter had turned her back on them, or she'd come to harm. Early in the investigation, they phoned me every day. Eventually I stopped picking up. I'm not proud of that."

"So your interest is twofold and self-serving. You want to clear your conscience and at the same time stick it to the cops."

"There's something else. I got a call at my office earlier this week. The voice sounded male, but I can't be sure. It was muffled by some sort of filter."

"Uh-huh."

"I'll spare you the colorful verbiage. Bottom line, the caller threatened to take me down by exposing my past to the media unless I backed off on the Gamble-Lovette thing."

"And you said?" I kept my voice neutral to hide my skepticism.

"Nothing. I hung up."

"Did you trace the number?"

"The call was placed on a throwaway phone."

"Your explanation?"

"The body in the landfill. The story in the paper."

Galimore's eyes again swept the restaurant.

"Someone out there is getting very, very nervous."

17

"What do you propose?"

"I did some checking. Fries was in the wind for a while, reappeared about five years back, and now lives outside of Locust. He's in his eighties, probably senile."

Offended by Galimore's broad-brush dismissal of the elderly, I snatched up the bill. He didn't fight me.

"You intend to question him?" I asked curtly.

"Can't hurt."

While digging for my wallet, I spotted the page of code I'd torn from Slidell's spiral. I withdrew both.

When Ellen left with my credit card, I unfolded and read Rinaldi's notations.

"This mean anything to you?" I rotated the paper.

"What is it?"

"It's from Rinaldi's notes on the Gamble-Lovette investigation."

Galimore looked at me. "Rinaldi was a stand-up guy," he said.

"Yes."

The emerald eyes held mine a very long moment. When they finally dropped to the paper, my cheeks were burning.

Jesus, Brennan.

"Wi-Fr. That's probably Winge-Fries. Rinaldi was curious about the contradiction between their statements."

I felt like an idiot. I should have seen that, but then I'd just learned of Fries.

"OTP. On-time performance?"

"Seriously?"

"Onetime programmable? You know, like with some electronic devices."

"Onetime password? Maybe the rest is a password for something."

"Could be." Galimore slid the paper to my side of the table. "The rest, I've no idea. Unless FU stands for the obvious."

My eyes were still rolling when Ellen returned. I signed the check, collected my card, and stood.

Galimore followed me out to the parking lot.

"You'll let me know what Fries says?" I asked in parting.

"Shouldn't this go two ways?" Slipping on aviator shades, though the day was cloudy. "You must have something on that John Doe by now."

Oh yeah. The ricin. The confiscation and destruction of the body. The Rosphalt. No way I could share that information.

"I'll talk to Dr. Larabee," I said.

"I'm good at this, you know." The aviators were fixed on my face. "I was a detective for ten years."

I was weighing responses when my iPhone overrode the traffic sounds coming from East Boulevard.

Turning my back to Galimore, I moved a few paces off and clicked on.

"Yo." Slidell was, as usual, chewing something. "This will be quick. Got two vics capped, another bleeding bad, probably not gonna make it. Looks like the gang boys are unhappy with each other."

"I'm listening." Sensing Galimore's interest, I kept my response vague.

"Owen Poteat." I waited while Slidell repositioned the foodstuff from his left to his right molars. "Born 1948, Faribault, Minnesota. Married, two daughters. Sold irrigation systems. Canned in 'ninety-five. Two years later the wife divorced him and moved the kids to St. Paul. Dead in 2007."

"Why was Poteat at the airport?"

"Going to see his *madre*, who was checking out with cancer."

"How'd he die?"

"Same as Mama."

Failed job. Lost family. Dead mother. Though far from unique, Poteat's story depressed the hell out of me.

"Looks like I'm out on Lovette-Gamble for now. With the bangers on the warpath, the chief's reined us all in."

"I understand."

"I'll jump back aboard when things cool down."

"Focus on your investigation. I have another lead."

"Oh yeah?"

Moving farther from Galimore, I told Slidell about Fries.

"Where'd you get that?"

"Cotton Galimore."

"What the fuck?" Slidell exploded.

"Galimore participated in the original investigation. I thought he might have useful information. Which he did."

"What did I tell you about that asswipe?"

"He claims he was framed."

"And Charlie Manson claimed he was just running a day camp."

It was exactly the reaction I'd expected. "I don't plan to date him," I snapped.

"Yeah, well. Word is Galimore wasn't exactly humping back in 'ninety-eight."

"What does that mean?"

"That investigation went bust. Why's that, I ask myself. I come up with no explanation makes sense. So I float a few questions."

"To whom?"

"Cops been around the block."

"They suggested that Galimore obstructed the work of the task force?"

"They inferred as much."

I ignored Slidell's misuse of the verb. "Why would he do that?"

"I ain't his confessor."

"Did they cite examples?"

"All I'm saying. Galimore's a reptile. You chum with him, I'm out."

Dead air.

"I'm guessing that was Skinny."

Furious with Slidell, I hadn't heard Galimore approach. Shifting my face into neutral, I turned.

"He's pissed that you're talking to me."

I said nothing.

"And ordering you to be a good girl and send me on my way."

"He was reporting that he'd be tied up for a while."

"So we're on our own."

"What?"

"Just you and me, kid." Galimore winked. Ineffective, given the unnecessary lenses.

I dropped my phone into my purse and glanced up at him. As before, my stomach performed a wee flip.

I looked away. Quickly.

Two cats were tearing at something in a patch of grass by one corner of the restaurant. One was brown, the other white. Both had sinewy shadows overlying their ribs.

"I know you're curious about Fries," Galimore said.

I was.

"And Bogan." Cale's father.

"You're heading to talk to them now?" I asked, still looking at the cats.

"I am."

A zillion brain cells clamored that it was a bad idea. I waited for opposing views. Heard none.

"I drive," I said.

North Carolina is loaded with little pockets that have managed to remain on the far side of rural. Fries had found one of them. Or someone had found it for him.

Following Galimore's directions, I'd taken the outer beltway, then gone east on NC 24/27. Just before Locust, I'd cut north on 601, then made several turns, ending up on a stretch of gravel that hardly qualified as a road.

For several minutes we both assessed the scene.

If Galimore's information was correct, Eugene Fries lived in the seediest trailer I'd ever seen. Its hitch rested on a boulder, keeping the thing more or less horizontal.

The trailer had no wheels, its flip-open windows were rusted shut, and a mound of debris rose halfway up the side facing us. BOLER was barely legible on its sun-fried aluminum.

A brand name? The owner's name? A name given to the

trailer itself? Whatever. I suspected Boler had been parked sometime this millennium and never again moved.

The trailer occupied most of a small clearing surrounded by hardwoods and pines. Along its perimeter I could see more trash heaps.

Behind and to the trailer's right stood a shed constructed of haphazardly nailed two-by-fours. A dirt path circled from the trailer's door around the hitch and boulder toward the shed. Straight shot to the can. Though gray and weathered, the outhouse seemed of more recent vintage than Boler.

To the trailer's left loomed an ancient oak whose trunk had to be eight feet in diameter. Its gnarled limbs stretched over both trailer and shed. In its shadow, the earth was dark and bare.

Four feet up the oak's trunk, I spotted two bolts. Clipped to each was a chain, now hanging slack. The stainless-steel links looked shiny and new.

My eyes traced the chains downward, then out across the bare ground. As I feared, each ended in a choke-collar clip.

"There might be dogs," I said. "Big ones."

"Yeah." Galimore's tone suggested he shared my apprehension.

As one, we lowered our windows.

And heard nothing. No birdsong. No barking. No WKKT Kat Country music twanging from a radio.

I sorted smells.

Damp leaves. Moist earth. An organic pungence that suggested garbage rotting in plastic.

Galimore spoke first. "You stay here. I'll see if anyone's home."

Before I could object, he was out of the car. Couldn't

say I was unhappy. My mind was conjuring images of Rottweilers and Dobermans.

Galimore took two steps, then paused.

No slathering canines came charging forth.

Looking left and then right, Galimore headed across the ten feet of open space between the road and the trailer. A backward crooking of his right elbow told me he was armed.

Striding with purpose, he went directly to the trailer's only door. His voice broke the stillness. "Mr. Fries. Are you in there?"

No response.

Galimore called out again, louder. "Eugene Fries? We'd like to talk to you."

Nothing.

"We're not going away, Mr. Fries." Pounding the metal door with the heel of his left hand. "Best you come out."

Still, no one answered.

Galimore stepped back to recheck his surroundings. And made the same observation that I had. The only path in the clearing was the one leading to the outhouse.

I watched Galimore circle the boulder and hitch, then disappear behind the trailer.

Time passed.

I checked my watch. Three-twenty-seven.

How long had Galimore been gone?

My eyes roved the clearing. The edge of the woods. The trailer.

Three-thirty-one.

I drummed anxious fingers on the wheel. Where the hell was he?

Three-thirty-four.

A yellow jacket buzzed the windshield, tentative. Landed. Crawled, antennae testing.

The tiniest breeze rustled the leaves overhead.

Three-thirty-six.

Thinking Galimore might have called to tell me to join him, I dug out my mobile. Checked for messages. Found none. Verified that the ringer was turned on. It was.

Impatient, I leaned toward the passenger-side floor and snatched up my purse.

When I straightened, the cold steel of a muzzle kissed my left temple.

18

Icy fear traveled my spine.

In the corner of my eye, I could see a dark figure standing outside the car. He or she held a shotgun tight to my skull.

Through the open window, I heard growling and thrashing.

Terror froze me in place. I was in the middle of nowhere. Alone. At the wrong end of dogs and a gun.

Dear God, where was Galimore?

"State your business."

The wheezy voice snapped me back. Low and deep. Male.

I swallowed. "Mr. Fries?"

"Who the hell's asking?"

"Temperance Brennan." Keep it simple. "I'm a friend of Wayne Gamble. Cindi's brother."

The growling gave way to snarling and scratching. The Mazda lurched.

"Down, goddammit!"

The earsplitting bellow sent a new wave of adrenaline flooding through me.

"Rocky! Rupert! Asses to the dirt!"

I heard the dull thud of a boot hitting flesh. A yelp.

My heart pounded in my chest. I didn't dare turn my head. Who was this lunatic? Had he killed Galimore?

The gun muzzle prodded my skull. "You're going to get out now. Real slow. Keeping your hands so's I can see 'em."

I heard the sound of a latch, then the door swung open.

Hands high, I thrust out my legs and stood.

Rocky and Rupert were the size of elk, black, with brown crescents above eyes that were fixed on me. Though a low growl rose from each massive throat, neither dog made a menacing move.

Their master looked about as old as a human can look. His skin was pale and tissue-paper thin over a prominent forehead, chin, and nose. His gaunt cheeks were covered with prickly white whiskers.

Though the day was muggy, the man wore wool pants, a long-sleeved flannel shirt, an orange hunting cap, and a windbreaker zipped to midchest.

His Winchester followed my every move. Its condition suggested an age equaling that of its owner.

The old man studied me with rheumy blue eyes, his gaze as steady as his grip on the gun.

"Who sent you here?"

"No one, sir."

"Don't you lie to me!"

As before, the vehemence of the outburst caused me to flinch.

"Move." The gun barrel arced toward the far side of the clearing.

I held ground, knowing that entry into the trailer would limit my options.

"Move!"

"Mr. Fries, I—"

The muzzle of the Winchester jammed my sternum, knocking me backward. My spine struck the edge of the open car door. I cried out in pain.

The dogs shot to their feet.

The man lowered a hand, palm toward them.

The dogs sat.

"I said move." Cold. Dangerous. "That way."

Again he gestured with the gun.

Seeing no alternative, I began walking, as slowly as I felt my captor would allow. Behind me, I heard panting and the crunch of boots.

Desperate, I sorted options. I saw no phone or power lines. My mobile was in the car. I'd told no one where I was going.

My heart thudded faster.

I was marooned.

With a madman.

And Galimore nowhere in sight.

Outside the trailer, I stopped and tried again. "Mr. Fries. I mean you no harm."

"You take one step, you get a load of shot in your head."

The man circled me, then snapped his fingers at Rocky and Rupert. "Down!"

The dogs dropped to their bellies, mouths open, purple tongues dangling over yellowed teeth.

Keeping the Winchester cradled in one arm and pointed at my chest, the man bent, snatched up one chain, and clipped it to either Rocky or Rupert. He'd just secured the second chain when I noticed a flicker in the shadows beyond him.

Galimore struck like a ninja.

Firing around the trailer's far end, he arm-wrapped the old man's throat, dragged him clear of the dogs, and yanked the gun from his grasp. The hunting cap went airborne and landed in the dirt.

The dogs flew into a frenzy.

Terrified, I backpedaled as fast as I could.

Confused and enraged, Rocky and Rupert alternated between lunging at Galimore and me, muscles straining, saliva stringing from their gums and jowls.

"Call them off!" Galimore's command barely carried over the furious barking.

A gagging sound rose from the old man's throat.

"Sit them down or I shoot them!"

"Break." Barely above a whisper.

Galimore released the old man. He doubled over, coughing and spitting.

The dogs grew even more frantic.

The old man straightened and tried again, louder, one trembling hand extended toward his animals. "Break."

The dogs dropped to the ground, bodies tense, eyes on their master, clearly dubious about his directive.

"What's your name?" Galimore demanded.

"Eugene Fries." The old man's Adam's apple seemed ready to pop out of his throat. "This is my place. You got no right to bully me."

"You were pointing a shotgun at the lady's heart."

"I weren't gonna shoot no one."

"You had me fooled. Her, too."

No shit. The lady's heart was still hammering against her ribs.

The old man leaned over and hawked an impressive gob.

Galimore cracked open the Winchester. Seeing it was unloaded, he snatched up the hunting cap and smacked it back and forth against one thigh.

"Got a couple of questions for you, Mr. Fries." Galimore parked the cap on the bald old head. "Then we're on our way."

Fries said nothing as Galimore urged him in my direction, staying carefully outside the reach of the dogs.

Fries's eyes rolled to me, then refocused on Galimore. Still on edge from the dogs and the gun, I let Galimore do the talking.

"We're interested in two kids who went missing from the Charlotte Motor Speedway back in 'ninety-eight. Cale Lovette and Cindi Gamble. You know who I'm talking about?"

"I know *what* you're talking about. Never knew either one of 'em."

"You stated that you served Gamble and Lovette at a concession stand around eight p.m. the night they disappeared. Is that correct?"

Fries nodded.

"How did you know it was them?"

"The cops showed me pictures. Lovette was easy to remember because of the tats."

"A lot of guys get inked."

"OK. I knew of Lovette by reputation."

"How's that?"

"He was tight with a bunch of militia types. Word was they were real bad actors."

Galimore thought about that. Then, "You know Grady Winge?"

"He's an idiot."

"According to Winge, Gamble and Lovette left the Speedway around six that night."

"Like I said, Winge's an idiot."

"How could you be so certain about the time?"

"I was checking the clock."

"Why was that?"

"A certain lady was coming to see me at nine."

"She show up?"

"No. Look, I told all this to the cops back then. Nearly got my ass killed."

"What does that mean?"

"Means I nearly got my ass killed."

Galimore drilled Fries with a look.

"Right after I talk to the cops, I get a call. Guy says my life turns to shit if I don't change my story."

"Who was it?"

"If I'd known that, the prick would be fertilizing a patch of forest."

"What did you do?"

"I told him to fuck off. A couple days later, my dog turned up dead on my porch."

"Maybe it just died."

"She sure as hell did. From a slug in her brain. Two days after that, my house burned down."

"You think the caller actually followed through on his threats?" I was shocked.

"No." Fries turned to me, contempt drawing his thin, flaky lips into a downward U. "It was Al Qaeda recruiting me to the cause."

"Then what did you do?" Galimore asked.

"What the hell would you do? I quit my job and headed west. Few years back, my brother offered me this trailer. I figured enough time had passed, so I come home."

"You've had years to think about it," Galimore said. "You must have your suspicions."

Fries didn't answer for a very long time. When he did, his scraggly white brows were drawn low over his lids. "All's I'll say's this. Word on the street was Lovette and his pals were trouble."

"You're talking about the Patriot Posse?"

Fries nodded.

"Why would they threaten you?" I asked.

"What?" The brows shot up. "I look like a cop? How the hell would I know?"

I asked the same question I'd asked of the others.

"Mr. Fries, what do you think happened to Cindi Gamble and Cale Lovette?"

"I think Lovette and his asshole buddies either killed someone or blew something up. Then he and his girlie split."

"Where the hell were you?" Buckling my seat belt, adrenaline still pumping through me.

"Checking a path behind the trailer. I didn't want Fries coming up on us from the woods."

"Good job."

I spent the first few miles concentrating on the road. And my nerves.

Galimore seemed to understand. Or was focused on thoughts of his own.

We were on I-485 when I finally felt calm enough for conversation. Exhilarated, almost. Being rescued from a shotgun-toting maniac and his hounds will do that, I guess.

Nevertheless, I kept it professional.

We debated the significance of Fries's story. Galimore

thought the old geezer was probably exaggerating about the threats and harassment. I didn't think so. His house either burned or it didn't. Easy enough to check. Why lie?

We were still confused by the contradictory statements given back in 'ninety-eight. Had Lovette and Gamble left the Speedway at six, as Grady Winge reported? Or had they left later, as Eugene Fries insisted? Had one of the two been mistaken? Or had one intentionally lied? If so, which one? For what purpose? I was putting my money for accuracy on Fries.

We discussed theories concerning the fate of Gamble and Lovette. Currently there were five.

One: Cale and Cindi left voluntarily, either to join a militia elsewhere or to marry. This was the finding of the task force. I didn't buy into the run-away-to-marry theory. Even a halfhearted investigation would have uncovered that.

Two: Cale killed Cindi, then went into hiding. Wayne Gamble thought his sister had dumped Lovette and feared for her life. Lynn Nolan suspected Lovette was abusing Cindi.

Three: Either Cale or Cindi was working undercover for the FBI. The Patriot Posse learned of this and killed them both. This was Slidell's suggestion.

Four: Learning that Cale or Cindi had been compromised as a CI, the FBI had pulled and routed them both into witness protection. This had been my idea.

Five: Cale did something illegal with the Patriot Posse, then he and Cindi went into hiding. Eugene Fries had concocted this scenario based largely on rumor.

Still, I was bothered by the effectiveness of the disappearances. In all those years, not one phone call. Not a single slipup. That seemed to discredit the runaway theory.

Except for Owen Poteat. His sighting suggested a mistake on someone's part.

I remembered my conversation with Slidell. Wondered if he'd learned anything more about Poteat other than that he was dead.

As we pulled into the lot at Bad Daddy's, Galimore proposed dinner. Though tempted and hungry, I decided against it.

Galimore confused me. He was egotistical, infuriating, and of dubious moral character. But his actions proved he was a definite asset in a fight.

Bottom line: I found him smoldering hot.

Puh-leeze!

"No, thanks," I said. "I have a skull waiting for me."

Galimore looked at his watch. "It's going on six."

"I do some of my best work at night."

Stupid!

Before Galimore could jump on the opening, I slammed it shut. "Alone."

Winking, Galimore opened his door. "See you, Doc."

In minutes I was at the MCME.

Bad mistake.

I was about to take a quadruple volley.

19

Not a pathologist or receptionist on site. The board showed one death investigator present. Joe Hawkins.

My phone's message light was blinking. After getting a Diet Coke from the kitchen, I put the thing on speaker and picked up a pen.

Special Agent Williams, sounding annoyed. It was urgent that I call him back. I jotted down the number.

Wayne Gamble, sounding anxious. He knew who was following him and intended to confront the guy.

Earl Byrne, the mushroom-shaped reporter from the *Observer*, sounding eager. He wanted to write a follow-up to his original article and wondered what was taking so long with an ID on the landfill John Doe. Delete.

Special Agent Williams. Delete.

Special Agent Williams. Delete.

Cotton Galimore, sounding, what? Flirtatious? The dinner offer was still on the table. Also, he intended to visit Craig Bogan in the morning. Did I want to come along?

I was scribbling Galimore's number when a shadow fell across my desk. I looked up.

Hawkins was standing in my doorway, a half-dozen forceps in one hand.

"Hey, Joe."

"That Cotton Galimore?" The scowl on Hawkins's face would have frightened small children.

"Sorry?"

"Galimore." He jabbed the forceps toward my phone. "You talking to him?"

"Mr. Galimore was involved in the search for Cale Lovette and Cindi Gamble back in 'ninety-eight."

"You need to stay away from him."

"Excuse me?"

"The man's not to be trusted. You've got no business being anywhere near him."

"How I choose to conduct an investigation is of no concern—"

"The man's corrupt."

"People change."

"Not him."

"That's a bit rigid."

"Galimore worked that case, all right. Wouldn't surprise me if he took part in the cover-up folks are talking about. He's probably jumping in now to protect his sorry ass."

"Or he has a genuine interest in finding out what happened to his investigation?"

Hawkins was in full rant mode and in no mood to listen.

"Why the interest now after all these years? Could it be you're getting to the truth and he wants to keep you close? Whatever Galimore's motive, he's acting solely in the interest of one person. Cotton Galimore."

At that moment my phone rang.

Snorting his disgust, Hawkins turned and strode down the hall.

Without thinking, I picked up the receiver.

"Dr. Brennan. I'm glad I caught you."

"I was just about to leave." Not true. But I didn't want another sermon. Especially from the likes of Special Agent Williams.

"I'll keep it brief."

"Why did you confiscate the landfill John Doe?" I decided to take the offensive.

"I explained the bureau's reasoning to Dr. Larabee."

"Ricin contamination."

"Yes."

"The ricin toxin isn't contagious."

"It was not my decision."

"Was it your decision to cremate the body?"

"That was an unfortunate error."

"What about my bone plugs?"

"What about them?"

"Were those samples also destroyed?"

"It is my understanding they'd been placed in the same body bag."

"Could it be the bureau doesn't want this man ID'ed?"

"That's ridiculous."

"Ted Raines turn up yet?"

Williams knew what I was asking. Did the bureau suspect that the landfill John Doe was the missing man from Atlanta?

"Not that I know of."

"Odd coincidence. Raines working for the CDC. The John Doe showing evidence of ricin poisoning."

"Indeed." I heard what sounded like a ballpoint pen

being clicked repeatedly. "I understand you talked to J. D. Danner."

"Nice hair."

"What did you tell him?"

"I could handle the groceries myself."

A beat. Then, "I have been authorized to reveal certain sensitive information. Dr. Larabee already has it. He asked me to share it with you."

I waited.

"In 1996 the Patriot Posse came to the attention of the FBI. The group was small and strictly local, but intel was that certain members were becoming radicalized, perhaps plotting acts of violence."

"Which members?"

"That's not relevant."

"Danner?"

The pen. *Click. Click. Click.*

"Lovette?"

"No."

"What was their alleged target?"

"This information is strictly confidential."

"Oh. Wait. I'll cancel my tweet."

"According to our source, the posse was planning to contaminate the water supply of a nearby town."

"Why?"

"Two gripes. The presence of a women's clinic that provided abortions. The election of a black woman as mayor."

A mélange of anger and disgust soured my stomach. I reached for the Diet Coke.

"At the time Cindi Gamble and Cale Lovette vanished, the posse was under surveillance," Williams went on.

"You had someone inside?"

"I can't tell you that."

"Was it Lovette? Gamble?"

Williams ignored my questions. "Our intel also suggested that members of the group may have had ties to Eric Rudolph."

"Did they?"

"We were unable to establish that fact with certainty."

Click. Click. Click.

"The posse disbanded in 2002, but the bureau has continued to track some of its members."

"J. D. Danner?"

"Danner now heads a much bigger organization called the Loyalist Movement. The group has several thousand followers throughout the Southeast."

"Who are they?"

"Extremists who believe that the federal government deliberately murdered people at Ruby Ridge and Waco, and that door-to-door gun confiscation could begin any day. Their ideology is less white-supremacist than in the nineties, though many have now turned their venom toward followers of Islam. What holds the group together is anger at the government."

I pictured the Tommy Bahamas, the sapphire ring, the RX-8. "Danner looked pretty flush."

"The Loyalist Movement is well funded, and Danner skims a big chunk off the top. But make no mistake. Though he lives well, Danner is committed. The guy's cunning as a fox and dangerous as typhoid."

"Why are you sharing all of this now?"

"To keep you in the loop."

"You want nothing in return."

"Normal professional consideration."

"Uh. Huh."

With that, we disconnected.

Right, I thought. Who's the fox?

After chugging the dregs of my Diet Coke, I got MCME 239-11 from the cooler.

The I-485 creek-bed skull was covered with moss and missing its entire face and most of the base. Copper staining, remnants of adipocere, tissue turned crumbly and waxy due to the hydrolysis of fats, and the presence of a shriveled mass of petrified brain told me I was probably looking at an old coffin burial. Without more contextual information, there was little I could say.

I was jotting a request to Hawkins for information about cemeteries in the vicinity of the creek bed, when my iPhone rang.

Katy.

I clicked on.

"Hey, babe. What are you up to?"

"Working late." Her tone suggested a need to vent. "As usual."

"Same here. Anything interesting?"

"Mind-blowing. I can hardly stay in my chair."

"Oh?" I ignored the heavy sarcasm.

"Some guy's in the running for most flagrant tax-fraud artist of the year. I get to plow through boxes and boxes of his papers."

"Getting any good ideas?"

"With my salary? What would be the point of tax evasion?"

"Will you finish tonight?"

"I won't finish until I'm ready for Medicare—one of the few systems this creep didn't scam. Here's a good one.

He'd buy first-class airline tickets, then turn them in for a full refund and buy coach. But he'd submit the first-class receipts for tax purposes."

"Not all that original."

"OK. How about this one? He set up some sort of tax free bank accounts for his kids' education. But before they went to college, he drew out all the money. And never told Uncle Sam."

"Isn't the IRS able to track that sort of thing?"

"I'm probably missing something. It was complicated. And just one of the many cons el creepo got away with for years."

I heard an intake of breath. Assuming Katy had more to say, I waited.

"Um. Have you talked to Ryan lately?"

"He's pretty tied up with Lily."

"How is she?"

"Eh."

"How about Charlie Hunt?"

"He's busy composing the world's most brilliant closing argument."

There was a moment of hesitation. Then she blurted, "I think he's seeing this other lawyer in the office. They work late a lot. Together. And they just left. Together. All chatty and smiley."

I felt a cool fizz in my chest.

"That's fine. Charlie and I have no commitment to each other."

"Have you heard from him?"

"No."

A little beep told me another caller was trying to get through.

"Gotta go, sweetie."

"Come by my cubicle sometime. Reach in and take my pulse."

I was still chuckling when I clicked over to call waiting. The sobs put a choke hold on my mirth.

"Tempe, I do hope it's OK to call you." Tremulous. "I didn't know where else to turn."

"I'm at the ME office, Summer."

"I am super, super sorry. You have such a kind nature, and I fear I am abusing it."

Thinking decidedly unkind thoughts, I began gathering my things.

"The wedding is now a complete disaster."

When I tossed my purse onto the desk, my wallet popped out. The page with Rinaldi's code stuck out like a bookmark.

"Pete's ideas are completely worthless. He chose green napkins. Green? Can you imagine?"

"Mm."

Desperate for distraction, I teased the paper free and spread it flat with one palm.

ME/SC 2X13G-529 OTP FU

Wi-Fr 6–8

"One of my bridesmaids is pregnant and can't wear the dress. That's Mary Gray. How could she *do* that to me?"

Galimore's interpretation of the second line made sense. Rinaldi was interested in the contradiction in time line presented by Grady Winge and Eugene Fries. I focused on the first line.

"Sarah Elizabeth can't get to Charlotte in time for the rehearsal. How can you have a wedding without a rehearsal?" Warbly.

163

Summer blew her nose loudly. "I don't know why I'm surprised. Sarah Elizabeth has always been horribly thoughtless."

My lower centers sat up.

What? Napkins? Pregnant? Rehearsal?

I stared at the alphanumeric string, only half-listening to Summer's whining.

Mary Gray.

Sarah Elizabeth.

My mind strained, on the verge of a breakthrough.

"I swear." More wet sniffling. "I just want to go to sleep and never wake up."

I ran through my conversation with Katy.

IRS? Airline tickets? Bank account?

I dug deep.

Dots connected.

I knew what was needed to decipher Rinaldi's note.

20

After hustling Summer off the line with some vague promise of support, I phoned Slidell. Got voice mail. Left a message. Urgent. Call me.

I tried Galimore. Voice mail. Same message.

Frustrated, I tossed my Diet Coke can into the recycling bin, grabbed my purse and laptop, and headed out.

Something was happening at the NASCAR Hall of Fame that night. I averaged about four miles a decade crossing uptown.

The bumper-to-bumper crunch changed my supper plan. No way I'd divert to Price's for fried chicken. A salad made from produce in my refrigerator would have to do.

I was finally heading south on Providence Road when my iPhone sounded.

Galimore.

"I think I know what concerned Rinaldi," I said.

"You're breaking my heart." Galimore sounded, what? Coy? "I thought you'd changed your mind about dinner."

"What was Owen Poteat's middle name?"

"I can check."

"Poteat had two daughters, didn't he?"

"That sounds right."

"Get their names, too."

"Yes, ma'am."

Ahead, the light turned red. I stopped at the intersection. To my left, Providence Road cut south. To my right, it became Morehead Street.

"What about bank records? Tax records?" I asked.

"Whose?"

"Any account bearing Poteat's name."

"It would help to know the bank."

The light went green. I proceeded straight on what was now called Queens Road. See. I wasn't kidding.

"Start with Wells Fargo," I said. "Work backward to 1998."

"I've got sources who can do that. What are you thinking?"

"How long will it take?"

"The names, a matter of minutes. Tax and financial records, that's tougher. Why aren't you getting this through Slidell?"

"He's either tied up or ignoring my calls."

"Don't expect Skinny to come around easily. The guy's a champion grudge-holder."

I turned in at Sharon Hall.

"I'm at my town house. I've got to go."

"A quiet meal at home alone?"

"I'll be dining with my cat."

Birdie had other thoughts. Upon hearing me enter the kitchen, he retreated to a dining room chair.

I knew what was up. The feline coolness was a comment on the lateness of the hour. Normally Birdie eats at six.

I checked my phone, hoping for a message from Ryan

or Charlie.

Neither had called.

Disappointed, I flipped on the TV. Two overly keen sports analysts were discussing potential lineups for the upcoming Coca-Cola 600. One predicted Sandy Stupak's #59 Chevy would start near the front.

Hearing an unhappy meow, I went to the dining room, reached under the table, and stroked Birdie's head.

"Sorry, Bird. I've been wicked busy."

The cat didn't budge.

"Cut me some slack. I've been to Concord and Locust all in one day. Slidell berated me. Hawkins lectured me. Ryan and Charlie have apparently dumped me. Katy and Summer both whined in my ear. Oh yeah. And an old coot held me at gunpoint with a Winchester."

The cat remained obstinate.

After filling Birdie's bowl, I went upstairs to shower. Then I threw on shortie-PJ bottoms and an old tee. No bra or panties. The freedom was exhilarating.

Back to the kitchen.

The tomato was flaccid, the cucumber slimy, the lettuce limp and black on the edges. So much for a salad.

Plan B. Something in a can.

I was rooting in the pantry when the back doorbell chimed. Wary, I peeked out.

Galimore was standing on the porch, face bathed in a yellow wash from the overhead bulb.

I closed my eyes. Tried to wish myself gone.

I heard the cadence of the evening news. The cat crunching Iams.

But gone where? What did I really wish for? To let Galimore in? To send him away?

Both Hawkins and Slidell disliked the man. Were they bitter that Galimore had made mistakes?

Had Galimore betrayed the badge? Were their concerns justified?

Had Galimore really taken a bribe? Or had there actually been a frame-up back in 1998? A frame-up in which police officers participated?

Had Galimore impeded the Gamble-Lovette investigation? Was he trying to do so now? Or was he genuinely interested in righting a wrong to the Gambles, which he saw as partly of his making?

Ryan wasn't exactly burning up the phone line. Nor was Charlie Hunt.

Did I just need a booster? What was this peculiar attraction I felt for Galimore?

I sneaked another look.

Galimore was holding a flat square box. DONATOS was visible in big red letters.

My eyes drifted to the tomato and cuke. Which were now oozing liquid across the sideboard.

What the hell.

I crossed and unlocked the door.

Galimore smiled. Then his gaze dropped.

Too late, I remembered my lack of undies. One hand rose, pointlessly, to my chest.

Galimore's eyes snapped up. "Totally loaded." He raised the pizza. "Hope you like anchovies."

I gestured toward the table. "Let me throw on some clothes."

"Not on my account." Galimore winked.

A flush rose up my neck.

Oh, yes, cowboy. On your account.

When I returned in jeans, a sweatshirt chastely concealing my bosom, the table was set. A small bottle of San Pellegrino sat beside each wineglass.

Out of courtesy to me? Or was Galimore also a nondrinker. Given his past, it seemed likely.

Before taking my place, I muted the TV.

"What did you learn?" I started off, wanting to set the tone.

"Not yet." Galimore slid an overloaded slice of pizza onto my plate. "First, we eat. And enjoy the lost art of conversation."

In the course of three helpings, I learned that Galimore lived alone uptown, had four brothers, hated processed food, and besides auto racing, enjoyed football and opera.

He learned that I had one daughter and a cat. And that the latter was inordinately fond of pizza.

Finally Galimore bunched his napkin and leaned back in his chair.

"I know where you're going," he said. "And I think you're dead-on."

"What was Owen Poteat's middle name?"

"Timothy."

"And his daughters?"

"Mary Ellen and Sarah Caroline."

"Yes!" I performed the "raise the roof" pantomime with both hands.

"What I can't figure is how you got that."

"First, I spoke to my daughter earlier this evening. She talked about a man who opened tax-advantaged savings plans for his kids' educations.

"Second, I have a friend who is getting married. Right after my conversation with Katy, she phoned to complain about her bridesmaids."

"Condolences."

"Thanks. Both bridesmaids go by double first names."

"True maidens of Dixie."

"As I listened to Summer, I was studying Rinaldi's code."

"Summer is the lovely bride-to-be?"

"Do you want to hear this?"

Galimore raised apologetic palms.

"The plan Katy described is named after Section 529 of the Internal Revenue Code. 529s are investment vehicles designed to encourage saving for the future college expenses of designated beneficiaries."

"OK. How do they work?"

"A donor puts money in and can take it any time he or she wants. The main benefits are that the principal grows tax-deferred, and that distributions for higher-education costs are exempt from federal tax."

Pete and I had considered a 529 when Katy was small. Never followed through.

"A side bennie is that the assets in a 529 plan are not counted as part of the donor's gross estate for inheritance tax purposes," I added.

"So a 529 can be used as a sort of estate planning tool, a way to move assets outside your estate while retaining control if the money is needed in the future."

Galimore was a very quick study.

"Yes," I said.

"How much is a donor allowed to put in?"

"Thirteen thousand per year."

Our eyes met.

"Get the code." Galimore sounded as jazzed as I was.

I dug the spiral page from my purse and unfolded it on the table.

Silently, we both translated the first line.

Mary Ellen. Sarah Caroline. Two times thirteen thousand into a 529 plan. Owen Timothy Poteat. First Union.

"First Union National Bank became Wachovia, then Wells Fargo," I said.

Galimore cocked a brow.

"Right. You knew that. When can you get your hands on Poteat's financial records?"

"Now that I know what I'm looking for, the job will be easier."

"Tomorrow?"

A waggled hand. Maybe yes, maybe no.

"So." Galimore gave me a high-beam smile.

"So." I smiled back.

"Why did Rinaldi think it was worth writing down?"

"Poteat is the single witness who claimed to have seen Cale Lovette after the night of October fourteenth. The man has no job and no assets. Suddenly he parks twenty-six thousand in accounts for his kids?"

"Someone paid him to lie." Galimore was right with me.

"Or at least Rinaldi thought so."

"Who?"

I'd given the question a lot of thought. "The FBI? The Patriot Posse? A party wanting to make it look like Lovette and Gamble were still alive?"

Galimore leaned back and took a swig of his San Pellegrino.

Moments passed. In the dining room, Gran's clock bonged nine times.

"Big weekend coming up." Galimore's eyes had drifted to the TV behind my back.

"Want audio?" I asked.

He shrugged.

As I crossed to turn up the sound, the station cut to a commercial.

We are the champions, my friends . . .

"That's what we are." Galimore laughed. "The DOD's going to be recruiting our asses to join some secret cryptography unit."

"Yep," I agreed. "We dazzle."

Shooting to his feet, Galimore sang another line of Queen. "'No time for losers!'"

"'Cause we are the champions,'" I joined in.

Galimore caught me in a waltz hold and swirled me around.

We finished the lyrics together.

"'Of the world!'"

More swirling.

I laughed like a kid at a carnival.

Finally we stopped. The emerald eyes caught mine. Our gazes locked.

I smelled Galimore's sweat and cologne. Traces of tomato and garlic on his breath. I felt his body heat. The hardness of muscle below his cotton shirt.

I experienced a sudden, almost overwhelming yearning.

A memory flashed in my brain. Andrew Ryan and I dancing in this same room. A little black dress dropping to the floor.

Yearning for whom? I wondered. Galimore, who was here? Ryan, who was so far away?

Heat rushed up my face.

Palm-pushing from Galimore's chest, I turned toward the TV.

A kid from Yonkers was singing about heartbreak, hoping to be America's next idol. He hadn't a chance.

As the kid crooned, a crawler appeared at the bottom of the screen. For distraction, I read the words.

My hands flew to my mouth.

"Oh my God!"

21

"You OK?" Galimore's hand was on my shoulder.

I gestured at the TV.

"Holy shit. Wayne Gamble's dead? At my friggin' speedway?"

Galimore grabbed his phone. Flicked a button. Messages started pinging in. Ignoring them, he jabbed keys with his thumbs.

I said nothing. I was already hitting speed dial myself.

Larabee answered on the first ring. Background noise suggested he was in a car. "I was just about to call you."

"What happened to Gamble?" I asked.

"Some sort of freak accident. I'm heading to Concord now. You'd better join me."

I didn't ask for a reason.

"I'll leave right away."

"Thanks." A beat. Then, "Everyone's looking for Galimore. Any idea where he is?"

Great. Hawkins had told Larabee about the message he'd overheard. Undoubtedly embellished.

"I'm sure he'll turn up," I said.

When I disconnected, Galimore was no longer in the

kitchen. Through the window, I could see him on the porch, talking on his mobile. Exaggerated gestures told me he was upset.

In seconds the door opened.

"I gotta go." Galimore's face was taut.

"Me, too. Larabee wants me at the scene."

"That doesn't sound good."

"No."

"See you there."

For the second time that day, I made the long trek out to the Speedway.

As the finding of the landfill John Doe demonstrated, the Charlotte media monitor police frequencies. And word spreads fast.

Every local station was there, one or two nationals, each positioned to provide an appropriately cinematic backdrop for sharing news of tragedy. A major NASCAR event is in full swing. Violent death strikes the pit crew of a favored son. I could hear the lead-ins in my head.

I had no doubt other reporters were barreling toward Concord. By morning not a millimeter of space would remain unoccupied.

I showed ID at the main gate. Was asked to wait. In moments a deputy climbed into my passenger seat. Wordlessly we looped around the stands toward the tunnel.

Along our route, reporters spoke into handheld mikes, expressions grim, hair and makeup perfect under portable lights. Others waited, smoking alone or sharing jokes with their camera and sound technicians. Media choppers circled overhead.

Barricades had been erected since my morning visit.

Sheriff's deputies, Concord cops, and Speedway guards manned them to keep the frenzy at bay.

On the infield, campers stood beside tents or atop trailers, talking in lowered voices, hoping for a glimpse of a celebrity, a shackled suspect, or a body bag. Some held flashlights. Some drank from cans or longneck bottles. Curving high above the gawkers, the glass-fronted luxury suites loomed dark and empty.

The deputy directed me toward the Sprint Cup garage area. In my mind's eye, I pictured Wayne Gamble. In my office at the MCME the previous Friday. In Sandy Stupak's trailer with Slidell just twelve hours earlier. Now the man was dead. At age twenty-seven.

Gamble had reached out to me, and I'd ignored him. Failed to return his call.

The guilt felt like a cold fist squeezing my chest.

Shake it off, Brennan. Focus. Help find what he wanted to tell you.

Once past the Media Center I could see the usual grouping of cruisers, civilian cars, and vans. One of the latter was marked CRIME SCENE UNIT. The other was our own morgue transport vehicle. Behind the wheel was a silhouette I knew to be Joe Hawkins.

I parked off to one side and got out.

The night was still and muggy. The air smelled of rain, gasoline, and concession-stand grease.

"I need to find Dr. Larabee," I said to my escort.

"I'll take you to him."

Grabbing my recovery kit from the trunk, I followed the deputy.

On the edge of the hubbub, a man leaned against a Cabarrus County Sheriff's Department cruiser, face pale in the pulsating blue and red lights. He appeared to be trying hard for composure.

I knew from the logo on his shirt that the man was a member of Stupak's crew. I guessed from his expression that he'd been the one who found Gamble.

Larabee was outside Stupak's garage, talking to a guy in a shirt and tie whom I didn't recognize. Experience told me they were standing at ground zero.

Every scene shows the same people-dispersal pattern. You can read it like a map. The ME near the vic, maybe a detective or death investigator nearby. Moving outward, the uniforms, speaking to no one. Sitting in or near their trucks, the CSU and morgue techs, idle and bored until called into action.

Despite the oppressive humidity, Larabee was wearing a Tyvek jumpsuit. Behind him, in the garage, I could see the #59 Chevy, its trunk end raised at an odd angle. The painted-on taillights looked dull and flat in the garish illumination of the overheads.

"Tempe," Larabee said upon seeing me. "Thanks for coming."

"Of course."

Larabee tipped his head toward the shirt-and-tie guy. "Mickey Reno. He's with Speedway security."

Reno had seen too many barbecues and too few barbells. Once muscular, his body was stalwartly moving toward fat.

I offered a hand and we shook.

"Why am I here?" I asked Larabee.

"You got a suit?"

I raised my kit in answer.

"Put it on. And bring what you need. It's tight in there."

Larabee's tone told me it was bad.

Placing the metal suitcase on the ground, I flipped the

levers, pulled out and zipped a jumpsuit over my clothes. After hanging a camera around my neck, I stuffed latex gloves, plastic specimen containers, Ziplocs, tweezers, and a Sharpie into one pocket.

Satisfied, I nodded that I was ready.

"I'll go in on the left, you go on the right," Larabee directed.

Tight was an understatement. The garages assigned to NASCAR drivers at tracks are microscopic. The car takes up most of the space. The crew works around and under it.

Larabee entered and sidestepped toward the garage's far end, his back to the wall. I did the same, opposite and facing him, the Chevy between us.

I noted familiar smells blending with the stench of gasoline and oil. Urine. Feces. A sweet coppery odor.

Again, icy guilt gripped my chest.

Shake it off.

I'd gone maybe five feet when I felt slickness below the soles of my sneakers.

I looked down.

It seemed more blood than could come from one human body. The pool stretched from wall to wall and half the length of the floor.

Breathing through my mouth, I continued.

When I reached the car's hood I understood the reason for the hideous carnage. And the reason for my presence.

Wayne Gamble's body lay off the right front tire, supine, legs crooked to his left, arms outstretched and tossed to his right.

Wayne Gamble's head had been detached when the Chevy fired forward with great speed and force, slamming his head and neck into the garage's back wall, crushing them. On impact, bone and brain matter had exploded in all directions.

Feeling a tremor beneath my tongue, I swallowed and drew several deep breaths.

Emotions in check, I dropped onto my haunches for a better look. Larabee did the same on the other side of the car.

I could see stuck to the mangled metal that had been the Chevy's hood and engine front more bloody tissue, tufts of hair, isolated teeth, and bone fragments that included segments of upper and lower jaw, with dentition in place, and several large sections of skull.

"No chance of a visual ID," Larabee said.

"No," I agreed.

"He got family?"

"Not that I know of. His parents are dead."

As Larabee watched, I took photos.

"I wouldn't let them move the car until you'd had a chance with this mess."

"Good call," I said, pulling on the latex gloves. "If there's no relative who can provide DNA for comparison, the dentition might be critical for a positive ID, even though we have anecdotal evidence who this is. What happened here?"

"Gamble was working with another mechanic, performing some test where you lift the rear wheels up, then rev the accelerator to hell and back. I forget what it's called, but apparently it really stresses the engine."

Larabee watched me tweeze up a molar and place it in a Ziploc.

"The other guy left to pee and grab coffee. Says he was gone maybe twenty minutes. When he got back, the car was against the wall, Gamble was down, and his brain was hamburger. His phrasing, not mine."

"The rear wheels must have made contact and engaged, and the car fired forward, smashing Gamble's skull against the concrete."

"Yeah. Body position suggests he was leaning over with his head between the wall and the front grille. Only the guy says there's no way something like that can happen. Says he and Gamble run this test before every race. Swears it's safe."

"So is swimming. Still, people drown."

"Amen."

Every few minutes Reno would shout through the open door, anxious to cue the tow truck.

"What's with Reno?" I asked Larabee, voice low.

"Stupak's people no doubt want immediate access to the car to see if it can be repaired for the race or if they need to go to a backup."

"Seems cold. What time was he found?"

"Just past nine."

"Jesus. Word travels fast."

"You've got that right. News teams were already shouldering for real estate when I arrived. Apparently some reporter cold-called Stupak's trailer and questioned one of his kids who happened to be there."

"That's ghoulish."

"You need me for anything?"

"Anything new on Ted Raines?"

"Not yet. Legally we can't get dental records until an MP actually turns up dead. But Raines's wife allowed the Georgia authorities to search his computer's hard drive and his cell phone records."

I nodded. My thoughts weren't really on Raines at that moment.

"I'm good here," I said.

"I'm going to step out to talk to Hawkins."

For the next hour and a half, I collected what I could reach, gently teasing teeth and bone shards from the engine block, or plucking them from the wheels, undercarriage, walls, and ceiling.

As I tweezed, packaged, and jotted identifying information for each specimen, sound bites looped in my mind. Gamble insisting he was being followed. Claiming someone had broken into his trailer. Saying he was about to confront his pursuer.

Had this been an accident? Or were we looking at a murder?

It was one a.m. when I finally emerged from the garage. My work was done. Larabee would now continue with examination and recovery of the remains.

While I'd been collecting what remained of Gamble's head, the assemblage outside had grown. Galimore had arrived with the Speedway's director of operations and several more security personnel.

Sandy Stupak had also appeared. He, Hawkins, and Larabee were discussing ways to tow the Chevy with the least amount of damage.

As I listened, it became clear that their concerns differed. Larabee and Hawkins were eager to preserve the body and its surroundings. Stupak was worried for his #59 car.

I was placing my jars and Baggies in the transport van when I heard the crunch of tires, followed by the thunk of a car door.

I turned.

And couldn't believe who was walking toward me.

22

Williams and Randall wore the same blue suits and ties, white shirts, and stern expressions they'd featured when ambushing me on Saturday.

"Evening, Special Agents," I said when they were ten feet out.

Both looked surprised. I think.

"Dr. Brennan." As before, Williams did the talking. "Nice to see you. Though not under these circumstances."

"What *are* these circumstances?" I asked.

"That's what we're here to ascertain."

"Good word, 'ascertain.'"

"Yes. May I ask why a forensic anthropologist was needed here?"

"I managed to get most of Gamble's head." I hooked a thumb toward the van at my back. "The small pieces are in Ziplocs. The big hunks are in jars."

Randall lost control. Blinked.

Williams's face remained carefully neutral. "Could you elaborate?"

I did.

After a long pause, Williams spoke again. "You've been in recent contact with Mr. Gamble, isn't that correct?"

"He came to my office last Friday, wondering if the landfill John Doe could be his sister. He phoned me several times after that, but we only spoke once. Detective Slidell and I interviewed him here around nine this morning."

"As part of your reinvestigation of the Gamble-Lovette disappearances?"

"It's hardly a formal reinvestigation."

"Yes. Did Mr. Gamble say anything to lead you to believe he might be despondent?"

"Despondent? How is that relevant to what we have here? You're not seriously suggesting he could have killed himself?" I wasn't believing the question.

"I'm not suggesting anything. During your conversations, did Mr. Gamble express concern about anything? Other than his sister, of course."

"He felt there might have been a break-in at his trailer. And that he was being followed."

Again I felt the gut-wrenching guilt.

"Go on," Williams urged.

"Today he left a message saying he was going to confront the guy."

"Had he discovered the identity of the person surveilling him?"

"Obviously he thought he had. Otherwise, how could he confront the guy?"

"Do you recall anything else?"

"Not really."

"Think, Dr. Brennan."

I shrugged. "He was feeling lousy."

"How so?"

"He thought he had the flu."

Did I imagine it? Or did Williams and Randall both stiffen?

"May I ask why the FBI was needed here?" I borrowed a line from Williams's playbook.

"As I stated during our initial conversation, the FBI very much wants to know what happened to Cale Lovette and Cindi Gamble. The young woman disappeared under suspicious circumstances. Her brother has now met a violent death. Shortly after you reopened her case."

"I haven't the authority to reopen a case." It came out more defensive than I intended.

"You take my meaning."

I did. And couldn't disagree. So I said nothing.

"While the bureau has confidence in the competence of local authorities, Special Agent Randall and I have been asked to remain active in the investigation. Any help you can offer will be much appreciated."

Williams let that hang out there a moment, but I didn't bite.

"Thank you. We'll want to see you and Dr. Larabee when he's finished the autopsy."

"So you can steal Gamble's body?" Snarky, but the guy's prim superiority was pissing me off. And I was exhausted.

"I assume that will take place tomorrow?"

"I don't determine Dr. Larabee's schedule."

Williams did that maybe-smile thing with his lips. Then he and Randall strode into the crowd, blue and red lights slashing their somber dark suits.

Before leaving, I told Larabee about Williams and Randall. He said he planned to autopsy Gamble first thing in the morning. I said I'd be there.

While I was driving home, then lying in bed, different scenarios played in my head. Most, when prodded, showed serious fault lines.

Gamble killed himself. But how could he drop the wheels from the position in which he was found? Plus, the man had given no indication of suicidal intent. He was actively pursuing his job and seeking to learn about his sister.

Gamble fell, dislodging the car from its jack. But I'd read that a NASCAR cup car must weigh a minimum of 3,400 pounds. How could something that heavy accidentally be knocked loose? And it was the rear wheels that had to hit the ground for the car to surge forward. Gamble was at the front.

Gamble made an error. It happens. He was feeling unwell. But what kind of error?

Gamble's coworker had accidentally caused his death, then lied about being elsewhere. Why? Was the man afraid of losing his coveted position on Stupak's pit crew?

Gamble was murdered. He believed someone was following him, was intent on confrontation. Had his suspicions been more than paranoia?

One uncertainty blossomed again and again, drowning out other thoughts like a drunken uncle at a family gathering.

Was I somehow responsible for Wayne Gamble's death, or at least responsible for a killer remaining unknown, because I had not returned a call in which Gamble might have identified the person?

The next morning I woke crazy-early, the same questions swirling in my brain. While making coffee, I turned the TV to the morning news. Flicked channels. Every station was reporting on Gamble, speculating less on how he had died than on how his death would affect the upcoming race and season.

To calm my nerves, I took my coffee to the garden to watch daybreak over the roof of Sharon Hall. It wasn't much of a dawn. The sun was just a fuzzy bronze disk behind overstuffed clouds. Looking at the anemic performance, I thought not even Kipling could turn it into poetry.

At seven I left for the MCME.

And again encountered the Fifth Estate. Cars and vans packed the lot, and reporters and news crews stood talking in small clusters. I recognized the locals. WBTV. WSOC. WCCB. Others were anyone's guess.

I noticed that Larabee's car was parked in its usual slot. Hawkins's truck was also present.

When I got out of my Mazda, cameras went to shoulders and mikes went to mouths. I heard murmured words, my name, then the questions began.

"Dr. Brennan, can you tell us anything about what happened?"

"When will Dr. Larabee finish the autopsy?"

"Why were you at the Speedway?"

"Word is Gamble's body was mutilated. Can you comment—"

Ignoring the onslaught, I wormed my way through the crowd, hurried up the steps, and entered the building. The glass door swung shut, cutting off the barrage of voices.

Larabee had Gamble on a table in the main autopsy room. He and Hawkins were already finishing the external exam.

"You were up with the birds," I said.

"Some dickhead called my home at five this morning."

"How did he get your number?"

Above his mask, Larabee's eyes made the point that my question was stupid. It was.

"You've heard of high-profile?" Larabee said. "This one's going to be in the stratosphere."

"Any issues with ID?"

"Not really. Gamble's wallet was in his pocket. The other mechanic was right there with him. Guy's name is Toczek. Still, I'd like you to reconstruct as much of the dentition as you can. We'll shoot X-rays, do a comparison just to be safe."

"You have dental records?"

"They're coming."

"Any reason to doubt Toczek's story?"

"Williams and Randall didn't think so. They grilled him so hard I thought the poor bastard would puke on his shoes."

"I suspect we'll have the pleasure of their company in the very near future."

I was right. Mrs. Flowers announced their arrival at eleven-fifteen.

I was placing the last of Gamble's cranial fragments into a boiler basket for final removal of flesh. Hawkins was shooting X-rays of his teeth. Larabee was stitching the Y on his chest.

Williams and Randall cooled their heels in reception while the boss and I showered and changed from surgical scrubs. The four of us then gathered in Larabee's office.

Our visitors wore identical frowns. Annoyed at having to wait? Unhappy with developments in the investigation? With life in general? Because of their arrogance, I couldn't have cared less.

Larabee's face was also unnaturally stiff. Lack of sleep? Or had the autopsy revealed something disturbing?

As usual, Williams lasered straight to the point. "What did you find?"

Larabee stiffened at the man's brusqueness. "Death due to exsanguination resulting from massive cranial trauma and decapitation."

"Did the body show any defensive injuries?"

If the question surprised Larabee, he didn't let on.

"I observed bruising in the right wrist area and a slight abrasion on the back of the right hand. Both injuries appeared to have occurred shortly before death. I cannot conclusively attribute them to any specific cause."

"Anything else?"

"The stomach and intestinal linings were severely inflamed. I noted internal bleeding, widespread irritation of the mucous membranes, and early signs of vascular collapse and multiorgan failure. The stool that I collected contained blood."

"So Gamble was sick."

"He was probably suffering from excessive thirst, a sore throat, perhaps difficulty swallowing. He may have had nausea, abdominal cramping, vomiting, diarrhea, or a combination of these symptoms. It's possible he was experiencing general weakness, perhaps drowsiness and disorientation."

"What's your diagnosis?" Williams asked.

"The configuration could mean many things. I've taken samples. Until I have tox results, I can't be sure."

Larabee paused a moment before continuing.

"What I find noteworthy is that the pathological fingerprint presenting in Wayne Gamble is identical to that which presented in the landfill John Doe."

What the flip? The landfill John Doe had been poisoned with ricin. Was Larabee suggesting the same thing had happened to Gamble?

The special agents locked eyes for what seemed a very long time. Finally Williams nodded.

Randall withdrew a paper from the pocket of his really dark suit. Half rising, he tossed it onto the desk.

As Larabee read, my mind flew in a zillion directions. I pictured the empty water bottles, the tissues, and the Pepto in Gamble's car. The man had called me and I'd blown him off. Once more, I had to hammer back the guilt.

"So." Larabee looked up and gave a slow roll of his shoulders. "What now?"

23

"Gamble's symptoms fit with abrin poisoning, am I correct?"

Abrin? I was expecting ricin.

"Yes," Larabee said.

"What can you tell me about it." Williams laced his fingers and dropped his hands onto his genitals.

"Abrin is also known as agglutinin or toxalbumin. It's a highly toxic lectin found in the seeds of *Abrus precatorius*, the rosary pea."

"How does it work?"

"Like ricin, abrin attacks cells from the inside, inhibiting protein synthesis and causing the cells to die. As the toxin penetrates the body, more and more tissues are destroyed. This leads to organ failure and eventual death."

"How quickly?"

Larabee shrugged one shoulder. "Hours or days. It depends on the dose and the route of exposure."

"Route of exposure?"

"One could touch a surface on which abrin particles or droplets have landed, or particles or droplets could land on the skin or in the eyes. One could inhale abrin if it's in the form of a mist or powder. One could ingest it if it's in food or water."

"That's it?"

"I suppose pellets, or abrin dissolved in a liquid, could be injected into a person's body."

"How common is accidental exposure?"

"Not common, though it happens."

"Give me a scenario."

"Rosary pea seeds are used to make jewelry and percussion instruments, mostly in India or Indonesia. I think the products are illegal in this country. Anyway, there have been cases in which broken seeds have exposed the wearer."

"So, in all likelihood, it would take a deliberate act to obtain abrin, either from rosary pea seeds or from some other source, and use it to poison someone?"

"In all likelihood. Now, I want to know—"

"If ingested, how much is required to kill a human being?"

"Very little."

Williams curled his fingers in a "give me more" gesture.

"One seed would probably do it." Larabee tapped the paper on his blotter. "Now. My turn. How was this sample obtained?"

Williams answered with carefully chosen phrasing. "Early this morning, Special Agent Randall and I entered an unlocked vehicle licensed to Wayne Gamble and collected a coffee mug clearly visible through an open window."

"Your lab has an amazingly fast turnaround time." I couldn't help myself.

"This case has top priority."

"Why is that?"

"The FBI has obtained information that"—Williams

paused for another vetting—"bumped our request to the front of the queue."

"This is your interpretation of normal professional exchange?" Disdain chilled my words.

Larabee had had it. Before Williams could respond, he jumped in. "Dick with this office, you'll wish you were working a coal mine in Guizhou province."

Williams and Randall exchanged another of their *Men in Black* glances. Then Williams graced us with a crumb of an explanation.

"Ted Raines works at the CDC but supplements his income with part-time employment at Emory University. The project on which he is a lab technician is funded by the U.S. Army Zumwalt Countermeasures to Biological and Chemical Warfare program. The project's research focuses on the fate and mobility of environmentally dispersed phytotoxins."

"Such as ricin and abrin," I said.

"Yes."

"So Raines has access to these substances."

"Theoretically."

For a full minute we all let that percolate. Down the hall, I heard my office phone ring.

I broke the silence. "The landfill John Doe showed signs of ricin poisoning. Wayne Gamble shows signs of abrin poisoning. Cindi Gamble and Cale Lovette disappeared in 1998. Ted Raines has now vanished. You believe these facts are interrelated?"

"That is correct."

"How?"

"The FBI would very much like to know."

"Why did the *FBI* order my John Doe torched?" Larabee

spat the letters as though they were a bad taste on his tongue.

"That is hardly a fair assessment."

"Why was the Lovette-Gamble file confiscated?" I asked.

"I cannot confirm bureau involvement in that."

"You had that one all loaded up." Larabee was growing more steamed with each of Williams's evasive replies. "Tell me, then. What is the *FBI* doing to resolve this whole mess?"

"The bureau is working with local law enforcement to determine Mr. Raines's whereabouts."

"Probably six feet under, like Gamble and Lovette and the poor slob from the landfill."

Williams ignored Larabee's outburst.

"With the consent of Mr. Raines's wife, experts are searching the hard drive from his home computer. Unfortunately, his laptop goes with him when he travels. Mr. Raines's cell phone records are also under scrutiny."

"Unfortunately, his cell phone goes with him when he travels." Larabee's sarcasm had the atomic weight of lead.

"We have established that Raines's mobile was not used after Monday last week. A call was made from Charlotte to the Raines's home landline. We are also looking at the GPS on Raines's second vehicle."

"Which, *unfortunately*, was in his driveway when the poor schmo fell off the planet." Larabee stood, anger barely in check. "This is bullshit. Get back to me when you're ready to share what you learned by stealing my stiff."

Williams and Randall rose, smiled tightly, and took their leave.

Back in my office I had not one but two phone messages. Both were unexpected.

I returned the calls in the order in which they came in. And slammed into yet more anger.

"Galimore." Curt.

"It's Dr. Brennan."

"Oh. Sorry. Didn't check the caller ID."

"I was surprised to hear from you. Figured you'd be completely jammed up with the situation at the Speedway."

"They've turned me into a goddamn traffic cop!" Galimore sounded furious. "The bastards won't let me anywhere near the garage area. Did you know there's some question Gamble died by accident?"

"Yes."

"Hallelujah! Everyone's in the loop but the head of security!"

"Williams and Randall were here."

"The freaking FBI. This happened on my patch. And what do I get to do? Freaking crowd control!"

"You going to break down now?"

"What?"

"It's manly and all. But I'm not good with tears."

"What the hell are you talking about?"

"Getting in touch with your feminine side."

For a moment I heard nothing but background noise. Then Galimore chuckled. "You're a real wiseass, you know that."

"Yes. Why did you call?"

"While my people play mall cop, I'm going to do some real police work. You want to meet Craig Bogan?"

I did.

Gamble's cranial fragments wouldn't be ready for analysis for twenty-four hours. I had no other cases.

Hawkins would disapprove. Ditto Slidell.

Screw Hawkins and Slidell.

"I'm at the MCME," I said. "Where shall I meet you?"

"Right outside. I'll be there in thirty."

I disconnected and dialed again.

This time the anger was pointed at me.

"What the hell are you thinking?"

"Good morning, Detective. Going to be another hot one out there."

"Cotton Galimore is a slime-spewing, amoral, bastard of a scumbag."

I had to give Slidell credit. His prose was creative.

"Don't hold back," I said.

"You've got no business breathing air with that freak show. He'll use you, then ditch you like a snotty tissue."

"Perhaps I'm using him."

"Galimore's a booger that you can't flick off."

"That was good. The way you expanded the metaphor."

"What?"

"Why did you call?"

"The impending gang war turned out to be a cheating ex taking revenge on the love of his life. Killed her and the boyfriend, put the lady's brother in the ICU."

It is one of the most common causes of violence against women. The man threatens. The woman asks for protection, maybe gets a restraining order. Big help. The cops finally step in when Mr. Tough Guy actually batters or kills her. Every time I hear of a case like that, I feel the same outrage and frustration.

"If I can't have you, no one can," I said, voice coated with disgust.

"Yeah. Noble. Anyways, I've got a little downtime now, so I plan to check out the car Gamble and Lovette drove off in the night they disappeared."

"The 'sixty-five Mustang described by Grady Winge."

"Yeah. I'm thinking there couldn't have been many of those. Wish I had the original damn file. I'm probably reinventing the wheel."

"Are DMV registration records kept that long?"

"I'll let you know."

"Any mention of the car in Eddie's notes?"

"That's where I plan to start."

I told Slidell about Larabee's autopsy results. And about the abrin found in Wayne Gamble's coffee.

"What the hell's abrin?"

I provided a quick overview. Slidell saw the connection right away. "Like the shit what killed the landfill John Doe."

"We don't know if the man died of ricin poisoning. He'd also suffered head trauma."

"Guess you could say that about Gamble."

"But it's not just the abrin," I said.

I told Slidell about Gamble's calls to me, about his anxiety, and about his decision to confront the person tailing him.

"So the FBI's thinking Wayne Gamble got iced. Why?"

"I don't know. But there's more."

I relayed what Williams had shared concerning Ted Raines.

"The feebs are fingering Raines?"

"No one's suggesting that Raines killed Gamble."

"Then what's the link?"

"I don't know."

"You're saying that a lot."

I hesitated, decided it was better to have everyone on the same page. Leaving out the part about the shotgun, I described the encounter with Eugene Fries.

"I'm telling you. Galimore is a snake."

"Let it go."

Angry air whistled in and out of Slidell's nose for several seconds. "Who would have threatened this guy Fries?"

"I've no clue. But they made an impression."

"Who's wrong? Fries or Winge?"

"Yes."

A beat.

"You think one of them lied?"

"I don't know. But I think Owen Poteat may have."

I walked Slidell through my interpretation of Rinaldi's coded note.

"Sonofafrigginbitch," he said.

"Sonofafrigginbitch," I agreed.

24

Galimore arrived bearing Chick-fil-A. His shirt was wrinkled and sweat-stained under the arms. His eyes were puffy, his cheeks unshaven. Not the sexy unkept look Bruce Willis sometimes features. The up-all-night-and-grungy version.

Though the food was good, Galimore's mood was not.

We ate in tense silence.

When I asked our destination, I got one word. Weddington.

As I bunched and rebagged my sandwich wrapper and waffle-fries carton, I considered briefing Galimore on the autopsy, the abrin, and the other info obtained from Williams and Randall.

Not yet.

"What does Bogan do?" I asked.

"I already told you."

"Indulge me."

"He grows vegetables."

"You look like you didn't get much sleep."

"I'm fine."

"I spoke with Slidell this morning."

"Always reason for rejoicing."

"He questions your motive for looking at the Gamble-Lovette case after all these years."

Galimore snorted.

"It wouldn't hurt to talk to him."

"I'd rather take a punch to the balls."

Okay, then.

Galimore turned from Providence onto Weddington Road, which soon veered southeast. Through my window I watched malls and subdivision entrances slide past. I pictured the pretentious homes beyond the flawlessly quaint signs, each trying to be Tudor, or Tuscan, or Provençal. A few years back the area had been farmland. Where had all the countryside gone?

Eventually we entered a stretch of woodland. Galimore made a right, then another, then a third into a driveway. An engraved wooden placard announced our arrival at CB Botanicals.

Through a stand of pines, I could see a bungalow, beyond it a greenhouse. Beside the greenhouse was a small pond.

The bungalow was old but well kept. The siding was blue, probably the kind that never needed painting. The door was red, the gutters and window trim white.

The gardens bordering the house were lavish with color. I recognized some flowers. Phlox, daisies, lilies, begonias. Most I didn't.

A kid was up on a ladder, pulling leaves from a gutter along the house's right side. He had wires coming from both ears and didn't look up at the sound of our car.

Galimore and I got out and followed a walk bisecting a luxuriantly green lawn. The air smelled of jasmine and fresh-cut grass. From somewhere, I heard the *tic-tic* of a sprinkler.

Galimore thumbed the bell. A muted chime bonged inside the house.

Seconds passed. Galimore was reaching out again when the door swung inward.

The woman was tall and weighed approximately the same as my purse. She wore black spandex shorts and an oversize tee atop a black sports bra. Which was not needed. She held a plastic water bottle in one hand.

"Yes?"

Galimore flashed some sort of badge, quickly jammed it back into his pocket.

"Sorry to disturb your workout, ma'am. We're looking for Craig Bogan." Sunny as could be.

"Why?"

"I'm afraid that's confidential."

"Then so are his whereabouts."

Galimore beamed a megawatt smile. "My bad. Let's start again."

The woman took a long slug from the bottle. "You think my tits are saggy?"

"Far from it."

"Craig does."

"Then Craig needs corrective lenses."

"He needs more than that." The woman stuck out a hand. "Reta Yountz."

They shook so forcefully, Reta's bracelet jumped like a string of ladybugs doing a conga.

"Craig would be Craig Bogan?" Galimore asked.

Reta nodded.

"Your husband?"

"Jesus, no. We just live together."

Reta tipped her head to one side and opened her lips

ever so slightly. Her face had a sheen of perspiration that made her cheeks shine.

"Maybe I'll get a boob job." Looking directly at Galimore.

"A totally unnecessary expenditure." Looking straight back.

I fought an impulse to roll my eyes.

As Galimore worked his charm, I studied Reta. Her hair was pulled carelessly up and held back by an elastic band. I guessed her age at around forty.

"We'd like to ask your boyfriend a few questions." Galimore was oozing charisma. "Nothing big."

"You'll come back and see me afterwards?" Reta used the hem of the tee to wipe her throat, exposing a rock-hard midriff.

"You can count on it."

"He's in the greenhouse."

The greenhouse was one of those glass and metal affairs that, from a distance, look like the skeleton of an actual building. This one was much larger than I'd expected, big enough to accommodate a couple of small planes.

When we entered, the heat and humidity felt like a living thing. The air was heavy with the smells of fertilizer, loam, and compost.

Overhead, the glass walls arched into a high dome. Underfoot, the ground was covered with gravel.

Rows of wooden planters shot the length of the building, each outfitted with pipes that ran upward into more pipes that I assumed were a central irrigation system. Baskets hung from hooks. Pots sat on the floor.

There was so much flora I could almost hear the photosynthesis going on around me. I knew some easy ones. Basil, impatiens, ferns, geraniums. The rest were a leafy green mystery.

We both looked around. Bogan was nowhere in sight.

Galimore called out, got no response.

When he called out again, a voice bellowed from beyond an open door at the greenhouse's far end. We walked toward it between stands of toddler azaleas. Already my hair was lank and my shirt was sticking to my back.

The owner of the voice was in a small room that appeared to function as some sort of prep area. He was kneeling beside a barrel and, on hearing our approach, swiveled, trowel in one hand.

Bogan's hair, once red, was now salmon-gray. Rosacea made it hard to tell where his pink face ended and his scalp began.

From Bogan's greeting, I guessed the greenhouse had few walk-in customers.

"Who the hell are you?"

Galimore did the quick badge-flip thing. "We have a few questions for you, Mr. Bogan."

"Questions about what?"

"Your son."

"You have news of my son?"

"No, sir. We were hoping you might."

I noticed a tremor in Bogan's hand as he lay down the trowel. Double-gripping the barrel rim, he slowly pulled himself to his feet.

The word "flamingo" popped into my mind. The coloring. The spindly legs. Bogan's upper body seemed far too bulky for his lower limbs to support.

"Who are you?"

"My name is Cotton Galimore. My associate is Dr. Temperance Brennan."

Bogan bounced a glance off me but asked no follow-up question.

"We've been looking into the disappearances of Cindi Gamble and your son, Cale."

"That was a long time ago."

"Yes, sir."

Bogan's eyes narrowed. "Do I know you?"

"I was on the task force back in 1998." Galimore left it at that.

Bogan seemed to consider, let it go. "The police have reopened the case?"

Galimore did not correct Bogan's misinterpretation that he was still on the job. "Last week a body was found in a landfill next to the Charlotte Motor Speedway. You may have seen media reports."

"I don't follow the news." A nod in my direction. "What's her connection?"

"Dr. Brennan examined that body."

Bogan turned to me. "Was it Cale?"

"I think it's unlikely."

"But you don't know."

"Not with complete certainty."

Bogan opened his mouth. Before he could speak, music burst from my purse.

Apologizing, I withdrew a few steps, dug out my mobile, and clicked on.

And immediately regretted ignoring the caller ID.

"Sweet baby Jesus, Tempe. My life's going to hell in a handbasket."

"I can't talk now, Summer." Hand-cupping my mouth.

"I'm going to die. I really am. No person on this earth—"

"I'll help you later."

"When?"

"Whenever."

"Really?"

"Yes."

"Tonight?"

"Yes."

"You really cross-your-heart will?"

"Yes," I hissed.

Behind me, I heard Bogan ask, "You on some sort of personal crusade?"

"Nothing like that," Galimore said. "I just always felt we left that investigation a little too soon."

Outside the glass, the pond looked flat and gray, a pewter disk compressed by the afternoon's oppressive heat and humidity.

"Say it," Summer whined.

"Yes."

"Say you promise."

"I promise."

"I've completely given up on Petey. I don't like passing judgment on other people's taste. But if you take my meaning—"

"I have to go."

I was turning back to the others when something velvety brushed my elbow.

A tarantula image replaced the flamingo.

My instincts acted without clearance from my higher centers.

My hand flew up.

The mobile shot skyward, then augured into the gravel

at Galimore's feet.

"I'll get it. I'm already covered with cow flop."

Before I could respond, Bogan scooped up the iPhone, stepped to a sideboard, and wiped each surface with a rag. "Good as new." Handing it back.

"Thank you," I said.

"Daytona's manners need improving."

At my confused look, Bogan pointed to a straight-back wooden chair beside the door. On it, a black cat sat grooming itself, one leg shooting the air like a Ziegfeld girl's.

"It's sticky in here," Bogan said. "Let's go to my den."

We walked single-file, Bogan, then Galimore, then I. Daytona abandoned his toilette to bring up the rear.

The house's interior was dim. And at least a zillion degrees cooler than the greenhouse.

The front door opened into a small foyer. Beyond, on the right, stairs rose to a second floor. Nothing fancy. No carved spindles or sweeping handrail. Just treads and banisters screwed into the walls.

Through the ceiling came muted thuds I assumed were footfalls on a treadmill. I had to credit Reta. She was booking.

Bogan led us down a central hall past amateur watercolors hung in cheap plastic frames. A landscape. A bowl of fruit. A gaudy bouquet.

In a few short steps we reached a kitchen, and the hall made a ninety-degree turn.

"I'll get some sodas." A skinny finger pointed to an open door. "Y'all go in there."

Galimore and I went left as directed and entered what had to be Bogan's den.

I could only stare in amazement.

25

The room held a scruffy leather couch and matching chair, a battered oak coffee table, and a flat-screen TV the size of a highway billboard. The rest of the room was a testimonial to NASCAR.

Display cases and shelving lined the walls, all crammed to overflowing. Above the cases hung framed posters, photos, and memorabilia. Freestanding items filled every unoccupied inch of floor space.

It was doubtful the Hall of Fame had more on exhibit.

My eyes roved the assemblage.

A hunk of asphalt carved into the numeral 3 and labeled as coming from turn one at Daytona. A life-size cutout of Denny Hamlin. A hunk of red sheet metal with some driver's name incised into the surrounding plastic casing. Autographed trading cards. Commemorative coins in velvet boxes. Flags. Sweatshirts. Caps. Die-cast models of hundreds of cars.

I guessed some of the items could be valuable. A black-and-white print that looked at least fifty years old. Team suits that seemed way out of date. A car door with the number 24 painted on the outside.

"Can you believe all this shit?" Galimore was equally stunned.

"The man is a fan," I said.

"More like a fanatic."

I crossed to look at some of the poster-size photos. Jimmie Johnson, kissing the ground after winning the 2007 Brickyard. Jeff Gordon, making a pit stop. Tony Stewart, raising an index finger at Watkins Glen.

I checked the old picture. It showed a man wearing goggles and high boots straddling an old-fashioned motorcycle.

"You know who that is?" Bogan was standing in the doorway holding three cans of Pepsi.

I studied the scrawled signature. "Erwin Baker?"

"Erwin 'Cannonball' Baker won the first race ever held at the Indianapolis Motor Speedway. That was in 1909, when the track was brand-new. Cannonball cycled back and forth across the country more than a hundred times, later served as commissioner of NASCAR. The guy was a legend."

Bogan held out a Pepsi. I took it.

"That was before the fancy-pantsification of stock car racing. Before diversification." He elongated the second syllable to show his disdain.

"Sorry?"

"Back in the day everyone knew whose sport it was. And drivers were tough."

"They're not tough now?"

"Back then men were men."

"Mister, we could use a man like Herbert Hoover again." Without mirth. I didn't like the vibe I was getting.

"What?'

"Never mind."

Bogan gave Galimore a Pepsi, then dropped into the chair and threw his bird legs over one arm.

Galimore and I sat on opposite ends of the couch. Almost immediately he slipped his cell from his pocket, clicked on, and spoke into it.

"Hold on." To us. "Sorry. Got to take this." Galimore set down his soda and stepped out into the hall.

"You're here because Wayne Gamble got himself killed, right?"

"I thought you didn't keep up with the news," I said.

"I don't. I watch racing. Gamble's an item because of the Coca-Cola 600. Stupak's a favorite. *Was* a favorite."

"Did you know Wayne Gamble?"

"Knew his sister." Bogan popped the tab on his can. "What do you want from me?"

"Your thoughts on what happened to your son."

"I've got none."

"Tell me what you remember."

"Diddly-squat. I hardly saw Cale once he hooked up with Cindi Gamble. Why ask me now? You've got my statement."

"Just trying to see if anything may have been missed. Did you try to find Cale on your own?" I opened and sipped my Pepsi. It was warm, but I wanted Bogan to feel at ease.

"I contacted everyone I could think of. Trouble was, I didn't know much about the kid's life. The only thing he and I ever shared was NASCAR."

"You and Cale were estranged," I said.

"He blamed me for his mother's death. Like I could have prevented it? The woman was an alkie and a crackhead."

"Do you believe your son left the area voluntarily?"

"Yeah. I can believe that."

"Why?"

"He and his girlfriend were all caught up in that movement."

"The Patriot Posse."

"Look, Cale had been living on his own for six years." Defensive. "He was twenty-four. I had no control over who he hung out with. Not that I disagreed with everything they were saying."

"Do you know Grady Winge?" I asked.

"Isn't he the guy who saw Cale and his girlfriend driving off in a 'sixty-five Petty-blue Mustang?"

"Yes."

Again, jazz erupted from my purse.

"I'm so sorry. I thought I'd switched it to vibrate also."

"Blame Daytona."

I reached in and flicked a button. When I sat back, Bogan was eyeing me oddly.

"Grady Winge?" I asked.

"I knew Winge to shoot the breeze. We talked gardening a couple of times. But I don't leave home to watch races anymore." He gestured at the TV. "Got a better seat right here."

"What about Eugene Fries?"

"Never heard of him."

"Fries was a concession-stand worker at the Speedway in 1998."

"That narrows it to a couple hundred people."

Galimore rejoined us. Again apologized for the interruption. I let him take over.

"Talk about Cindi Gamble."

Bogan screwed his lips to one side and shook his head.

"You didn't like her?"

"Wasn't much to like or dislike. The word I'd use is 'ordinary.' But she had some crazy-ass ideas."

"Such as?"

"The little girl wanted to drive NASCAR."

"Why was that crazy?"

"Cindi Gamble was as likely to drive NASCAR as I am to swim naked with Julia Roberts."

"She did well with Bandoleros."

Bogan snorted derisively. "I saw a couple of those races. That gal couldn't steer her way around a toilet bowl. Cale could outdrive her any day of the week."

Daytona chose that moment to stroll in and jump onto Bogan's lap.

"Look, I don't mean to be rude. But I've got bougainvillea needs fertilizing."

I looked at Galimore. He nodded.

I hit Bogan with my standard closer. "What do you think happened back in 'ninety-eight?"

Bogan shrugged.

"At the time, did you agree with the task force finding?"

"Who was I to disagree?"

"Do you still accept it?"

Bogan stroked Daytona for a while before answering.

"All those years, I kept waiting for a call, a letter, a telegram, anything to let me know that my son was alive. Every time I returned to this house, I checked the answering machine. Every time the mail arrived, I looked for Cale's handwriting. It became an obsession. Pointless, but I couldn't help myself. Then one day I stopped."

Bogan drew air into his nose, slowly released it. Then he looked me straight in the eye.

"I don't know what happened back then. Cale took off to

marry his girlfriend? Went into hiding? Got himself killed? You tell me. I gave up trying to figure it out."

"Herbert Hoover?"

Galimore and I were back in the car.

"I thought Bogan was going all Archie Bunker," I said.

"You're far too young to remember *All in the Family*."

"Save the enchantment for Reta."

"You think Bogan's a racist?"

"Did you hear how he pronounced 'diversification,' as though it were a dirty word?" I hooked quotation marks in the air. "'Back in the day everyone knew whose sport it was.' Give me a break."

"The man likes cats."

"A point in his favor. I also think Bogan's a homophobe." More quote marks. "'Men were men'? Did the dolt really say that?"

"The line was good enough for Archie and Edith."

"I know there are rumors, but has anyone in NASCAR actually come out?"

"Evan Darling. He's a Grand-Am driver. But most stay deep in the closet."

"If Bogan's attitude is typical, I can see why."

"There's a growing fan base among the gay community. Quite a few websites. Gaytona.com. Queers4Gears.com. GayWheels.com."

"Who knew?"

"You talked to Bogan more than I did. What was your take?"

"His grief over losing Cale seemed genuine. But his view of Cindi Gamble doesn't square with what I've heard from others."

"What others?" Galimore turned north onto Providence Road.

"J. D. Danner, the leader of the Patriot Posse. Danner thought Cindi had a good shot at driving NASCAR."

"Maybe Bogan was biased. Don't parents always think their kids are better athletes or artists or whatever compared to everyone else's kids?"

"Maybe." I thought a moment. "A teacher named Ethel Bradford said Cindi was highly intelligent. And Lynn Nolan, a high school friend, described her as scary-smart."

"Bogan wasn't saying Cindi was dumb. He was saying she was dull."

I remembered Galimore's phone interruption. "I hope your call wasn't bad news."

"It wasn't good. There's a feeding frenzy going on at the Speedway. I've got to get back."

I checked my watch: 3:20. No wonder I was hungry. There was nothing at home. I'd have to stop for groceries.

Suddenly I remembered something that had fallen through the cracks.

"Lynn Nolan mentioned another of Cindi's friends. Maddy Padgett. Slidell was going to try to locate her."

"Did he?"

"I forgot to ask him. When he called, we just talked about the Mustang."

We wound through town, my thoughts buzzing like wasps in a bottle. So many loose ends. So many unanswered questions.

"Did I tell you that Lynn Nolan thought Cale was abusive to Cindi?"

Galimore turned to me, surprise on his face. "Oh yeah?"

"She thought she spotted bruising on Cindi's arms."

"No shit."

"I think we should talk to Maddy Padgett."

"We can do that."

We were almost to the MCME when I remembered the call I'd ignored.

A red dot indicated voice mail.

I tapped the icon and listened.

And felt the tiny hairs on my neck go upright.

26

I sucked in my breath.

Checked the list of incoming calls.

"Shit."

Sensing agitation, Galimore glanced my way.

With a shaky finger, I rejabbed the icon.

Listened again.

"Jesus."

"What's going on?"

I hit speaker while extending the phone in Galimore's direction.

The voice was low and deep, the message short.

"You're next."

"Play it again," Galimore ordered.

I did.

"Again."

We listened to the same two words. Still the meaning was unclear.

"Is he saying 'you're next'? Or is he saying 'your next' and then getting cut off?"

"Yes," I said.

"Don't be a smart-ass."

Galimore was right. I was being a jerk. It's the game face I wear when frightened.

"If this is a threat, I intend to take it seriously."

"Thanks, Hulk."

"Christ, Brennan. Check the number."

"The call logged in as unknown."

"Do you recognize the voice?"

"No. Does it sound like the same guy who threatened you?"

"I can't be sure. But here's what you're going to do."

"I react poorly when people use that opener."

"Go home. Arm the security system. Stay there. I'll contact you when I'm done kicking ass at the Speedway."

"Can I admit strangers if they're really polite?"

My surgical strike for groceries ended up costing two hundred and forty bucks. But I had provisions to take me into the next millennium.

While I placed cans and boxes in the pantry, fruit in a bowl, and veggies and dairy products in the refrigerator, Birdie chased empty bags across the floor. Periodically, he'd roll to his back and claw the plastic with four upraised paws.

I ate a carton of yogurt, a peach, and two Petit Écolier cookies. Then I went upstairs to peel off my sweaty clothes and shower with my impulse purchase of pomegranate energizing body cleanser.

When I returned to the kitchen, pits, stems, and tiny globs of pulp littered the floor. Great. The little bugger had eaten three cherries and mangled four more.

While waiting for Galimore, I decided to see what I could scare up on abrin. An hour on the Internet taught me the following.

Abrus precatorius goes by many common names, including but not limited to Jequirity, Crab's Eye, Rosary Pea, John Crow Bead, Precatory Bean, and Indian Licorice.

The plant is a slender perennial climber that twines around trees, shrubs, and hedges. Its leaves are long and pinnate-leafleted. Its seeds are black and red and contain the toxin abrin.

Though native to Indonesia, *Abrus precatorius* is now found in many tropical and subtropical areas of the world, including the United States. When introduced to new locales, the species tends to become weedy and invasive.

Known as *Gunja* in Sanskrit and some Indian languages and *Ratti* in Hindi, *Abrus precatorius* is used as a traditional unit of measure, mostly by jewelers and Ayurved doctors. The seeds are valued in native jewelry for their bright coloration. In China, they are a symbol of love. In Trinidad, they are worn to ward off evil spirits.

Jewelry-making with *Abrus precatorius* is considered dangerous work. Death by abrin poisoning has resulted from finger-pricking while boring the seeds for beadwork.

Symptoms are identical in abrin and ricin poisoning. But abrin is more toxic by almost two orders of magnitude.

Abrin is a macromolecular complex consisting of two protein subunits termed A and B. The B chain facilitates abrin's entry into a cell by bonding to certain transport proteins on the cell membranes. Once inside, the A chain shuts down protein synthesis.

I was eyeballing pictures of the assassin legume when my iPhone started bouncing across the table. I'd forgotten to switch it from vibrate.

"You'll never guess what I caught."

"Scabies," I said.

"What the hell's scabies?"

"I'm good, Detective Slidell. How are you?" Why couldn't the guy ever open with a greeting?

"I was up, so I caught your NASCAR pal."

It took me a moment to translate. "You're working the Wayne Gamble investigation?"

"Concord asked for help in sorting the thing. You been watching the news? It's a shitstorm."

"Galimore said a lot of media were camped out at the Speedway."

Slidell did the throat thing. At mention of the media? Of Galimore?

Disregarding Slidell's censure, I recounted my visit with Craig Bogan.

"And?"

"I wouldn't be surprised if the guy keeps a spare bedsheet in his closet."

"Meaning?"

"I think he's a bigot."

"Who don't he like?"

"Anyone who's not white and straight."

"Uh-huh."

I described the phone threat. If it was a threat.

"Where was Galimore?" Stony.

"Right there with me."

As the words left my lips, I realized that was wrong.

"So what are you doing?"

I knew Slidell was referring to the call. Chose not to acknowledge.

"Researching abrin," I said.

"You know what you are, Doc?"

"Crafty on the Internet."

Slidell clucked disapproval but let it go.

"Looks like Gamble was doing some research of his own."

I waited for him to explain.

"Grady Winge talked about a 'sixty-five Mustang, right?"

"Right."

"I found a folder in Gamble's trailer. He'd traced every 'sixty-five Mustang registered in the Carolinas back in 'ninety-eight."

"Through NCIC?"

"Hell, no. That's just for people on the job. You gotta take a class, get a user name and password. It's mandated by the FBI. If the system was open to every Tom, Dick, and Harry—"

"What about DMV records?"

"No."

"So how did Gamble do it?"

"Maybe he had inside help. Maybe he requested the original file and was given access. Before some FBI spook snatched the bloody thing, of course."

"Did Eddie put anything in his notes?"

"Yeah. He tracked down eighteen 'sixty-five Mustangs tagged in North and South Carolina. Ran them all. Fifteen came up legit. The other three owners he could never locate."

"But Gamble found them."

"One car belonged to a dead woman. Her daughter-in-law ponied up for a tag every year without even asking questions. The dead lady no longer lived at the Raleigh address listed on the paperwork. Or anywhere else, for that matter."

"Where was the Mustang?"

"Rusting in a storage shed."

"The second car belonged to a collector with a Myrtle Beach address. Same deal. The guy's assistant relicensed annually, not knowing the thing was sitting in a warehouse somewhere with no wheels and no engine. The owner was living in Singapore."

"So his contact information was also useless."

"The third car belonged to a retired army sergeant. He'd moved the vehicle to Texas but kept the South Carolina plate. When Eddie tried to call, the line had probably been disconnected."

"So those three owners were effectively lost to the system back in 'ninety-eight."

"Yeah. But Gamble found them. And all three are dead ends."

"Like the other fifteen."

"You've got it."

"How could such a unique vehicle remain untraceable?"

"Good question."

"Could Winge have been wrong?"

"He was very specific." I heard paper rustle. "At the Speedway, he told us it was a 'sixty-five Petty-blue Mustang with a lime-green decal on the passenger-side windshield."

I felt a tickle deep in my brainpan. What?

Slidell shifted gears. "Your gut about Owen Poteat was right on target. In 'ninety-eight the guy was up to his eyeballs in debt. He hadn't worked in three years, and he'd dropped a ton fighting the little missus over custody. The poor bastard took out loans, eventually sold his house. Still lost his kids. Never again found gainful employment."

"But somehow he had twenty-six thousand to invest in their college educations."

"Winning lottery ticket?"

"What are the odds?"

After we disconnected, I spent a little more time on my laptop. And learned a few more disturbing facts.

Abrin is a yellow-white powder that can be released into the air as fine particles. If released outdoors, it has the potential to contaminate agricultural products.

Abrin can be used to poison food and water.

The fatal dose of abrin is approximately seventy-five times smaller than the fatal dose of ricin.

I checked another site. Got a figure. Did some math in my head.

Holy crap.

Abrin can kill with a circulating amount of less than 3 micrograms.

At seven p.m., I broiled a flounder filet and shared it with Birdie. Preferring a mayo-based sauce, he passed on the slaw. Or maybe he just dislikes storebought salads.

I then worked through my in-box.

Several e-mails concerned casework. A pathologist at the *LSJML* needed clarification on a report. A prosecutor in Charlotte wanted to schedule a meeting. LaManche wondered when I'd return to Montreal.

Others offered the deal of a lifetime. A Rolex watch for fifty bucks. Access to unclaimed funds in an African bank. A cleanser that would make my skin glow like that of a Hollywood star.

Katy was thinking of quitting her job to spend a year in Ireland. She had an offer to tend bar at a pub in Cork. Great.

Ryan had sent an uncharacteristically long message describing his latest therapy session with Lily. He was dismayed at the amount of anger his daughter seemed to harbor. Against him for being absent during her childhood. Against Lutetia for hiding from him the fact of her existence—and for recently abandoning her to return to Nova Scotia.

He wrote that he was discouraged, homesick, and missed my company. The tenor was so heartbreaking, it drilled a hole through my sternum.

But Ryan's message wasn't as sad as the one penned by Harry. Recently, my sister and I had received shocking news not dissimilar from that which had altered Ryan's world.

Harry's son, Kit, had fathered a child the summer he was sixteen and in Cape Cod at sailing camp. For reasons that would forever remain a mystery, the child's mother, Coleen Brennan, of an unrelated branch of the clan, had not disclosed to her summer love that he had a daughter.

Victoria "Tory" Brennan was now fourteen. Upon the sudden death of Coleen, Tory had relocated from Massachusetts and was now living with Kit in Charleston.

Harry had a granddaughter. I had a grandniece.

Harry was furious about all the lost years. And despondent over the fact that Kit, wanting to give Tory time to adjust, wouldn't yet allow his mother to visit.

I was dialing Harry's number when the front bell chimed. Thinking it was Galimore, I put down the handset and went to the door.

It wasn't my worst nightmare.

But it was close.

27

Pete and Summer were standing close but not touching. Both looked tense, like people waiting in line. Summer held a Nieman Marcus bag by its string handle.

Pasting on a faux smile, I opened the door. "To what do I owe this pleasure?"

Summer looked like the question stumped her.

"You sure you want to do this?" Pete sounded uncomfortable.

"Sure." Oh, no. "Come on in."

Pete was wearing flip-flops, khaki shorts, and a Carmel Country Club golf shirt. Summer had on wedge sandals, a silk tank, and designer camouflage pants that would have unnerved Patton.

Summer swanned straight to the dining room and parked the bag on the table. Pete and I followed.

"Can I get you anything?" I asked. Cyanide and Kool-Aid?

"Merlot would be nice if—"

"We won't be here that long." Pete shot me an apologetic grin. "I know you have more important things on your mind."

"See, Petey. That's your problem. Our wedding *is*

important. What could be *more* important?"

Finding a cure for AIDS?

Summer began lifting items from the bag and organizing them into clusters. Napkins. Swatches of fabric. Silver picture frames. A glass container that looked like a giant lab flask.

"Now. The tablecloths will be ecru. The centerpieces will be made up of roses and lilies arranged in these vases." A cherry-red nail ticked the flask. "These are the napkin possibilities."

She fanned out the stack. The choices included pink, brown, silver, green, black, and a shade that I took to be ecru.

"And these are the options for the fabric that will drape each chair back."

She arranged the swatches side by side below the lucky napkin finalists. Over her back, Pete's eyes met mine.

I crooked a brow. Seriously?

He mouthed, "I owe you."

Oh, yeah.

Summer straightened. "So. What do you think?"

You don't have the sense God gave a corn muffin.

"Wow," I said. "You've done a lot of work."

"Indeed I have." Summer beamed a smile that could have sold a million tubes of Crest.

How to maneuver the minefield?

Psychology. No chance muffin brain would catch on.

"How would you describe the floral arrangements?" I asked.

"Kind of pink and yellow. But *very* understated."

"So you want simple."

"But elegant. It has to make a statement."

"Clearly green is out."

"Clearly."

As Summer snatched up the first reject, I raised my brows to Pete.

"Very funny," he mouthed.

"Do you like a monochromatic look?"

Summer regarded me blankly.

"Things being the same color."

"I like more punch. Ah. I see what y'all mean."

The ecru napkin disappeared into the bag.

"Stark contrast?"

"Not so much."

"Then black is probably wrong."

"Totally."

Black. Gone.

"An earthy look?"

"Not for summer." She giggled. "Not me. The season."

"Then forget brown."

Gone.

That left silver and pink.

"Are you leaning toward one of the patterns?" I asked.

"I love this one." She stroked a swatch with ghastly pink swirls on a cream background.

I remembered the outfit she'd worn on her last visit.

Bingo.

I laid the pink napkin artfully across the swirly swatch of fabric.

"Yes!" Summer clapped in glee. "Yes! Yes! I agree! See, Petey? You just have to use good taste."

Petey held his applause.

"Now." Summer arranged the four silver frames in a row. "Every place setting will have one of these. So the guests now where to sit. Then they keep it as their gift. Clever, right?"

"Um."

"Which is your favorite?"

"They're all very nice."

As Summer pointed out the minutiae that set each frame apart, I noted that she took longer with one than the others.

"I like the dotted border," I said.

"So do I! Tempe, we are so much alike, we could be sisters!"

Behind his fiancée's back, Petey winced.

Summer was gathering her samples when my mobile sounded. Excusing myself, I stepped into the kitchen.

Area code 704. Charlotte. I didn't recognize the number. Preferring a sales pitch for funeral plans to further interaction with Bridezilla, I clicked on.

"Temperance Brennan?"

I heard a car horn in the background, suggesting the caller was outside.

"Yes."

"The coroner?"

I felt my scalp tighten. "Who is this, please?"

"You got Eli Hand at the morgue."

The voice was muffled, as though coming through a filter. I couldn't tell if it was the same one that had uttered the menacing two-word voice mail.

"Who is this?"

I heard a click, then three beeps.

"Damn!"

"Everything OK?"

I whipped around.

Pete was watching me, his face tight with concern. I was so freaked I hadn't heard him enter the kitchen.

"I"—I what?—"got an unexpected call."

"Not bad news, I hope."

"No. Just—" Adrenaline made it feel like crickets were trapped in my chest.

"Unexpected," he finished for me.

"Yes."

"You can remove the phone from your ear."

"Right."

"I want to thank you for"—Pete jabbed a thumb over one shoulder toward the dining room door—"that."

"You're welcome."

"She's really very bright."

"You've got to have a penis to hold that view."

Pete raised his brows.

I responded in kind.

"How's Boyd?" I asked.

"Talks about you constantly."

"I miss him."

"And the Chow feels likewise. He's crazy about you."

"That dog is an excellent judge of character."

"Recognizes rare qualities that others fail to appreciate."

I'd no idea what to respond. So I said nothing.

Pete studied my face for so long, the moment grew awkward.

"Guess you should be moving along," I said.

"Guess so."

"I doubt you'll be enjoying a chatty evening." I smiled.

"Perhaps not a bad thing." Pete didn't.

Uh-oh. Trouble in paradise? I knew Pete. And he sounded unhappy.

Back in the dining room, Summer had been joined by Birdie. The cat was on a chair, batting at a napkin she was dangling above him.

I narrowed my eyes at the little turncoat.

He gave me the cat equivalent of an innocent look.

"Good luck," I said as they made their way down the front steps.

I meant it.

As soon as they'd gone, I phoned Larabee. He'd just returned home from a ten-mile run.

"Do we have someone at the morgue named Eli Hand?"

"Not to my knowledge. Who is he?"

I told him about the call.

For a full thirty seconds no one spoke.

"You don't suppose—"

Larabee finished my sentence. "—it could be a tip about the landfill John Doe."

"That was my first thought."

"How do we find out about Hand?"

"Do you have contact information for Special Agent Williams?"

"Hold on."

I heard a thunk. After a brief pause, Larabee returned and read off a number.

"You think Williams will know something?" he asked.

"I think he'll know a lot."

"Keep me looped in."

Williams answered on the second ring.

I identified myself.

If my call surprised him, he didn't let on.

"Eli Hand," I said.

The silence went on for so long, I thought we'd been disconnected.

"What are you asking me?" Williams's tone was flinty.

"Was Eli Hand John-Doeing it at our morgue?"

"I can't comment on that."

"Why not?"

"Why are you asking about Eli Hand?"

"I got an anonymous tip."

"From what source?"

"See, that's the anonymous part."

"How did you receive this tip?" Terse.

"On my mobile."

"Was the phone able to capture the number?"

I gave it to him.

"Who is Eli Hand?"

"I'm not at liberty—"

"With or without any of that famous FBI cooperation, Dr. Larabee and I *will* find out who Eli Hand is. Or was. And we *will* find out if Hand turned up dead in a barrel of asphalt in the Morehead Road landfill. Should that prove to be the case, Detective Slidell *will* find out why."

"Back the attitude down a notch."

"Then give me some answers."

"I'll speak to you tomorrow."

Next I phoned Galimore.

Got no answer.

Between the anonymous threat, Summer's idiocy and Pete's gloominess, the call about Eli Hand, Williams's arrogance, and Galimore's disappearing act, sleep was elusive when I went to bed.

My mind kept juggling pieces, repositioning and twisting to make them interlock. Instead of answers, I ended up with the same questions.

I knew from Williams's reaction that the landfill John Doe would turn out to be Eli Hand. Who was he? When had he died? Why did his body show signs of ricin poisoning?

Abrin was found in Wayne Gamble's coffee. How had it gotten there? Surely Gamble had been murdered. By whom? Why?

Cale Lovette had associated with right-wing extremists. Had they helped him vanish? If so, how had he managed to skim under the radar all these years? Had they killed him?

Descriptions of Cindi Gamble did not jibe. Was she smart, with NASCAR potential, as Ethel Bradford, Lynn Nolan, and J. D. Danner suggested? Or dull, a poor driver, as Craig Bogan said? Was she in love with Cale Lovette? Or terrified of him?

Accounts given by Grady Winge and Eugene Fries disagreed. Was one of them simply in error? Was one of them lying? Why?

Had Owen Poteat actually seen Cale Lovette at the Charlotte airport ten days after he disappeared from the Speedway, or was this deliberate misinformation? If so, why? Had someone paid him? Who?

Ted Raines was still missing. Raines had access to ricin and abrin. Was Raines involved at all?

I kept trying to find a connection. Just one. That connection would lead to another, which would lead to another. Which would lead to answers long overdue.

When I finally drifted off, my rest was fitful. I woke repeatedly, then dozed, dreaming in unrelated vignettes.

Birdie, walking on a table set with glassware and swirly pink fabric. Galimore, driving a blue Mustang with a green sticker on the windshield. Ryan, waving at me from very far off. Slidell, talking to a man curled up in a barrel. Summer, teetering down a sidewalk in skyscraper heels.

When I last checked the clock, it was 4:23.

28

Exactly three hours later the landline jolted me awake.

"You good?"

"I'm fine."

"Last night turned ugly." Galimore sounded like he'd logged less sleep than I had.

"I'm a big girl. I'm fine."

"You hear back from that tool?"

"No. But I heard from someone else."

I told him about the Eli Hand call and about my conversation with Williams.

"You're going to stay put, like I said, right?"

"Oh, yeah. I'm waiting for a call from Oprah."

"You should put together an act. Maybe take it on Comedy Central."

"I'll think about that."

"But not today."

"Not today."

Galimore sighed in annoyance. "Do what you gotta do."

"I will."

I was making toast when the phone rang again.

"Williams here."

"Brennan here." Sleep deprivation also makes me flippant.

"The number you gave me traced to a pay phone at a Circle K on Old Charlotte Road in Concord."

"So the caller could have been anyone."

"We're checking deeds for properties located within a half-mile radius."

"That's a long shot."

"Yes."

"Who's Eli Hand?"

"Due to your recent involvement in the situation, I've been authorized to share certain information with you and Dr. Larabee. May we meet this morning?"

"I can be at the MCME in thirty minutes."

"We'll see you then."

It was take two of the previous day's scene. Larabee was seated at his desk. The specials were side by side in chairs on the left, facing him. I was to their right.

Williams began without being asked.

"Do you remember Bhagwan Shree Rajneesh?"

Williams was asking about a 1980s Indian guru who moved several thousand followers onto a ranch in rural Wasco County, Oregon, and established a city called Rajneeshpuram. The group eventually took political control of the small nearby town of Antelope and renamed it Rajneesh.

Though initially friendly, the commune's relations with the local populace soon soured. After being denied building permits for expansion of Rajneeshpuram, the commune leadership sought to gain political control by dominating the November 1984 county elections.

"The bhagwan and his crazies wanted to win judgeships on the Wasco County Circuit Court and elect the sheriff," I said. "But they weren't certain they could carry the day. So they poisoned restaurant salad bars with salmonella, hoping to incapacitate adverse voters."

"Exactly," Williams said. "*Salmonella enterica* was first delivered through glasses of water to two county commissioners and then, on a larger scale, to the salad bars. Seven hundred and fifty-one people got sick, forty-five of whom were hospitalized. The incident was the first and single largest bioterrorist attack in United States history."

"I remember," Larabee said. "They finally nailed the little creep right here in Charlotte. It was national news."

Larabee was right. Back in the eighties, few in the country had heard of a quiet southern city called Charlotte other than for its school integration and mandatory busing. The arrest conferred notoriety, and the citizenry got a kick out of it. *We Bagged the Bhagwan* T-shirts did a booming business.

"In 1985 a task force was formed, composed of members of the Oregon State Police and the FBI," Williams continued. "When a search warrant was executed, a sample of bacteria matching the contaminant that had sickened the town residents was found in a Rajneeshpuram medical laboratory. Two commune officials were indicted. Both served time in a minimum-security federal prison."

Williams looked pointedly at me. "A third disappeared."

"Eli Hand," I guessed.

Williams nodded.

"Hand was a twenty-year-old chemistry major at Oregon State University. In the spring of 1984 he fell under the influence of the bhagwan, dropped out of school, and moved to Rajneeshpuram."

"Just months before the salad bars were spiked."

"Hand was suspected of having helped orchestrate the poisonings. Following the bhagwan's arrest and deportation, Hand left the commune."

"And came east?"

"Yes. Convinced his spiritual master had been persecuted, Hand grew increasingly disillusioned with the government. He spent time in western Carolina, eventually joined a group of right-wingers called the Freedom Brigade. When that fell apart, he drifted to the Charlotte area, in time hooked up with J. D. Danner."

"And his Patriot Posse."

"Yes."

"So the FBI had Hand under surveillance?" Larabee asked.

"We were tracking a lot of people back then. Intel had it that Hand and his buddies hid Eric Rudolph for a while."

"Where is he now?" I knew the answer to that.

"Hand slipped off the grid in 2000."

"You never found him again," I said.

"No."

"But now you have."

Williams gave a tight nod. "An odontologist says it's a match."

That surprised me. "You found dental antemorts?"

"Hand's mother still lives in Portland. Eli had an orthodontic evaluation when he was twelve. She still had the plaster casts and X-rays. The odont said it was enough for a positive."

"Hand's prints weren't in the system?" Larabee asked.

"He'd never been arrested, served in the military, or held a job that required a security clearance."

"Let me guess," I said. "The FBI suspected Hand and the Patriot Posse were planning a bioterrorist attack like the one in Oregon, this time with ricin."

"Yes."

"That's why you were treading eggshells back in 1998."

"We couldn't risk setting them off."

"But it never happened."

"No."

"How would Hand get hold of ricin?" Larabee asked.

"We think he may have been producing the toxin himself."

"*Ricinus communis* grows in North Carolina?"

"Easily."

We all thought about that.

"So how did Hand end up in a barrel of asphalt?" I voiced the question in everyone's mind.

"Accidentally poisoned himself? Fell on his head? Got taken out by his pals? We honestly don't know."

"What happened to Cale Lovette and Cindi Gamble?" I asked.

"Same answer."

"Was either of them working inside for the bureau?"

"Not to my knowledge."

"Uh-huh."

I held Williams's eyes with mine. He didn't blink.

The small office filled with tense silence. When Williams broke it, his voice was elevated a microdecibel. It was as excited as I'd seen him.

"The long shot paid off, Dr. Brennan."

"Sorry?" The quick segue lost me.

Williams cocked his chin toward his partner.

One word and I knew why Randall spoke so rarely. His

voice was high and nasal, more suited to a Hollywood hairdresser than an FBI agent.

"Alda Pickerly Winge has owned a home on Union Cemetery Road in Concord since 1964. The property is less than a quarter mile from the Circle K from which the call was placed to your mobile last night."

I felt centipedes crawl my arms.

"Alda is related to Grady?" Stupid. I knew the answer to that one, too.

"He is her son."

"You think Grady Winge called in the tip on Eli Hand?"

"Winge's truck is currently parked at his mother's house. We believe it has been there all night."

"Who's Grady Winge?" Larabee asked.

"A Speedway maintenance worker who saw Cindi Gamble and Cale Lovette argue with a man, then enter a car shortly before they disappeared."

Again the troublesome tickle in my brainpan.

What?

"A 'sixty-five Mustang," Williams added.

Suddenly, the tickle exploded into a full-blown thought.

I shot upright in my chair.

"A 'sixty-five Petty-blue Mustang with a lime-green decal on the passenger-side windshield. That's what Winge told Slidell and me at the Speedway last Monday. Can you check his statement from 1998?"

The specials exchanged one of their meaningful glances. Then Williams lowered his chin almost imperceptibly.

Randall got up and went into the hall. In moments he was back.

"A 'sixty-five Petty-blue Mustang with a lime-green decal on the passenger-side windshield."

"You're sure that's what he said?"

"That was his statement verbatim."

"What are the chances a witness would use the exact same words and phrasing so many years apart?" I was totally psyched.

Williams appeared to consider that. "You think Winge made up his story? Practiced it to be sure he'd get it right?"

"It would explain why the Mustang could never be traced. Think about it. A car that rare?"

"Why would Winge lie?"

No one had an answer.

"He's not a smart man," I offered.

"Why tip you about Eli Hand?" Williams asked.

"Maybe Winge was involved in Hand's death and is feeling guilty," Larabee tossed out.

"After more than a decade?" Williams sounded skeptical.

"He claims to have found Jesus," I said.

"You believe him?"

I shrugged. Who knows?

"Maybe Winge was involved in what happened to Gamble and Lovette." Larabee was hitting his stride. "Maybe he killed them. Maybe he killed Wayne Gamble because the guy was figuring things out."

We all went still, realizing the implications of that line of reasoning.

Might Winge think *I* was figuring things out? Had he left me the threatening voice mail? Might he be planning a similar "accident" for me?

"We've got Winge under twenty-four-hour surveillance," Williams said. "If he changes his socks, we'll know about it."

Williams stood.

Randall stood.

"Until this is resolved, I'm going to ask the CMPD to run units by your town house on an hourly basis."

"Do you really think that's necessary?"

"Better safe than sorry."

Williams stuck out a hand. "Nice job on the Mustang catch."

"Thanks."

We shook. Randall did not join in.

"Perhaps it's best if you lay low for a while."

What the flip? First Galimore, now Williams.

I made a noncommittal sound.

"I'll phone if anything breaks," Williams said.

That call came very, very soon.

29

Galimore rang at nine-twenty. The weekend's races were fast approaching, and the media were growing hysterical for information on Wayne Gamble's death. He couldn't leave the Speedway for any reason.

Galimore sounded so rushed, I didn't take time to mention that the landfill John Doe had been identified. Or to explain how that had come about.

Slidell phoned around ten. I filled him in on recent developments. He promised to locate Maddy Padgett once he got done checking documents and a PC confiscated from Wayne Gamble's trailer.

Williams's call came at eleven-fifteen. I was in the stinky room gluing cranial fragments. Wayne Gamble's partially reconstructed skull sat in a bowl of sand at my elbow.

Williams sounded out of breath. "About the time we were leaving the MCME, Winge got into his truck and drove from his mother's house to the Stephens Road Nature Preserve. You know it?"

"It's between Mountain Island Lake and Lake Norman, right?"

"Exactly. Stephens Road cuts off Beatties Ford Road, winds past a housing development, then dead-ends in some fairly dense forest."

A voice called out.

"Hang on."

The air went thick, as though Williams had pressed the phone to his chest. In seconds, he was back.

"Sorry. Winge parked and walked into the woods. Agents found him about fifty yards north of the road. He was on his knees and appeared to be praying."

I felt my heart rate kick up a notch.

"The agents called me. They described an area of ground slump at the spot where Winge was kneeling. I instructed them to detain Winge and ordered a cadaver dog to the site."

My grip tightened on the receiver. I knew what was coming.

"The dog alerted at the depression."

"What's happening now?"

"CSU is on the way."

"So am I."

"I was hoping you'd say that."

The sun was low by the time the bones were fully uncovered. One skeleton lay on top of the other, the arm bones intertwined, as though the victims were embracing in death.

The grave was shallow, dug quickly, filled with haste. Standard. And Winge, or whoever had done the burying, had made the usual mistake of the uninformed. Instead of leaving the fill mounded over the pit, he, she, or they had stomped it flat. With the passage of time, soil compression had led to the telltale slump.

The temperature and humidity had been so high all afternoon, the forest seemed to be rendered lifeless. Trees, birds, and insects held themselves still and silent.

The dog had remained. Her name was Clara. Clara's handler had walked her past our excavation periodically. She'd scent, then sit, tongue dangling, saffron rays of sunlight tinging her fur.

Slidell had arrived shortly after I'd staked out a square and set up a screen. He'd watched silently as I instructed the CSU techs on how to trowel and sift dirt. They worked sluggishly, immobilized by the stifling heat.

When I asked Slidell why he was there, he said his sergeant was viewing the Wayne and Cindi Gamble deaths as related. He'd been told to hustle Gamble's laptop to the geek squad and get his ass to the burial site. From now on he was out of rotation, assigned strictly to their cases.

We'd sealed the scene with sawhorses and yellow tape, but it hadn't been necessary. The heat and the remoteness of the location had been enough. No one had come to gawk as we went through our macabre routine.

The remains we assumed to be those of Cindi Gamble and Cale Lovette lay on the surface now, zipped into two pitifully flat body bags.

I sat in a patrol unit on Stephens Road, sipping water from a plastic bottle. The radio crackled, and the usual motion swirled around me. I'd come to do my job, to be a professional. But I was finding it hard.

Had it really been less than a week since I'd learned of Gamble and Lovette? It seemed so much longer. I felt I knew them. I'd been so hopeful. Now the verdict was in. Death.

I tried to keep my brain blank. I didn't want to replay

the scene of the soil-stained bones emerging as the layers of dirt were peeled off. To visualize the skulls grinning up from the trench. To see the small round holes centered in the occipital bones.

I'd recognized the earrings instantly upon seeing them in the screen. Small silver loops with race cars dangling from one edge.

I pictured the little oval face. The pixie blond hair.

Push it away.

You didn't kill her, I said silently to Cale Lovette. *You probably tried to save her.*

I'd supervised the excavation, done preliminary bio-profiles on the skeletons. Then Slidell had taken charge of the scene.

I watched him emerge from the trees now. He conferred with Williams, then turned and walked in my direction.

Hitching a pant leg, Slidell squatted next to the car, one hand on the open door's armrest. His face was raspberry, and perspiration soaked his hair and armpits.

"Not the outcome we were looking for." Slidell's voice was a bit husky.

I said nothing.

Slidell reached behind his back and yanked a hankie from his pocket. His palm left a small saddle of perspiration on the vinyl armrest.

"You find anything down there with them?"he asked.

"Her earrings. Zippers. Some moldy shreds of clothing."

"Shoes?"

"No."

Slidell shook his head.

"You think they were killed here?" I asked.

"Hard to say. They could have been forced to take off

their shoes. Or their bodies could have been transported from somewhere else."

"They pick up anything with the metal detector?"

"Nothing useful." He knew I was asking about bullets or casings.

Behind Slidell, I could see two attendants carrying a stretcher. Together, they transferred both body bags to the morgue gurney and buckled the black straps.

When I looked back, Slidell was studying my face.

"Can I get you something? More water?"

"I'm good." I swallowed. "Did Winge do it?"

"Dumb-ass keeps mumbling he's sorry. Over and over. Sounds like a confession to me."

"Why?"

"I've never been able to understand how these mutants think. But trust me. We'll get everything he knows out of him."

The heat in the car was like hot syrup against my skin. I got out and lifted my hair to feel the breeze on my neck. There was none.

I watched the morgue attendants slam and secure the van doors.

And felt a sob build in my chest. Fought it back.

I spotted Williams walking toward us. *He says one thing to me and I'll rip his goddamn lips off,* I promised myself. I meant it.

Williams spoke to Slidell. "We about done here?"

"Yeah."

"Where's Winge?"

"Being booked."

For a few moments the three of us stood in self-conscious silence. Sensing strong emotion, the men didn't know how to act, what to say. I didn't feel like helping them out.

Avoiding my eyes, Slidell addressed Williams. "Meet me downtown. We'll grill this cocksucker."

On the drive home, my eyes burned and my chest heaved intermittently.

Don't cry. Don't you dare cry.

Somehow, I didn't.

A bubble bath and a change of clothes did wonders for my body. My spirits remained in the cellar.

Slidell's visit did nothing to lift them. Maybe it was his BO. More likely his report on Grady Winge.

"The prick's stonewalling."

"What do you mean?"

"He won't talk. Keeps his eyes closed and his lips moving, like he's praying."

"What did he say about the graves?"

"You listening to me?"

"You must have other interrogation techniques."

"Right. The rubber hoses slipped my mind."

"What about a psychologist?"

"We reminded Mr. Winge of the popularity of capital punishment in this state. Now we're letting him ponder that."

An image of the two skeletons fountained up in my mind. I felt anger and sadness. Pushed them away.

"Now what?" I asked.

"I'm going to squeeze Lynn Nolan a little harder. This time pop her at home."

"Why?"

"I want to know more about the guy Lovette was talking to at the Double Shot."

"You think Nolan was holding back?"

243

"Let's just say I want another run at her."

"Did Williams tell you the FBI confiscated the Gamble-Lovette case file?"

"No."

"He virtually admitted it."

"Yeah?"

I described my *aha!* moment regarding the statements Winge gave in 'ninety-eight and on the previous Monday.

"Randall made a call, confirmed that Winge's wording was identical. He must have had someone check the original file."

"Those arrogant pricks." Slidell's jaw muscles bulged, relaxed. "Don't matter. That sonofabitch is guilty and he's going down. The question is, who else?"

"Where does Nolan live?" I asked.

"The old hometown. Kannapolis."

It was obvious Slidell hadn't been home. His BO was strong enough to put down a horse. The prospect of a car ride together was not appealing.

"You're going now?"

"I thought I'd have a couple beers first, maybe catch a movie."

The clock said 9:20.

I desperately craved sleep.

"Hold on." I hurried to the study and grabbed my purse.

I'd overestimated the drive time. But underestimated the aromatics. By the time we got to Kannapolis, I craved another hot bath.

Nolan lived in a faux-colonial complex that looked like it had taken five minutes to construct. Her apartment was in the middle building, on the upper of two floors. Her unit and three others were accessed by the same iron and concrete staircase.

Slidell and I climbed to her door and rang the bell.

Nolan answered almost at once. She was wearing very little, most of it black and transparent.

"Did you forget your key, silly?"

Upon seeing us, Nolan's face fired through a series of reactions. In a heartbeat, her expression went from bewilderment to recognition and finally settled on fear.

"What are you doing here?" Hopping behind and peeking around the door.

"Is this a bad time, Mrs. Nolan?"

"Yes it is." Nolan was looking past us toward the staircase at our backs.

"There are just a few small points I don't understand." Slidell was doing Columbo.

"It's late. Can't we do this tomorrow?" The woman was nervous as hell. "I'll come downtown or whatever you want."

In the lot below, a car door slammed.

Nolan's expression morphed to terror.

Footsteps ticked up the treads.

"Don't come here!" Nolan called out. "Go back!"

Too late.

A man's head appeared above floor level.

At first I wasn't sure.

Then I was.

The man froze, then reversed and thundered down the stairs.

Slidell bolted after him.

I could only stare in confusion.

30

With his weak jaw and long test-tube nose, Ted Raines did in fact resemble a bottlenose dolphin. Adding to the effect, at the moment his forehead and cheeks were shiny and gray.

Raines was slumped across Nolan's sofa. Slidell stood glaring down at him, face sweaty and flushed. Both men were breathing hard.

Nolan and I were across the room in cheesy Kmart armchairs. She'd thrown a fuzzy blue robe over the naughty lingerie.

"What the fuck are you thinking?" No more Columbo. Slidell was furious.

Raines just kept panting.

"Do you know how many people are looking for you, you dumb shit?"

Raines's head turtled down between his shoulders.

"Your wife's got every cop shop in Dixie hunting your bony ass. BOLO dispatches are out in three states." Slidell was so keyed up, he'd slipped into police code. Be On the LookOut.

"Stop harassing him."

Slidell swiveled to face Nolan. "You got something to say?"

"Ted's wife is not a nice person."

"That so?"

"Ted needed some time out."

"Time out?"

Slidell closed in on her with two angry strides. Nolan shrank back, as though fearful of a blow.

Across the room, Raines seemed to collapse inward even more.

"Time out? That what you call this?" Slidell flapped an angry arm between Nolan and Raines.

"You're scaring me."

"Be scared. Be very scared."

"We haven't done anything illegal."

"Yeah? Well, you and lover boy are about to experience a busload of shit coming down on your heads."

"We're in love."

"That's so sweet I may puke."

"It's true." Petulant. "Besides, we haven't hurt anyone. Why are you being so mean?"

"Please don't blame her." Raines was still sucking air.

Slidell whipped around. "She thinks I'm mean? I'll tell you what's mean, you worthless piece of shit. Disappearing without a bump in your thoughts to enjoy a little poontang with Miss Sex Kitten Slut over here. Letting your wife and kid wonder if you're dead in a ditch, and letting a hundred police officers spend time searching for you."

"You can't talk to us like that." Nolan's fingers were twisting her robe sash so tightly the knuckles bulged white.

"Ever hear of alienation of affectation? Maybe we should all query Mrs. Raines. See if she thinks anyone's been hurt."

I cringed at Slidell's mangling of the legal term, but said nothing.

"Ted's going to ask for a divorce," Nolan said. "Isn't that right, sweetheart?"

Raines now looked like jelly on the couch.

"Ted?"

Raines's gaze remained pointed at his knees. Slidell charged back across the room and jabbed a finger at him.

"While you're here sharpening your Captain Winkie skills, you don't give a flying fuck what kind of shitstorm you might be causing?"

Slidell's face was now the color of claret. I thought it best to lower the intensity.

"Just for the record. How did you two hook up?"

Perhaps seeing it as safer ground than the topic of litigation, Nolan fielded my question.

"Ted's a research assistant on a project that studies how poisons get blown around by air. The company I work for does sort of the same thing. You know. You were there."

I nodded.

"Last January CRRI sent me to work the exhibit booth at a conference in Atlanta. Ted was there with his team. We met in the hotel bar."

"And fell in lust." Slidell's voice was thick with disgust.

"It's more than that."

"Touching."

"Where's your husband?" I asked.

"Afghanistan."

"We'll order a medal to hang in your window," Slidell snarled.

Nolan crossed her arms on her chest and puffed air through her nose, a look of blank insolence on her face.

"OK, lover boy." Slidell finger-flicked the top of Raines's head. "Let's talk poison."

Raines looked up, features gathered in a look of puzzlement.

"Let me tell you a little story." Slidell had regained his breath, and his tone was now dangerously calm. "Two bodies turn up at a morgue. One tests positive for ricin. The other's got abrin on board. As we both know, your average Joe can't lay his hands on stuff like that."

Raines's eyes narrowed in uncertainty. Or perhaps he was considering answers to create the best possible spin.

"Fast-forward. A guy's in the wind. Gets busted. Turns out this guy has access to abrin and ricin. You see where I'm going, Ted?"

"What are you saying?"

"I hear you've got a real interesting part-time job."

"What does that have—"

"That's a mighty big coincidence. You working with biotoxins."

"You're suggesting I killed someone?"

Slidell just looked at him.

"That's insane."

"Is it?"

"Who are these dead people?"

"Eli Hand and Wayne Gamble."

Beside me, I heard a sharp intake of breath.

"I don't know either of them. Why would I poison total strangers?"

"You tell me."

"The substances I work with are strictly controlled. You

can't just waltz out of the lab with a jar in your pocket. Every gram of powder, every fricking red seed has to be accounted for." Raines's voice was taking on an edge of alarm. "Call my supervisor."

"I'll do that."

"Do I need a lawyer?"

"Do you?" Slidell asked.

"I didn't do anything!" Shrill.

"Why are you in Charlotte?"

Raines's eyes bounced from Slidell to Nolan and back. He answered with a nervous snigger, conspiratorial, guy to guy. "Look, man. I was just getting a little on the side."

"Bastard!"

I eased Nolan back into her chair.

"Your girlfriend knew Wayne Gamble." Slidell kept his eyes on Raines as he spoke to Nolan. "Didn't you, Mrs. Nolan?"

"What?"

"You gonna tell him? Or should I?"

"I knew his sister. Like, centuries ago. Wayne was just a kid."

"Sweet God in heaven." Raines flopped back like a rag doll, hands covering his face.

Slidell peeled his glare from Raines and turned it on Nolan. "You aware Gamble's dead?"

"While Ted was *getting a little* . . ."—she spat the phrase at Raines—"we weren't exactly keeping up with the news."

"You don't look real upset."

"I haven't seen Wayne Gamble since he was twelve years old."

"Tell me what you overheard at the Double Shot."

Slidell's change of direction seemed to confuse her.

"I already did."

"Tell me more."

"Like what?"

"Describe the guy that was talking to Cale Lovette."

"Kind of tall and thin. Old."

"How old?"

Nolan shrugged. "Probably not as old as you. It was hard to tell because he was wearing a hat."

"What kind of hat?"

"Like a baseball cap. Red with a big number above the brim. Oh. And it had a button pinned to the side. The button had a picture of a cowboy hat." Nolan smiled, pleased with the brilliance of her recall.

I'd seen a hat like that. Where? Online? At the Speedway?

"What was the tenor of their conversation?" Slidell asked.

"Huh?"

"Friendly? Heated?"

"Like, they didn't look happy."

"What were they saying?"

"I already told you this."

"Do it again."

Nolan crossed her legs, raised her toes, and pumped one foot as she searched her memory.

"OK. The old guy said that thing about poisoning the system. Then Cale said something about it being too late. It was going to happen. Then the old guy said something about knowing your place."

We waited out an interval of rapid foot pumping.

"When I passed them again, Cale was telling the old guy to, like, quit carping. Then the old guy told Cale not to act so holy. Then something about a bloody hatchet. But there was a lot of noise. I couldn't really hear that part."

251

"Go on."

"Then I went back to the booth and sat with Cindi."

"And?"

"She was all in a wad because Cale was taking too long, so she walked over there. Cale put his arm around her waist. That was nice. But it was creepy the way the old guy looked at her."

"Creepy how?"

"Cold." Nolan's eyes did the saucer thing. "No. More than that. Like he hated her guts."

"Then what?"

"The old guy said something. Then Cale said something, all in the guy's face, like he was really mad. Then the old guy stormed out."

"When Cale came back to the booth, did you ask him who he was talking to?"

"He said a jackass he wished he'd never laid eyes on."

"You didn't pursue it?"

"What do you mean?"

"Ask again."

"Cindi told me to let it go. I mean, she didn't, like, say it. She gave me this look, and I knew what she meant. I'm not stupid."

Yes, I thought. *You are irrevocably stupid*.

"Honest to God, that's all I remember," Lynn whined. "I'm tired. I need to go to bed."

"How come you never mentioned this man's hostility toward Cindi before tonight?"

"Because no one ever asked me about, you know, what happened after. Just what they were saying at the bar."

I looked at Slidell. Your call.

"OK, honeymooners. Here's what's gonna happen."

When Slidell laid down the usual "don't leave town" spiel, Nolan shot to her feet and pointed at Raines.

"Fine. But I want this jerk out of my apartment. Mr. Get a Little on the Side is not staying here."

So much for true love.

En route to the Annex, Slidell and I shared impressions.

"They're both moral invalids."

"Yeah," Slidell agreed. "But Raines doesn't feel right for Gamble or Hand."

"Where was he living when Hand went into the landfill?"

"Atlanta."

"And what motive would he have for wanting Wayne Gamble dead?"

"Exactly. But I'm still going to give the dirtbag a real close look."

"Nolan's description of the old guy doesn't fit Grady Winge," I said. "Or J. D. Danner. Perhaps Eugene Fries, but he claims to be a victim."

"I plan to squeeze Winge first thing in the morning."

As we pulled in at Sharon Hall, a CMPD cruiser was pulling out. Slidell flicked a wave. The cop behind the wheel returned it.

"Guess we don't need stepped-up patrols no more."

"You're convinced Grady Winge killed Cindi and Cale?"

"You kidding? You saw him at that grave site."

"All that proves is that he knew where the bodies were buried."

"Then why's he so goddamn sorry?"

"What about Wayne Gamble?"

"Trust me. In a few short hours, Winge will be singing like a marching band."

Slidell's linguistic misadventures never ceased to amaze.

"The term is alienation of affection," I said. "It's a charge against the third party, not the spouse."

"Yeah. Well, I hope the wife cleans Nolan's shorts."

The clock read two-ten when I dropped into bed.

In the brief period before my brain shut down, I replayed what Nolan had said.

Who was the man arguing with Cale Lovette? What system did they intend to poison? A water system? Where? Obviously they hadn't done it. Or hadn't done it effectively. Such an attack would have been big news.

Something bugged me.

The hat? Where had I seen a cap like that?

Had Nolan read the man correctly? Had he truly regarded Cindi Gamble with malice? If so, why? Or had the look meant something else?

And what was the bit about a bloody hatchet?

Then I was out.

31

While I slept, my brain played with sounds.

Two phrases.

Bloody hatchet.

Maddy Padgett.

Suddenly I was wide awake.

Was that what Nolan had overheard? Were Cale Lovette and the old guy talking about Maddy Padgett?

The clock said six-twenty.

Too early to call.

Too jazzed to sleep.

I threw on a robe and went downstairs. Birdie opened one eye but didn't follow.

While Mr. Coffee cranked up to perk, I turned on the TV.

The local news was all about NASCAR. Qualifying for the Coca-Cola 600 had taken place the previous night. Jimmie Johnson had won the pole and would go off from the inside starting position. Kasey Kahne would share the front row.

Though farther back than predicted, Sandy Stupak had

also won good position. And big surprise, the tragic death of Stupak's jackman, Wayne Gamble, was no longer the lead B-story.

The secondary headliner was the weather. Periodic strong winds, thunder and lightning, and all-day rain were predicted for Saturday, so the Nationwide Series race had been moved up to Friday night. Unprecedented, but a necessary precaution to avoid cancellation and complicated rescheduling.

The new tertiary headliner was a big-ass crater.

As Speedway management was scrambling to make the accelerated timetable work, they learned that, overnight, a sinkhole had opened on the edge of the dirt track. Measuring forty feet long and thirty-five feet deep, the thing was a monster. Fortunately, no one had been injured.

The sinkhole's location made it unlikely that the evening's Nationwide Series event would be affected. Safety inspectors were on site. Officials had yet to announce if the race would begin at the newly designated time.

As I filled my mug, an officious expert presented this postmortem. The Charlotte Motor Speedway was built over an abandoned landfill, and thirty-five feet below the surface, an old drainpipe had deteriorated. In his opinion, the cave-in was the result of recent heavy rains, the burst pipe, and instability of the landfill substrate.

In awed tones, an anchorwoman explained that such incidents are not without precedent. Backed by footage of packed grandstands, she described a pothole that had delayed a Daytona 500 for hours.

Birdie strolled into the kitchen as I was pouring my second cup of coffee.

At seven, I finished my third.

Wired on caffeine, I dialed.

"Slidell." Gruff.

"Did I wake you?"

"Nah. I'm waiting for room service."

Easy, Brennan.

"Where are you?"

"Grabbing some java. I've been working Winge for over an hour."

"Is he talking?"

"Oh yeah."

"What's he saying?"

"Call my pastor. You're gonna love this. The Reverend Honor Grace."

"Did you call him?"

"I'm not in the mood for a gospel lesson."

"Did you ever locate Maddy Padgett?"

"Cindi Gamble's high school pal."

"Yes."

"Hang on."

I heard Slidell's chair squeak, a drawer open, more squeaking.

"Madelyn Frederica Padgett. Guess Padgett wasn't as crafty as Nolan at bagging Mr. Right."

"She's still single?"

"Eeyuh. Works as second engineer for Joe Gibbs Racing. Not sure what team. Maybe Joey Logano." He read off a Charlotte address.

"Do you have a phone number?"

"Just a landline."

I jotted it down.

"I'm going to squeeze Winge till he caves. Even if it takes all day and all night."

"You know what troubles me?" I said.

"What's that?"

"How could Winge get abrin to spike Wayne Gamble's coffee?" I pictured the holes in the back of the skulls dug from the nature-preserve grave. "And why would he do that? Cindi and Cale were both shot execution-style."

"Shrewd questions. For which I intend to get answers."

Maddy Padgett had a voice like my grandma Daessee, smooth and Southern as fatback gravy.

I apologized for the early hour, then gave my name and reason for calling. "I'd like to talk to you about Cindi Gamble."

"How did you get this number?"

"From a Charlotte PD homicide detective."

"Homicide?"

"Yes."

"Finally."

"What do you mean?"

"Honey, you tell me."

"I'd like to meet with you. Today, if possible."

"You follow NASCAR?"

"Sure." Sort of.

"You heard they moved the race forward to tonight?"

"Yes."

"And now there's a freakin' sinkhole."

"Yes."

"The new start time is causing major-league havoc, so Joey wants me at the Speedway all day. Garages open at nine. We'll be fine-tuning the car all morning. Joey's got an autograph session from one to two. Qualifying takes place at three, followed by a crew-and-driver meeting at the media center at six. The drivers are introduced at seven, then the Nationwide flag drops at eight. *If* it drops. What a nightmare."

"It's urgent that I speak with you."

I held my breath, hoping she wouldn't blow me off.

"I could give you a half hour around nine-thirty tonight."

"Tell me where."

"Come by Joey's garage. I'll arrange for a hot pass."

She gave me the location and we disconnected.

I phoned Galimore's mobile to tell him I'd be at the Speedway that night. As usual, he didn't answer the phone.

What the flip? Was he monitoring calls, ignoring mine? Or was he just too busy to pick up?

I considered dialing Galimore's office, instead left a message saying I'd be in the Nationwide garage area at nine-thirty.

After dressing, I went to the MCME to analyze Wayne Gamble's reconstructed skull. I noted in the file that all fracture patterning was consistent with failure due to rapid loading caused by compression between the Chevy's front end and the concrete wall.

I also updated the dossier on the landfill John Doe, adding that a positive identification had been made by the FBI based on dental records.

After lunch, I ran to SouthPark Mall to buy a birthday present for Harry. Then I returned home, washed several loads of laundry, and read the new issue of the *Journal of Forensic Sciences*.

At six I ate a dinner of lamb chops and peas. Then, out of ideas, I did a little more research on abrin. Printed out a few articles. Stuffed them in my jeans pocket in case I ended up having to wait for Padgett.

Throughout the endless day, I listened for the phone

to ring. It didn't. No Galimore. No Slidell. No Special or Special.

I also checked the clock. A lot. Each time, ten to twenty minutes had passed.

By seven, I was climbing out of my skin.

I decided to head to Concord early to see what all the fuss was about.

A mauve dusk was yielding to thunderheads mounding like enormous eggplants. The evening was electric with the feel of an impending storm.

The Speedway was another Hatter's tea party of noise and turmoil. The sweaty, buggy air reeked of hot rubber, exhaust, sunbaked flesh, and fried food. Amplified announcements barely carried over the ear-splitting whine of engines screaming around a mile and a half of asphalt.

My pass was waiting at the gate, as promised. Again I was taken to the infield by golf cart.

Slidell had been wrong. Maddy Padgett didn't work for Joey Logano's #20 Home Depot team. She was employed by a Nationwide Series driver named Joey Frank.

Joey as in Josephine.

Frank drove the #72 Dodge Challenger for SNC Motor Sports.

The race had begun at eight, as scheduled. Members of Frank's pit crew were listening to headphones, calling out adjustments, and frantically positioning gear. They looked like an army of droids in their red and black jumpsuits and black caps.

I spotted one form that seemed smaller than the others, maybe female. S/he was under a plastic canopy, inspecting a set of precisely stacked tires, each wider than my shoe size and devoid of tread. Not exactly "stock."

Not wanting to be in the way, I walked down pit row and peered through a gap between garages. The track looked surreal under its squillion-megawatt lights, the grass too green, the asphalt too black. The grandstands appeared as startling rainbow swaths. Crammed to capacity. I guess the word got out.

The race had been halted because of debris on the track. The cars waited two abreast, engines thrumming, hounds straining at their leashes to reengage in the hunt.

I'd never seen so much product promotion. On the vehicles, the uniforms, the enormous billboards surrounding the track. And I'm not talking one sponsor per team. Every door, hood, roof, deck lid, side panel, and person was plastered with dozens of logos. For some I couldn't see the connection to auto racing. Tums? Head & Shoulders? Goody's Fast Pain Relief? Whatever. One thing was clear. No one would confuse a NASCAR speedway with St. Andrews or Wimbledon.

The cars looked similar to the ones I'd seen in the Sprint Cup garages, maybe a little shorter. And they lacked the little shelf that projected from under the place where a front bumper would wrap a regular car. They also lacked the wing-looking thing the cup-series cars had, back where a car for street usage would have a trunk.

After a while I got the hang of the board indicating laps and driver positions. Why the crowd cheered or booed remained a mystery to me.

Just before nine-thirty, I returned to Frank's garage. A light rain had begun falling. The gracile figure was still under the canopy. Alone.

"Maddy Padgett?" I asked from six feet out.

The figure turned.

The woman's skin was the color of fresh-brewed coffee. Her eyes were huge, the pupils brown, the sclera white as overbleached cotton. Shiny black bangs curved from the brim of her cap to her eyebrows.

"No autographs now." Waving a distracted hand.

"I'm Temperance Brennan."

"Oh. Right." Quick glance at her watch. "OK. Let's do this. But it's got to be quick."

"How's she doing?" I asked.

Padgett smiled. "We'll win the next one."

"Tell me about Cindi Gamble," I said.

"Have you found her?"

"Yes."

"Is she . . . ?"

My look was enough.

"And Cale?" Afraid of the answer.

"Yes."

Padgett gave a taut nod. "On the phone, you mentioned homicide."

"Both had been shot."

Padgett went utterly still. Light sneaking under the plastic sparked droplets of rain on her shoulders and cap.

"Do the cops know who did it?"

"A suspect has been arrested."

"Who?"

"A man named Grady Winge."

"Why did he kill them?"

"Winge's motive remains unclear."

"Cindi could have done it, you know."

"Driven stock cars?"

"Been a NASCAR superstar. She had . . . " Padgett curled

her fingers, seeking the right word. "Flash!"

"That's a racing term?"

"My term." She smiled ruefully. "Cindi could make love to a car, could sweet-talk all that horsepower into doing whatever she wanted. And she was developing style. Yeah, she had flash. The fans would have worshipped her."

"Cale's father disagrees."

"Craig Bogan." Padgett snorted derisively. "There's a piece of work."

"You don't care for him?"

"I haven't seen that jackwagon in over a decade. Thank the Lord." Padgett tilted her head, throwing shadow from the cap's brim across her features. "Bogan hated me."

"Why was that?"

Padgett hesitated. Then gave me the full force of her big brown eyes.

"Sin of sins. I slept with his precious son."

32

"You were Cindi's friend."

"Yes. I was."

"Yet you betrayed her by sleeping with her boyfriend." I struggled to sound nonjudgmental.

"Awesome, huh?"

"More than once?"

She nodded.

Thunder rumbled, long and low.

"Lord almighty, I hope this weather won't cause a delay."

"How did that play?" I asked.

"It wasn't grand romance, if that's what you're thinking."

"What was it?"

She sighed. "The usual. I was sixteen. Cale was older, seemed worldly and sophisticated. We were both horny as hounds in heat."

"Did Cindi know?"

"I don't think so. She was a trusting person. Very sweet."

"But not putting out." Despite my resolve, disgust filtered through.

"You're right. I was a world-class bitch."

Rain was drumming the plastic canopy now. Padgett poked her head out, looked up at the sky, then at her watch.

"Bogan learned that you and Cale were cheating on Cindi," I guessed.

"Yes."

"How?"

"Does that really matter?"

Probably not.

"He resented you because he cared for her."

Padgett looked at me as if I'd said warthogs could fly. "How much effort have y'all put into this investigation?"

"I'm new to the case."

Padgett assessed me for a long moment. "Craig Bogan hated Cindi Gamble as much as he hated me. Maybe more."

"I'm sorry," I said. "I don't understand."

She spread her arms. "What do you see?"

"Ms. Padgett—"

"Seriously." She held the pose.

Though the jumpsuit was far from slimming, I could tell Padgett's body was fit and trim. She wore a string of red beads around her neck, probably coral. The subtle touch of femininity showed a flair for fashion that I've always admired but never possessed.

Padgett's makeup was understated and skillfully applied. And completely unnecessary.

"You're a beautiful woman—" I began, slightly embarrassed.

"Black woman." She dropped her arms to her sides. "A beautiful black woman."

"You're saying Craig Bogan is a racist?"

"The man is a Neanderthal."

As I'd suspected.

"And Cale wasn't?"

Padgett shook her head. "Honey, I'm not kidding myself. Wasn't then. There was no way Cale was going to put a ring on my finger. And my game plan didn't involve settling for a high school drop-out. We were both just sowing our oats."

Rain was coming down hard. As Padgett continued, I pulled a windbreaker from my purse and slipped it on.

"But it wasn't totally sex. Cale and I talked. I came to understand his way of thinking. He started out buying in to his old man's racist horseshit. Why wouldn't he? As a kid, he'd been brainwashed. And Bogan had a wicked temper. It was good Cale put distance between them."

"You're saying Cale became more liberal after getting away from his father?"

"He took up with me, didn't he?"

"Why the change?"

Padgett didn't hear my question. She was listening to an announcement coming over the loudspeakers.

"Son of a buck." She kicked the tires in irritation. "They've raised the red flag."

"The race is on hold?"

"Yeah. I'm going to have to cut this short."

"If Cale wasn't a white supremacist, why did he belong to the Patriot Posse?"

"He was quitting. I told all this to the cops back then."

"Which one?"

"Big guy, dark hair."

"Detective Galimore?" I felt a tickle of apprehension.

"I don't remember the name."

"Help me understand. You're saying Bogan hated you because you're black. What did he have against Cindi?"

"You didn't catch my second meaning?"

I was lost.

"Black. Woman."

"You're saying Bogan hates women?"

"Only us uppity ones." Delivered with an over-the-top black-girl cadence.

"Meaning?"

"Females who defile the hallowed and sacred."

"I'm sorry, Ms. Padgett. I'm not following you."

"I can't speak for now, but back when I was seeing Cale, Craig Bogan lived and breathed NASCAR. Went to all the races. Schmoozed all the drivers. Decked out like a honky fool in all the gear. I think he landed the contract here because he never went home."

Padgett's eyes shone with an emotion I couldn't define. I didn't interrupt.

"Bogan was obsessed with NASCAR staying true to its roots. The redneck cracker opposed even the tiniest suggestion of change, despised anything or anyone who might"—she hooked finger quotes—"pollute the system."

"The ladies and the less than white."

"You've got it, girlfriend."

"Bogan disliked the idea of Cindi driving NASCAR."

"Loathed the very thought of it."

"How did Cale feel?"

"He was resentful that Cindi could afford to participate in Bandoleros and he couldn't." She smiled at the irony of an old memory. "Made me happy. While Cindi was at the track in Midland, Cale and I were free to get it on."

"Did you ever see Cale act abusive toward Cindi?"

Padgett shook her head. "He was nuts for that girl. Even as he was screwing me, Cale was crazy in love with Cindi."

I was about to ask another question when the #72 Dodge

roared into its pit. Padgett yelled to be heard over the noise of the engine.

"I've got to go."

"Can we talk again later? I'm willing to wait."

"Come back when the race ends. Joey won't be hitting Victory Lane after this one."

"Where?"

"At the hauler. We'll be loading up."

Pulling my hood over my head, I walked back to the gap where I'd stood earlier. Thunder and lightning were putting on quite a performance. Strong winds were whipping the rain into horizontal sheets.

Many fans had abandoned the stands for cover. Those who remained in their seats huddled under umbrellas or sat swaddled in brightly colored plastic ponchos.

Some drivers were still on the track. Others, like Frank, had opted for pulling into the pit.

I looked around for a dry spot to wait out the storm. Seeing few options, I decided to seek sanctuary with Galimore.

As before, he didn't answer his mobile.

Annoyed, I resolved to find the security office on my own.

As I walked, head down, shoulders hunched against the downpour, disjointed data bytes ricocheted in my brain.

Slidell was certain Grady Winge had murdered Cale Lovette and Cindi Gamble and buried their bodies in the nature preserve. But what motive did Winge have? And why would he kill Wayne Gamble? To cover up his earlier crime? Gamble hadn't died from abrin. He might have eventually, but had someone decided his death needed to be immediate?

Winge had the IQ of a brussels sprout. How had he gotten his hands on abrin? And why use it? Cindi and Cale had been shot, not poisoned.

Eli Hand had been poisoned. With ricin. But had that killed him? Larabee's autopsy had also revealed head trauma.

Did Hand accidentally poison himself while experimenting with ricin? Were he and other crazies planning to use the toxin in some sort of terrorist assault? Was that what Cale Lovette and the old guy were discussing at the Double Shot?

Winge had access to the track, the barrel, the asphalt. Was he also responsible for Hand's death?

Had Cindi and Cale discovered that Winge killed Hand? Was that why he shot them?

Had Winge truly been born again? If so, did his conversion spring from guilt?

Waterlogged fans crammed every shelter and filled every canopied or awninged foot of dry ground. At least a hundred huddled under the portico at the Media Center. Dozens had crawled under picnic tables outside concession stands.

Seeing a foot of space between a woman in a tissue-thin Danica Patrick tee and a shirtless old geezer in nothing but cutoffs, I darted under the overhang of a cinder-block restroom building. Thunder boomed as I dialed Slidell's number.

Sweet Mother of God. Didn't people answer their phones anymore?

Fine.

I punched 411. Made my request.

A robotic voice provided a number. Even dialed it for me.

"Reverend Grace." The voice sounded a thousand years old.

"Am I speaking with Honor Grace?"

"Yes, ma'am. Are you troubled? Is your soul in need of salvation?"

"No, sir. Are you aware that a member of your congregation has been arrested for murder?"

"Oh, my, my. Oh. Who is this, please?"

I identified myself, then cut off inquiry into the specifics of my authority by asking if a Detective Slidell had called.

"No. But I've been ministering to the sick all day and have yet to check my answering machine."

"Are you familiar with Grady Winge?"

As I spoke, the Danica Patrick girl waved madly and shrieked, "Oh my God! Oh my God! Artie!"

"Are you all right, miss?" Grace sounded worried.

"I'm at the Speedway. Some fans are very energetic. Grady Winge?"

"Of course. Brother Winge has been a member of my church for many years. Is it he who is accused of this sin?"

"Can you comment on Winge's whereabouts on Tuesday night?"

"Without reservation. Brother Winge was right here with me."

I felt a chill that didn't come from the rain.

"You're certain?"

"Brother Winge comes every Tuesday to help prepare for Wednesday prayer meeting. This week I was taken ill. I don't know if it was something I ate or a bug—"

"Winge was there for how long?"

"He arrived at six, as is his habit, and stayed all night. It wasn't necessary. I was well by morning. But I was very thankful for his presence. The Lord does work—"

"Thank you, sir."

I clicked off and pressed the phone to my chest. Beneath my curled fingers, my heart pounded.

Grady Winge hadn't murdered Wayne Gamble.

Gamble's killer was still out there.

I closed my eyes. Breathed deeply.

Did that mean Winge hadn't shot Cindi and Cale? If not, who had?

Water ran from the eaves and ticked the gravel at my feet. People jostled and joked around me.

Wayne Gamble was killed at Stupak's garage. Who could get past the barriers surrounding the Sprint Cup garage area?

Suddenly the whole wet world tilted.

Galimore had access to the entire Speedway complex.

Hawkins distrusted Galimore. Slidell hated him. Veteran cops suspected him of impeding the Lovette-Gamble investigation back in 'ninety-eight. But what involvement would Galimore have had with ricin or abrin? Was Galimore in league with others?

Galimore had been missing when I received the threatening call on my mobile at Craig Bogan's house. He'd been missing when Eugene Fries put a gun to my head.

He was missing now. Had been since yesterday morning.

I remembered Padgett's comment about Cale Lovette quitting the Patriot Posse. She said she told a cop back then. A big guy with dark hair.

Had that statement made its way into any report?

The chill spread through my body.

33

I stood paralyzed with indecision. If the killer was still free, was I in danger? I continued to puzzle over Galimore. Ricin-abrin would not be his thing, but had he been protecting others? As a member of a group? As a hired hit man?

That made no sense. Had he simply colluded years earlier to protect the shooter? What was going on today? Was there a new plot in the works that Gamble was going to stumble upon?

Meanwhile, the rain. Where to go?

The security office. Galimore might be there, but so might others. Besides, he knew where to find me. He was not likely to snatch me from his own office.

My sneakers were soaked. My jacket was molded to my torso and head. Though the night was warm, goose bumps puckered my neck and arms.

"Oh, shit." Slurred, from my right.

The Danica Patrick girl was swaying drunkenly. Dropping her can of Miller High Life, she doubled over and moaned.

I tried shifting left. The shirtless guy was right at my shoulder.

Lightning streaked. Thunder cracked.

Vomit hit the ground at my feet.

Any place was better than here.

Lowering my head against the deluge, I set out for Joey Frank's hauler.

I was halfway down the Nationwide row when my iPhone vibrated.

Finally. Slidell returning my call.

I stepped between two enormous transporters and dug the phone from my pocket. Tugging my sleeve as low as possible for protection against the rain, I raised the device to my ear.

"Brennan—"

Something ticked my exposed fingertips.

Instinctively, I shook my hand to dislodge the insect.

My thumb accidentally hit the disconnect button, ending the call.

I punched redial. My finger slipped on the wet screen. I noticed that my skin was burning where I'd been stung.

Shoving the phone inside my jacket, I wiped moisture off the screen with my shirt.

I heard movement to my left, glanced sideways. The upraised hood blocked my peripheral vision.

I was dialing again when footsteps squished in the muddy grass. Hurried. Close.

As I raised my head, a viselike arm wrapped my throat.

The phone flew from my hand.

My head was yanked backward. Something snapped in my neck. Rain pummeled my upturned face.

I struggled.

Rapid breathing in my ear blocked all other sounds.

A noxious blend of oily hair, wet nylon, and stale cigarette smoke filled my nostrils.

Terrified, I kicked back with one heel. Connected.

The arm tightened, squeezing my trachea and cutting off air.

I gagged. Clawed.

I saw rain slicing diagonally across the sky. An antenna. A light on a pole.

Dark spots.

Lightning sparked.

Then the world went black.

The rain had stopped. Or had it?

Overhead I heard pinging, like nails hitting tin.

My mind groped for meaning.

I was inside. Under a roof.

Where?

How long had I been here?

Who had brought me to this place?

Angry vessels pounded the inside of my skull.

My mind offered only disconnected recollections.

Synapse: *A narrow gap between haulers. Footsteps in the dark.*

I raised my head.

My stomach lurched. I tasted bitterness and felt a tremor beneath my tongue.

I eased back down.

I smelled loamy earth. Vegetation. Felt cold hardness beneath my cheek.

Synapse: *A body pressed tight against my back.*

A real-time sensation intruded. Heat on my right ring finger.

I moved my hand. Tested the surface on which I lay.

Solid. Sandpaper-rough.

Concrete.

Synapse: *A chokehold squeezing my throat. My fingers clawing, my lungs desperate for air.*

I breathed deeply.

Opened my eyes.

Saw nothing but variations on darkness.

Using both palms, I raised one shoulder and shifted my hips.

Before I could sit, nausea overwhelmed me. I hung my head and threw up until my stomach muscles ached.

When I'd finished, I backhanded my mouth, rolled, and rose to all fours.

And vomited again until I could only spit bile.

I sat back on my haunches, listening.

Over the drumming rain, I heard what sounded like grinding gears, the thrum of an engine. Muffled by walls.

And another sound. Soft. Barely audible.

A moan? A growl?

Close.

Dear God!

Some other being shared my prison!

I felt a flutter in my chest, as if my heart had broken free and was beating at my rib cage.

I strained my ears. Heard no movement. No further sign of another presence.

Was I mistaken?

I rose to my knees and waited for my eyes to adjust. The only break in the inky blackness was a hairline strip of gray at floor level off to my left. Too little light to dilate my pupils.

I got to my feet. Paused again.

My gut cramped once more, but there was nothing left to purge.

Arms extended, I inched blindly toward what I hoped was a door.

My fingertips soon brushed something hard and smooth. Metal. Vertically ribbed.

I stepped to my right. The steel ribs now ran horizontally.

I felt around, found a discontinuity. Traced it up, over, down to the floor. A rectangle.

Aiming my shoulder at what I assumed was the rectangle's center, I lunged.

Metal rattled, but the door held.

I tried again and again until my shoulder ached. Then I dropped to my back and kicked with my feet.

My efforts were useless. I hadn't the strength of a toddler, and the door was metal.

I lay on the floor, limbs trembling, breath rasping in and out of my lungs.

My mouth was a desert. My head pounded. My gut was on fire.

Get out! Find the bastard who put you here!

The orders came from deep in my brain.

I rose again on rubber legs.

Dizziness sent the world spinning and triggered new nausea.

When I finished dry-heaving, I lurched forward once more.

And followed the wall. In ten feet, it met another. At the intersection, on the floor, slumped large plastic sacks.

I pressed my thumb to the nearest. The contents felt heavy but grainy, like oatmeal. I drew my nose close. Sniffed. Smelled a mixture of soil, clay, and dung.

Turning ninety degrees, I edged through the dark.

Two feet from the corner, a shovel hung from a hook roughly a yard above my head. Beside the shovel was a pitchfork. Then a hoe, another spade, a hand tiller, a hedge clipper, and a pruner. Below the tools were three coiled hoses.

My mind processed. An outdoor storage shed. Galvanized steel. One door. Bolted from the outside.

Tears threatened.

No!

The shed's interior was relatively cool. I knew that wouldn't last. When the rain stopped and the sun rose, the heat inside the windowless metal box would become unbearable.

Move!

Eight feet down, the second wall met a third.

I made the turn.

I'd taken two steps when the toe of my sneaker nudged an object on the floor. I prodded with my foot.

The thing felt firm. Yet yielding.

Familiar.

Another image fired up from my gray cells.

A corpse.

I shrank back.

Then, heart pounding, I squatted to examine the body.

34

I worked my way up the torso toward the throat.

It was a man. His chest was broad, and his cheeks were rough with stubble.

I pressed my fingers to the flesh beneath his jaw.

No sign of a pulse.

Again and again I shifted my hand, searching for the throb of a carotid. Or jugular.

Nothing.

The man's flesh felt cool, not cold. If he was dead, it hadn't been for long.

Sweet Jesus! Who was he?

With trembling hands, I braille-read the facial features.

Shock sent adrenaline firing through me.

Galimore!

Breath frozen, I pressed my ear to his chest. A faint murmur? The rain was so loud, I couldn't be sure.

Please God! Let him be alive!

I shivered. Then felt scalded.

My thoughts splintered into even tinier shards. Nothing made sense.

Galimore had not locked me in the shed. If he was a murderer or had partnered with a murderer, what was he doing here himself? Was he dead?

Galimore and I had a common enemy.

Who?

A wave of dizziness forced me down to my bum. I slumped back against the wall. Muddled words and images tumbled through my mind.

Two skeletons embracing in a makeshift grave. Two skulls with bullet holes centered at the back.

Grady Winge praying in the woods. Sitting at a table in the Speedway Media Center.

A 'sixty-five Petty-blue Mustang with a lime-green decal on the passenger side. Winge said it in 'ninety-eight. Repeated the exact phrase over a decade later.

Maddy Padgett standing by a pile of tires.

Padgett had been Cale Lovette's lover. She was black. Lovette planned to quit the Patriot Posse.

A neon-lit bar. Slidell, yanking a man by his beard.

A cheesy Kmart apartment. Lynn Nolan wearing a tacky negligee.

The old guy said that thing about poisoning the system. Then Cale said something about it being too late. It was going to happen. Then the old guy said something about knowing your place.

Maddy Padgett, face tight with emotion.

Craig Bogan was a racist, a sexist. Cindi Gamble had flash.

Again the bones.

Flash and bones.

A photo of a girl with a blond pixie bob and silver loops in her ears.

Craig Bogan in an armchair, stroking a cat.

Bogan said 'sixty-five Petty-blue Mustang.

Not "a Mustang." Or "a blue Mustang." A 'sixty-five Petty-blue Mustang.

Ted Raines cringing on a couch.

Every fricking red seed has to be accounted for.

Red beads peeking from the neckline of a jumpsuit.

Galimore talking to a woman in sweaty black spandex. Reta Yountz. A handshake. Yountz's bracelet jumping like a string of ladybugs doing a conga.

The world slid sideways.

I sucked in my breath.

Was that the message my id had been whispering?

Summoning what little strength I had left, I crawled to the door. Still on hands and knees, I pulled a paper from the back pocket of my jeans and unfolded it on the concrete. In the thin strip of light, I could see the picture and most of the text.

The article was titled "Rosary Pea: *Abrus precatorius.*" The image showed small red seeds with jet-black spots at one end. The text described them as resembling ladybugs.

In my delirium, atoms collided. Meshed.

Reta Yountz was wearing a bracelet made of rosary pea seeds.

Abrin comes from the rosary pea.

Wayne Gamble was poisoned with abrin.

Maddy Padgett made reference to a contract between Bogan and the Speedway. CB Botanicals. I was in a garden shed.

Padgett described Bogan as a redneck cracker who despised the idea of women and blacks in NASCAR. A man with a wicked temper.

Cindi Gamble was determined to race stock cars. Bogan

had watched her race Bandoleros and knew that she could do it.

Nolan's "old guy" at the Double Shot was Craig Bogan!

Bogan and Lovette weren't planning a terrorist act. They were arguing about Cindi's failure to know her place. The system being poisoned wasn't a water supply. It was Bogan's twisted vision of NASCAR.

The brutal truth slammed home.

Craig Bogan shot Cindi Gamble to stop her from driving NASCAR. He killed his own son because he and Cale were estranged, and he knew Cale would finger him as a suspect. He murdered Wayne Gamble because Gamble was asking too many questions and prodding the authorities to start a reinvestigation for discovery of new facts.

My vision blurred. My legs trembled.

I reached out to brace myself.

At that precise moment, a bolt slicked sideways.

Grating loudly, the door winged left.

I wobbled but didn't topple.

A dark figure loomed in front of me, backlit by two powerful beams.

I drew in my arm and shielded my eyes.

Two muddy boots swam into focus.

"Well, well." Bogan's tone was bloodless. "Aren't you the rugged one."

I sat back on my haunches. Looked up.

Bogan was a black silhouette. One elbow angled out. Something in his hand. "Guess I underestimated you, little lady."

Bogan shifted. Spread his feet.

Light glinted off a semiautomatic pistol pointed at my head.

Adrenaline-pumped blood made the rounds of my body. I felt a new surge of strength.

"The police are already searching for us." To my pounding ears my voice sounded slurry.

"Let them search. Where you're going, no one will find you."

"We found Cale and Cindi."

The razor face hardened into cold stone.

"You've already killed three people," I said. "I suppose you don't care about one more?"

"You forgetting your buddy over there?" Bogan flicked the gun toward Galimore.

I kept my mind pointed at one thought. *Stall*.

"Takes a special kind of man to shoot his own son."

Bogan's fingers tightened on the Glock.

"How'd you rope Winge in? Threaten to fire him? Appeal to his Patriot Posse loyalties?"

"Winge's a fool."

"Don't have Grady to do your dirty work this time? To lie for you? To bury your dead kid and his girlfriend? You know he'll break and implicate you."

"Not if he wants to live, he won't. Besides, it's only the word of an accused suspect. There's no evidence connecting me."

"Good cover. The stranger in the Mustang. How long did you have to coach him to get it right?"

As we sparred, I tried looking past Bogan. The double beams were blinding. Headlights?

I listened for sounds. Heard no engines. No amplified voices. I assumed the race was long since over. Or else we weren't at the Speedway.

"Your kind just can't be happy with what you got."

Bogan's face was pinched with loathing. "Always wanting more."

"My kind? You mean women?"

I knew I should quit piling on words. Couldn't stop myself.

"We scare the shit out of you, don't we, Craig?"

"That's it. You're history."

Before I could react, Bogan lunged, yanked me to my feet, and spun me into another chokehold. With a gloating laugh, he jammed the Glock into my ribs.

"Now who's scared shitless?"

Bogan dragged me toward the lights, gouging the muzzle deeper with every forced step. It was the scene at the haulers' all over again. Only this time my muscles were mush. I was like a moth flailing at a screen.

Rain was still falling. The ground was slick underfoot.

I heard traffic in the distance but couldn't lower my eyes to check for landmarks.

We passed the source of the double beams. Headlights shone from a backhoe with enormous front and rear shovels.

Ten yards beyond the backhoe, Bogan halted, shifted the gun to my occiput, and forced my head down.

I blinked into a yawning wound in the earth.

The sinkhole!

The gears of my mind jammed with terror.

"Enjoy eternity in hell." Bogan's voice was pure venom.

I felt his body tense. The pistol was no longer jammed against my head. Hands clamped onto my shoulders.

"Kiss my ass!" I screamed, twisting and writhing with adrenaline-stoked terror. "You worthless piece of shit!"

Bogan's right hand slipped on my wet nylon jacket. Slithered down the sleeve.

I wrenched my upper body sideways.

Bogan squeezed so tight, I thought my bones would shatter.

I cried out in pain.

Sliding the shoulder hand down my other arm, Bogan flexed both knees, lifted, and sailed me out over the edge.

My body flew sideways, then dropped. Time froze as I plummeted into inky blackness.

I hit hard on my right side, against an embankment partway down. The force of the impact sent me pinwheeling farther down, through muck and rubble. In seconds, I hit water.

Putrid liquid closed over me. I drew my knees to my chest and prayed that the pool was shallow.

Using my battered arms, I flayed the water and stopped my forward motion. I stroked my body vertical and extended my legs.

My sneakers touched bottom. I tested.

Terra not so firma. But solid enough so my feet were not sinking.

I stood in stagnant water up to my chest.

I smelled the sour reek of mud and rotten humus, the brown stench of things long dead.

Around me was tomblike darkness. Far above me the sky was a slightly paler black.

I had to get out. But how?

I waded to the point where I thought I'd entered the water. Explored with shaking hands.

The sides of the sinkhole were sharply angled. And slimy with sludge and putrid garbage.

Facing the bank, I lifted a leg that weighed a thousand pounds. Positioned my foot. Stretched my hands high and curled my fingers into claws.

Then I was spent.

My leg crumpled.

I collapsed and lay with my cheek and chest pressed to the mud.

A minute? An hour?

Somewhere, in another universe, an engine sputtered to life.

Gears rattled.

The engine grew louder.

The sinkhole seemed to wink.

I lifted my head.

Twin beams were slicing the darkness overhead.

My brain groped for meaning.

Steel screeched.

The engine churned.

Metal clanked.

I heard rumbling, like potatoes rolling down a chute.

A massive clod of dirt hit my back.

The wind was knocked from me.

As I fought the spasm in my chest, more soil avalanched down from above.

I tucked my head and wrapped my arms around it.

Bogan was filling the sinkhole! The monster was burying me alive!

Get to the far end!

I was dragging myself sideways along the bank when the engine backfired.

Muffled voices drifted down.

Or was I hallucinating?

The backhoe popped again.

Gears rattled.

The engine groaned, then cut off.

A small beam shot down from the lip of the sinkhole. Was joined by another. The small ovals danced the water, the muddy banks, finally settled on me.

"She's here."

"Sonofafrigginbitch."

Slidell's voice had never sounded so sweet.

35

I didn't get the full story until Presbyterian Hospital cut me loose three days later. By then Mark Martin had beaten twenty-to-one odds to win the Coca-Cola 600. Sandy Stupak had finished at number nineteen.

Completion of the Nationwide race had been postponed Friday night due to rain and the possibility of tornadoes. The following day Joey Frank crossed the line at number twenty-seven.

And the sun finally came out.

Katy had visited my bedside daily. Larabee dropped in. Charlie Hunt. Pete, sans Summer.

Hmm.

The sting on my finger wasn't from a biting insect. Bogan had hit me with an abrin-coated dart. My mobile rang at the precise moment he aimed his little blow tube at my neck. Either the movement of my hand, the phone, or my jacket sleeve deflected the hit.

Karma? Fate? Blind-ass luck? Whatever. That kind of help is welcome any time.

Here's a bit of irony. The caller was Summer. Another bout of wedding hysteria had saved my life.

The trace amount of abrin that had penetrated my skin caused vomiting, fever, headache, and disorientation. But I lived.

Galimore had also been poisoned. The prognosis was that, although further hospitalization was required, his recovery would proceed without complications.

Doctors figured either the abrin was degraded, incorrectly processed, or Bogan had put too little on the dart. Or maybe rain had diluted the toxin before or during delivery. Bottom line: the dosages were too low to be lethal to either of us.

Padgett was right. Bogan had been supplying flowers and greenery to the Speedway for years. After darting us, he'd locked our "bodies" in one of his gardening sheds, waiting for the right moment to dump them.

The sinkhole had been a stroke of luck. Bogan's offer to deal with the inconvenience had been gratefully accepted by frantic Speedway personnel. He intended to load us onto the backhoe, deposit us thirty-five feet below ground level, then shovel tons of fill over our corpses. Finding me alive had forced him to modify his plan. He'd drop Galimore after he got some dirt over me.

My epiphany in the shed was dead-on. Bogan had killed Cindi and Cale, then threatened Grady Winge with the loss of his job if he didn't help a fellow posseman dispose of a couple of bodies.

The Gambles and Ethel Bradford would be vindicated. The task force finding was indeed flawed. The couple hadn't run off to get married or to join an extremist group out West.

288

Lynn Nolan and Wayne Gamble were also wrong. Cale hadn't killed Cindi, then gone into hiding for fear of being caught.

Slidell and I had not been any more accurate. Cale wasn't an FBI informant and hadn't been murdered by members of the Patriot Posse. Nor had he and Cindi been piped into witness protection.

Eugene Fries's theory was also off base. Cale hadn't fled to avoid arrest for a terrorist act.

It was Tuesday, one week after Wayne Gamble's death. Slidell, Williams, Randall, and I were drinking coffee in my study.

Slidell was being Slidell.

"You clean up pretty good, Doc. Last time I saw you, you looked like something climbed out of an unflushed toilet."

"Thank you, Detective. And thanks for the flowers. They were very thoughtful."

"I tried hiring baton twirlers, but everyone was booked."

"That's OK. It would have been rather crowded in here."

It was tight anyway. Skinny was at the desk. The specials were in chairs dragged from the dining room. I was on the sofa, with Birdie curled on my quilt-covered lap.

"Bogan's going to make it?" I asked.

"Not because I wasn't aiming. The peckerwood hunkered down in the backhoe just as I fired."

The pops I'd heard weren't backfires.

"How did you know I'd gone to the Speedway?"

"A tip from a man of the cloth."

"Reverend Grace?" Of course. I'd mentioned my whereabouts in our phone conversation.

"Hallelujah, sister." Slidell waggled splayed fingers.

"Why did you go to the dirt track?"

"I learned that Bogan was supposed to fill the sinkhole. I hauled ass out there, saw the headlights, heard you cursing like a sailor on shore leave."

"Thank God you finally called Winge's pastor."

"Big Guy had nothing to do with it. And I didn't call Grace. He called me around ten, all in a twist because we'd collared one of his flock. I was still sweating Winge."

"Grace persuaded him to talk?"

"Yeah. Told him that salvation would be his only if he bore witness to the truth. Or some bullshit like that. According to Winge, Bogan killed the girl and his own kid, then told Winge they'd been agents of an anti-patriot conspiracy and ordered him to bury the bodies, or both his membership in the posse and his job were toast."

"Two years later, Bogan used the same arguments to force Winge to help dump Eli Hand."

Williams's comment was news to me.

"It was like a damn pyramid scheme," Slidell said. "Danner was squeezing Bogan. Bogan was squeezing Winge."

"J. D. Danner? The leader of the Patriot Posse?" Clearly I'd missed a lot while incapacitated.

"The head wrangler," Slidell said.

"After events at the Speedway, the bureau decided it was time to bring in some individuals we'd had under surveillance," Williams explained.

"Round 'em up." Slidell circled a finger in the air.

"Danner's lawyer allowed him to cooperate in exchange for immunity from prosecution. The DA agreed to a deal covering criminal acts prior to 2002."

"The year the Patriot Posse disbanded."

"Yes. As you know, Grady Winge is not the sharpest knife in the drawer. And he was still drinking back in 'ninety-eight. Winge let slip to others in the posse that Bogan had killed Cale and Cindi. According to Danner, certain group members used that knowledge to blackmail Bogan."

"They made him their whore," Slidell said.

"When Eli Hand died, higher-ups in the posse pressed Bogan into service to dispose of his body," Williams said. "As with Cindi and Cale, Bogan forced Winge to do the dirty work."

"Conveniently, at the time they were filling potholes at the Speedway," Slidell said.

It seemed incredible that a person, even one with Winge's limited IQ, could be pressured to do such a thing.

"How do you get someone to cram a corpse into a barrel, cover it with asphalt, and haul it to a landfill?" I asked.

"Bogan told Winge if he refused to dump Hand, he'd make sure Winge took the fall for Cindi and Cale. And he threatened to burn Mama Winge's place to the ground."

"It was Bogan who killed Eugene Fries's dog and torched his house," I guessed.

Williams nodded. "And it was Bogan who was stalking Wayne Gamble."

I considered that. "When Gamble first came to see me at the MCME, he offered to locate Cale Lovette's father and give him a call. He must have done that."

"Freaked Bogan out." Slidell was playing with a water globe I keep on my desk, a gift from my nephew Kit.

"Bogan used his usual MO to try to dissuade Gamble from pursuing the reopening of his sister's case," Williams said. "But this time intimidation didn't work."

I remembered Gamble's calls to me, the anger and fear in his voice as he talked of his stalker. Again felt the heavy weight of guilt.

"It was Bogan who threatened Galimore," Williams added. "And you."

I thought back to the day at CB Botanicals. The greenhouse. Daytona.

"His cat startled me, and I dropped my iPhone. Bogan probably got my number while pretending to clean it. But he was with me when the call came in."

"When Bogan went to the kitchen for sodas, he phoned an employee, offered fifty dollars, and provided your number and the message to be delivered or left on voice mail."

The kid on the ladder cleaning the gutters: Bogan's call must have beeped in while he was listening to music on his cell phone. Fifty bucks? Sure. The kid hit a few keys. Done.

"That a bird?" Slidell was holding the globe up to the light, squinting at the object sealed inside.

"It's a duck. Please put it down. How did Eli Hand die?"

"Danner claims it was accidental self-poisoning," Williams said.

"The prick pricked himself."

I ignored Slidell's witticism.

"Hand's skull was fractured."

"Danner speculates he may have fallen." Williams shrugged. "No witnesses. We may never learn the truth on that one."

He cleared his throat and looked straight at me. "The FBI confiscated Hand's body out of legitimate concern for ricin contamination."

"And destroyed it for what reason?" I kept my gaze steady on his.

"The cremation was accidental."

"And stealing our goddamn file? That accidental, too?" The base of the water globe smacked the desktop.

"I have been asked to formally apologize to Dr. Brennan and Dr. Larabee for the destruction of Eli Hand's remains. Requesting files from the top level of local law enforcement is routine." Williams coolly flicked a speck from his perfectly creased pants leg even as he directed the same coolness toward us. "The bureau is in possession of information concerning the Loyalty Movement that I am not—"

"Yeah, yeah. At liberty to divulge. You're bloody James Bond."

"I can tell you this. Members of the Patriot Posse also blackmailed Bogan into experimenting with abrin." Williams's calm was unshakable.

"Why?" I asked.

"In Danner's words, certain elements were not morally opposed to acts of civil disobedience. Ricin had its drawbacks. They wanted something better."

"The bastards were thinking of killing people," I said.

"But not Danner. He's Peter frickin' Pan."

"Wayne Gamble wasn't paranoid." I ignored Slidell's sarcasm. "The FBI did have his family under surveillance back in 1998."

Williams nodded.

I turned to Slidell. "What about Bogan? Is he talking?"

"Like Danner, he's looking to cut a deal. Bogan's got shit to offer, so the DA's offering zilch." The chair creaked ominously as Skinny leaned back and stretched his legs. "I'm floating some legal jargon his way. Stuff like 'lethal injection.' 'Shank.' The ever popular 'bend over, punk.'"

"Is Bogan impressed?"

Slidell laced his fingers behind his head.

"He will be."

36

The next afternoon Birdie and I were relaxing on the terrace. I was reading a book on the history of NASCAR. He was batting a mangled cloth mouse around on the brick.

We were both enjoying a Dr. Hook CD. The cat's favorite. He actually stops to listen when "You Make My Pants Want to Get Up and Dance" plays.

Hearing a car, I glanced to my left.

A blue Taurus was cruising past the manor house on the circle drive.

"Heads up, Bird. Our day is about to be filled with sunshine."

The cat stayed focused on his burlap rodent.

The Taurus disappeared behind a stand of magnolias, reappeared, and pulled in beside the Annex. Seconds later, Slidell hauled himself out.

I closed my book and watched Skinny trudge up the walk. He really is a very good trudger.

"Glad to see you're following doctor's orders." Sun shot from the lenses of Slidell's mock Ray-Bans.

"One more day," I said. "Then back to work."

"Yep. The lady's stubborn as belly fat."

"Is Bogan talking?" I shifted the subject away from my health.

"Like a cockatiel with a crack pipe."

Slidell's metaphors truly are something. Or was that a simile?

"Why?"

"He's gambling the DA will go south a bump on the charges."

I raised spread fingers. And?

"The night they died, Cale told his old man he and Cindi were getting out of Dodge. She had some kind of offer down in Daytona. Bogan flew into a rage. Get this. He's justifying the shooting, saying he was provoked because a broad was taking his son away from him. The son he hadn't said ten words to in years."

"And I suppose Wayne Gamble called him mean names?"

"Eeyuh. Hard to sell temporary insanity on that one. Want to hear a sick sidebar?"

I wiggled my fingers, indicating I did.

"Bogan kept their shoes."

"What?"

"Before the shooting, he made Cindi and Cale take off their shoes and walk down to the pond."

"The one by his greenhouse."

"Yeah. All these years, he kept their shoes in a box in his closet."

I could think of nothing to say to that.

"Has Bogan said how he murdered Gamble?" I asked.

"He was watching, saw the other mechanic leave the garage. When Gamble bent under the hood, Bogan released some thingamajig that dropped the jack. The engine was cranking full throttle, so when the wheels hit the floor, it was sayonara."

"Bogan had been poisoning Gamble. Why kill him in the garage?"

"Several triggers. First, Bogan was frustrated because the abrin wasn't working the way he'd expected. Probably because the dumb shit screwed the stuff up."

"Or the toxin was old and degraded."

"Or that. Second, Bogan was getting nervous because Gamble seemed to be making progress. You and Galimore showing up at his greenhouse scared the crap out of him."

"He didn't let on."

"No. But he recognized Galimore, both because of the task force back in 'ninety-eight and from seeing him at the Speedway. He knew who Galimore was, felt things closing in."

"Why didn't Galimore recognize Bogan?"

"Bogan got the landscaping contract before Galimore hired on at the Speedway. Since he already had his security clearance and employee ID, the two never intersected. Bogan kept an eye on Galimore but never really entered his orbit. Bogan's on-site man was Winge."

"So Galimore had little opportunity and no reason to notice Bogan."

"Bingo. Third, Gamble had confronted Bogan earlier that day, threatened to clean his clock if he didn't knock off the bird-dog act. Bottom line, Bogan saw an opportunity at the garage and grabbed it. Figured Gamble's death would pass as an accident."

Guilt vied with the anger knotting my gut.

Shoving both aside, I asked another question.

"According to Maddy Padgett, Cale was planning to quit the Patriot Posse. Was that true?"

"Eeyuh. And Cale knew a lot of their dirty little secrets. He and Cindi were crapping their shorts to get out of town. They feared posse hardliners might use muscle to keep them from leaving. Or worse."

"That's why she had the locks changed. She was afraid of the posse, not Cale."

"Bogan also gave it up on Owen Poteat. We were right. He paid Poteat to lie about seeing Cindi and Cale at the Charlotte airport."

"How did Bogan recruit him?"

"Before he got canned, Poteat sold Bogan a sprinkler system for his greenhouse. One day he was checking out a problem and they got to talking. Poteat needed money. Bogan needed the cops thinking his kid was alive and well and living somewhere with his girlfriend. Bogan undoubtedly gave some innocent-sounding reason for wanting to place the two of them at the airport. Poteat bit."

Reflections from the magnolias moved in shifting patterns across the dark lenses covering Slidell's eyes. I suspected his emotions were paralleling mine.

"It's hard to believe a man could murder two young people, one his own flesh and blood, over an outmoded definition of what a sport should be. But I guess with him, it wasn't a sport. It was a religion carried to the point of fanaticism."

"There was a time we lobotomized freaks like him."

"Those were the days."

Slidell missed my sarcasm. "Well, that's last season's pennant race. Here's a good one. Bogan's almost sixty, and the asshole's never left the Carolinas."

"I guess stock car racing was all the universe he needed. That and his plants."

Slidell shook his head.

"I keep seeing Bogan's den in my mind," I said. "The place was a shrine to NASCAR. Model cars, auto parts, clothing, signed posters, a zillion framed pictures. Yet not a single snapshot of Cale."

"Freak," Slidell repeated.

"Here's the craziest part. The dumb wang claims to love NASCAR history but knows little of it. Women have been pushing the accelerator since before Bogan was born."

"Yeah?"

"Sara Christian drove in the inaugural Strictly Stock race at the Charlotte Motor Speedway. You know what year that was?"

Slidell shook his head.

"1949. Qualified at number thirteen, finished fourteenth in a field of thirty-three."

"Get out."

"Janet Guthrie participated in both the Indianapolis 500 and NASCAR. In the late seventies she drove in thirty-three cup-level races. At the 1977 Talladega 500, she outqualified the likes of Richard Petty, Johnny Rutherford, David Pearson, Bill Elliott, Neil Bonnett, Buddy Baker, and Ricky Rudd. And not one of them said anything derogatory or resentful, at least not publicly."

"She win?"

"Turn one, first lap, another car's driveshaft went through Guthrie's windshield. After it was replaced, the engine blew."

"Ouch."

"Louise Smith. Ethel Mobley. Ann Slaasted. Ann Chester. Ann Bunselmeyer. Patty Moise. Shawna Robinson. Jennifer Jo Cobb. Chrissy Wallace. Danica Patrick. And that's hardly the full list. Women drivers are still a small minority, but they've always been there. And the numbers are growing each year. Did you know that approximately forty percent of NASCAR fans today are female?"

"How'd you get to be such an authority?"

I waggled my book.

"Ain't that grand."

"What's going to happen to Lynn Nolan and Ted Raines?" I asked.

"Shacking up for naughty boom-boom is adultery for him, alienation of affection for her, but those gripes are largely for family courts. No one ever prosecutes."

"She and lover boy were the unfortunate victims of bad luck and bad timing."

Neither of us laughed at my joke.

Slidell toed the pansies bordering the brick walk. Suspecting he had more to say, I waited.

On the boom box, Dr. Hook segued into "Freaker's Ball."

"What the hell is that?"

"Birdie's favorite group."

Slidell shook his head at the puzzle of feline taste, then, "Just FYI. Padgett didn't tell Galimore about Lovette quitting the Patriot Posse."

"She didn't?"

"The guy she talked to was FBI. Retired now. It's in the file."

"They finally let you see it?"

"Ain't the specials special?"

"I'm still not clear on how Galimore ended up in that shed."

"Bogan saw him poking around Gamble's trailer before the race Friday night. He told him he'd remembered something that could shed light on what happened back in 'ninety-eight, said Galimore had to go with him to see it. Galimore had no reason to be suspicious, so he went along. In the shed, Bogan nailed him with a dart. The dose was enough to knock Galimore out but not enough to kill him, as Bogan intended."

"Thanks for letting me know that Padgett's dark-haired cop wasn't Galimore."

"Don't mean the guy ain't a douchebag."

"Galimore is aware he failed a lot of people. Says he was focused on his own problems back then."

"A cop don't get that luxury."

"No. And he's beating himself up with guilt."

Slidell didn't respond.

"I understand how you feel." I spoke gently. "But it is possible that Galimore has changed."

A moment passed as Slidell studied the pansies. Then, "I did a little checking. When Galimore got tagged, there was a guy living in his building name of Gordie Lashner. Two months after Galimore went down, Lashner got popped for dealing smack, ended up doing a fifteen-year swing."

"You think it was Lashner's money in Galimore's storage bin?"

"All I know is Lashner's a lowlife."

"You'll look into it?"

"I ain't saying I think Galimore was framed."

"Just the unfortunate victim of bad luck and bad timing."

Same joke. Same reaction. Not so much as a smile.

Slidell watched a cyclist pedal past Myers Park Baptist across the way. He made no move to leave.

Dr. Hook started singing about Sylvia's mother.

When Slidell spoke, his words surprised me.

"I took a fern by the hospital."

"For Galimore?"

"No. For Dr Friggin' Pepper."

"That was a very nice gesture," I said.

"I didn't visit his bedside or nothing like that."

"Still, it was a considerate thing to do."

A beefy finger shot the air. "The fern business stays between you and me."

I pantomimed a key on my lips.

"Don't want people thinking I'm going all gooey."

"Bad for the image."

Slidell pulled an object from his pocket and tossed it to me.

"Galimore had that sent over to my office. Note said it was something you asked him for. Said he never had a chance to give it to you."

The object in my lap was a NASCAR cap. On its bill was a signature scrawled in black Magic Marker. *Jacques Villeneuve*.

A grin tugged the corners of my mouth. Lieutenant-détective Andrew Ryan, Quebec cop and Villeneuve groupie, would be thrilled.

"So." Slidell straightened his phony cool-guy shades. "Erskine Slidell still your favorite badass?"

"Yes, Detective." My grin widened. "You are still my favorite Charlotte badass."

FROM THE FORENSIC FILES OF DR. KATHY REICHS

In this bonus Q & A, the scribe behind Tempe Brennan takes questions on NASCAR, extremist groups, Tempe's love life, and the difference between writing a novel and penning a script for the TV show Bones *on FOX.*

1. *Flash and Bones* begins with the discovery of a body in a barrel of asphalt in a dump next to the Charlotte Motor Speedway, and characters from the racing world become implicated in the drama. What drew you to NASCAR as a backdrop? Are you yourself a racing fan?

Prior to writing *Flash and Bones*, I had only passing knowledge of auto racing, having attended one event way back in the gray dawn of history. But almost every Charlottean knows a player in the game—be it a team owner, a mechanic, a sponsor, or a driver. It's hard not to get caught up in the excitement each May and October when hundreds of thousands converge on our burg for big races. Like Daytona or Darlington, Charlotte is an epicenter for the sport. And, as Tempe explains in the book, stock car racing originated with bootlegging in the Carolina mountains during Prohibition.

I ended up writing NASCAR into the novel because

of my longtime friend Barry Byrd, himself a huge racing enthusiast. Each time I began a new Temperance Brennan novel Barry would suggest that NASCAR would provide a rich background for a story. I finally realized he was right. Barry offered to introduce me to Jimmy Johnson and his team, to take me to the track, to include me with the gang attending the All-Star Race and the Coca-Cola 600.

Barry followed through on his promises. I met track owners and managers, sports journalists, pit crew chiefs, and fans who had driven their Winnebagos from Portland, Houston, Teaneck, and Nashville. Thanks to Barry and the Smith family I enjoyed a top to bottom tour of the Charlotte Motor Speedway. My fascination with the adjacent landfill was, I fear, a source of some dismay.

2. *Flash and Bones* takes place entirely in Tempe Brennan's hometown of Charlotte. *Spider Bones,* on the other hand, begins in Montreal, where Tempe occasionally works, then moves to Hawaii. Other books have taken Tempe to Chicago, Israel, and Guatemala. How do you decide where to set your next novel? In what city do you spend most of your own time these days?

Setting is a living, breathing part of each story I write. When Tempe travels, her destination is always a place that I know well, one in which I have plied my trade or spent time doing research.

I work and live in Charlotte, so Tempe does, too. Like her, I am a commuter, shifting regularly from North Carolina to Quebec, where I consult to the Laboratoire de sciences judiciaires et de médecine légale in Montreal. Yep. I have the mother lode of frequent flier miles.

In *Spider Bones* Tempe heads to Hawaii to pursue a case

for JPAC, the Joint Prisoners of War, Missing in Action Accounting Command, the U.S. military facility dedicated to identifying the remains of servicemen and -women who have died far from home. Easy choice. I consulted for this lab for many years.

In *Grave Secrets* Tempe exhumes a mass grave in Guatemala. In the year 2000 I was invited to do the same by the Guatemalan Foundation for Forensic Anthropology.

In *Bones to Ashes* a case takes Tempe to Tracadie, New Brunswick. This setting was suggested by an exhumation and analysis I performed for an Arcadian family living in that province.

In *206 Bones* Tempe flies to Chicago. Another no-brainer. That's where I was born.

You get the idea. It's better to observe firsthand than to make things up.

3. Another dominant theme of *Flash and Bones* is right-wing extremism, a subject about which you've written before. Members of a white supremacist group figure as suspects in the book. How did you become interested in these factions of American society?

Extremist ideas do not offend me. In my view, people are free to believe what they will. Extremism that hurts others offends me greatly.

In *Cross Bones* I wrote of religious extremism—belief systems that refuse to accept the legitimacy of differing worldviews. In that story events take Tempe to Israel and bring her into contact with fringe groups who use violence to impose their ideologies and customs on others.

Political extremism can be equally dangerous, whether coming from the left or the right. In recent years hatred and intolerance have led to deadly attacks by domestic terrorists in the United States. Ted Kaczynski, the Unabomber; Timothy McVeigh and Terry Nichols, the Oklahoma City bombers; Eric Rudolph, the Olympic Park Bomber. Such individuals choose to kill their fellow citizens based on their own warped definitions of morality.

After years on the run, Rudolph was arrested while digging through a Dumpster in western North Carolina, about a four-hour drive from Charlotte. I wondered who else might be hiding in the woods and back roads of my state. In *Flash and Bones*, I imagine a group of people who come from the extreme mold of Eric Rudolph and his narrow-minded brethren.

Preferring comfort in numbers, some right-wing fanatics form clubs or militias. That's the case in *Flash and Bones*. Tempe is drawn into the world of an extremist group and must learn their philosophy and decipher their code of conduct in order to determine their role in a cold case that disturbs her greatly.

4. Over the course of *Flash and Bones*, Tempe develops a flirtatious relationship with Cotton Galimore, the head of security at the Charlotte Motor Speedway. Her old flame Lieutenant-détective Andrew Ryan and sometime suitor and Charlotte attorney Charlie Hunt only make minor appearances in the story. How do you decide what Tempe's romantic life is going to be like in each novel? Can you give readers any hints about where it might go in the future?

It's true. Tempe's love life is in a bit of a muddle. Andrew Ryan is preoccupied with his daughter, Lily, who is in drug rehab. And miles away. Charlie Hunt is absorbed in a complex legal case. Miles away in another sense.

Enter Cotton Galimore, strong, intelligent, and smoking hot. Sadly, Galimore's past isn't exactly spick-and-span. Joe Hawkins distrusts him. Skinny Slidell loathes him. And the guy is cocky as hell.

But the heart wants what the heart wants. Inexplicably, Tempe is drawn to the disgraced ex-cop. Is Galimore really as bad as her colleagues say? Should she steer clear as everyone advises?

Nope. No spoilers here.

5. *Flash and Bones,* as with all your books, contains unique forensic twists: the body found at the dump is lodged in a barrel of asphalt, which Tempe must painstakingly dismantle. Later, chemical tests at the CDC reveal the presence of a surprising toxin in the remains. What was the inspiration for these forensic discoveries? Have you seen such corpses in your real-life work, or, in writing your novels, do you imagine the strange possibilities of homicides you haven't yet encountered?

I am like a scavenger, always on the lookout for a snack. But instead of food, it's criminal twists I'm after. I keep my eyes and ears open for interesting characters, bizarre case elements, and cutting-edge science. A Temperance Brennan plot may derive from any number of sources.

Starting point. I draw ideas from forensic anthropology analyses that I perform myself. My own cases.

Move one circle out. The LSJML (my Montreal gig) is a full-spectrum medico-legal and crime lab. While there I am able to observe what goes on around me, to learn about the newest thing in ballistics, toxicology, pathology, or DNA.

Continue outward. Forensic scientists love to talk to each other about their cases. Colleagues often suggest ideas for Temperance Brennan stories based on investigations in which they have been involved.

Occasionally a plot twist is inspired by a presentation I attend at a professional conference. The annual meeting of the American Academy of Forensic Sciences provides particularly rich fodder. Articles in research journals also get the old brain pumping.

From my own caseload, and then from conversing, listening, watching, and reading, I get what I think of as "nugget" ideas, my core story concepts. Then, for both legal and ethical reasons, I change everything—names, dates, places, personal details. I then play the "what if?" game, and spin the nugget off into multilayered fiction.

6. In addition to writing the Temperance Brennan novels (and now the young adult novels featuring Tempe's niece), you've also written a script for the FOX series *Bones,* based on your books. How does writing a TV script differ from writing your novels? Is one harder than the other?

I am a producer on *Bones*. One of many. Just look at our credits. Mainly, I work with the writers, answering questions, providing bone clues, correcting terminology. Over the course of six seasons, I have read more than one hundred and thirty scripts. Though a television script is quite different from a book, there is some commonality.

For me the similarity between a Temperance Brennan novel and a *Bones* teleplay lies in structure. My books typically have a lot going on—an A story, a B story, maybe even a C. Ditto a *Bones* episode.

In *Flash and Bones* Tempe is asked to identify a body found in a barrel. That's the A story. Simultaneously, she is drawn into the search for a missing teenage couple. The B story. And, all the while, there's her complicated love life. C story.

In the season five *Bones* episode that I wrote, "The Witch in the Wardrobe," two sets of remains are discovered in a burned-out house. The witch in the wardrobe turns out to have been dead for quite some time. A story. The witch under the foundation is identified as a recent homicide victim. B story. Angela and Hodgins go to jail (and love rekindles). C story. The structures are very similar, you see.

On the other hand, a novel and a script differ in many ways. For example, with film or television there's no need for detailed description of setting or action. Those features are right there in front of your eyes. A screenplay or teleplay is all about dialogue, character, and story line.

Another difference involves the creative experience. When I write a novel, I am the stereotypical loner working at my keyboard in isolation. No one helps me. No one approves or disapproves my work. Not so the television writer.

Once a story idea (kind of like my "nugget" concept) is accepted, the next step is called "breaking the story." For one to three weeks the entire *Bones* writing staff brainstorms together, hammering out an outline act by act, scene by scene, working on erasable white boards that cover the walls of the writers' room. The process is collective, and it is exhilarating.

(The *Bones* writing team is awesome. Josh Berman, Pat Charles, Carla Kettner, Janet Lin, Dean Lopata, Michael Peterson, Karine Rosenthal, Karyn Usher. Thanks for your patience, guys.)

The completed script outline is then "pitched"—in the case of *Bones* to Hart Hanson, our genius creator and executive producer.

Once the outline is approved, the writer then "goes to script." That means back to the lonely keyboard to produce what is called the writer's draft. That stage takes one to three weeks. Unless the show is behind schedule. In that case, well, good luck.

Then there are rewrites. And more rewrites. Studio draft. Network draft. Production draft.

In the end it is amazing to see your episode actually being shot, with all the actors, the director, the gaffers, the grips, and the best boys. Lights! Camera! Action!

Almost as amazing as seeing your baby on the printed page.